ON YER BIKE, SCHWEIK!

ON YER BIKE, SCHWEIK!

Eric Davidson

WARNER
BOOKS

A *Warner* Book

First published in Great Britain in 1993
by Warner Books

Copyright © Eric Davidson, 1993

The moral right of the author has been asserted.

A CIP catalogue record for this book is
available from the British Library.

ISBN 0 7515 0867 5

Printed and bound in Great Britain by
Clays Ltd, St. Ives plc

Warner Books
A Division of
Little, Brown and Company (UK) Limited
Brettenham House
Lancaster Place
London WC2E 7EN

To Adam, Eve and the kids

The trouble with Man is not Original Sin but Butterfingers

New Proverb

Contents

Contents

Contents

Prelude

Our father – *'with chart in Heaven'* – left behind him three shiny medals, one tiny map of Flanders, and a well-thumbed roll of poems – all of which my mother buried with him.

'Now then, children,' she said, standing tight-lipped and black-booted in front of the table bearing the embroidered heads of my great grandmother, 'I want each of us to take a last look.'

There were two campaign medals 'for active service' in France and the Western Desert, and one 'for bravery' at Monte Cassino. The map was pocket-sized, folded in four, and bore slender red-ink lines that meandered across Belgium and northern France tracing his Regiment's dreary progress from the flatlands of Valenciennes to the beaches of Dunkirk. The roll was a sheaf of fading foolscap pages, brittle, dog-eared and spent, which he had bound together with his army-issue lanyard.

'They are going with him,' she said, as we gazed down helplessly at the humble gifts, 'so we shan't be seeing them again.'

During the six months from his return home until he died, my brother and sister and I had been allowed to finger, fondle, polish and play with the trio of beaming medals; to scout out and track down the wavering routes across the withering chart; and to contrive giggling sounds from impossible names like Armen-

1

tières and Ypres, Millonfosse and Séclin. But we were never allowed to examine what lay within the secret bundle – only to glimpse that the pencilled lines never went right across the page, confirming that his writing was, as he always insisted, 'mostly margins'.

'War poet?' My mother pondered my brother's final question. 'Yes, I suppose in a way he was.'

One

'Very complicated business, botching,' said our father, easing over on to another wound in his sick-bed, which was at least well enough to take his great frame, his five wounds and his roll of poems. And each time he changed over my brother twisted hard on his copy of the *Adventure*, my sister concentrated harder on some symbol on the Flanders map, and I dug the medal with the King's head deeper into the palm of my hand. 'Takes a lot of working out.'

Because I was born in September 1939, the month the War broke out, and because my father went 'off to it' early in October and didn't return from 'Frogland' until the following June ...

and because he sailed for the 'Middle-and-Off East' on my first birthday to spend the rest of the war 'straight-driving mosquitoes and Jerries' over the Western Desert and 'lifting Eyeties' all the way to the boundary of Italy and France before being 'retired hurt' through 'the rear Pavilion door' ...

and because he came home after five years' absence to spend his last six months in the upstairs bedroom at the back of the house with his sunburnt poems, his Gold Flake and our yellow canary, to die of the combined effects of five separate wounds which 'was more than I got medals for' ...

because of all these things, we never saw much of
him.

Dearly Beloved:

But we heard him:

*And the legions built a mighty tavern-acle within the city
to give them shelter and succour, whilst all about them
Jerry Miah got on with the business of tearing down the
walls of Maginot ...*

Right through the War he compiled his

BUMPER BOOK OF BOTCHERS

or rather, we did: from the tales he sent home as letters,
or the letters he sent home as tales, of the magnificent
legion of Botchers who tried so desperately to help him
not win the war:

*being the bewitching legends of belligerent botching
called war*

as the *Wizard* would have put it.

'Not just us,' he said. '*Every* bugger. Eyeties. Jerries.
Japs. Wops. Wogs. Frogs. Yanks. Diggers. The lot. All of
them. All of us. That's all we ever were – Botchers.'

*And they were in the desert seemingly all the days of
their lives, but they remembered the places whence they
had come and rejoiced in the news brought them from
home by Apolling, the sunburnt messenger from Field
Post Office.*

He didn't always write like the Bible. But it *sounded* as
if he did.

Every Thursday evening during the war we gathered
together to hear the weekly *READINGS* – the sound of
our mother's voice reading aloud from the latest edition
of flimsy, rustling pages which he sent home each
week. Despite having to fight a whole war on his own

and put up with 'Eyeties and Jerries, mud and flood, heat and feet, dunes and prunes, bully beef and Botchers', he managed to jot down something every day – sometimes sheets, sometimes only a page, sometimes no more than a line: 'God Bless you and keep you. Tomorrow we're moving it.' He wrote 'before shut-eye' every night and sent off 'a batch of Botchers' every week.

And lo, an uncertain Botcher named Long, son of Short, who was sorely troubled in spirits, awoke from his dream to find his gourd of nectar nicked, and called out for his beloved Sergeant, saying …

The letters always started with a bible-style passage which set the tone and mood and gave them a certain 'desert air', although he had used this practice from various barracks in England and France long before he 'hit the dunes'. Unlike his fragile roll of poems, the pages were not patterned as in verse but lavishly spread with words that flowed right across the flimsy, blue-lined paper which felt to the touch exactly like the Bible – 'which it is in a way'.

Propped up on his pillows in the bedroom upstairs, scribbling away at his secret scroll of poems, he said that it had all come to him in a flash of revelation at the Recruiting Office in Damascus Road, Clapham.

'There was this Regimental Sergeant Major, see, decked out in emperor's clothes and full regalia, like a cross between Moses and Rasputin. The Tzar's Gent, we called him.' He moved over to another wound. 'It was like the beginning of the world again,' he said. 'And the Word was with the Sergeant and remained so all our days.'

It was as if someone was forewarning that the description of the coming conflict would need its own particular voice. And that voice would be the sound of the Bible. Everything was in place from the beginning, from the barren desert to the Apocalypse of Cassino:

hope and glory at the start, fear and despair in the
middle, faith and triumph at the end.

'We could hear the sound of it coming – and the
music.'

And everybody in it a loser, 'from Adam to Jesus', all
bogged down in themselves and great wadies – stuff
heavy enough 'to make even Lamentations sound like a
whimper'.

*And behold, a certain Corporal named Bone – he whom
the disciples named Trom on account of the solace in his
voice – went forth into the desert to distribute among the
hordes the haversack rations, calling unto the heavens:
BACKSHEESH! And ever higher: BACKSHEESH!*

Nothing about the war itself. Only about the legion of
hapless Botchers who did their damnedest to stop him
winning it.

*And lo, in the seventh month of their tribulations a great
plague swept across the land, and the legions girded their
groins and hastened back to shelter again in the Wadi
from whence they had come. And they appointed a
certain sentry named Nodd to keep watch over their
knackered flock …*

'Well,' he said, balancing precariously on the margin
between one wound and another, 'that's war, isn't it?'

And there were Botchers on both sides.

'They're all over the bloody place! The Fault of the
Earth, they are – just bewildered by being down here in
the first place.'

But the responsibility for the war lay with a particular
kind of stunted Botcher called a 'Boche', who dwelt in
'the Abodes of the Guilty'. He always wrote of the
enemy as Jerry or Eyetie, not exactly *affectionately* but as
if he had no particular grudge against them. But when
they did something that really 'got right up the snifters',
he wrote abruptly and disparagingly of the snapped-off

version Boche – 'a sort of *incomplete* Botcher'. You could hear the difference.

'Remember, always leave Botchers big enough margins.'

We didn't see much of his poems, or whatever it was that lurked unsung between the whacked leaves of the brittle bundle he nurtured more carefully than his wounds, but we heard them – not the words, but the honing of them.

After he came home he sat up in bed whenever he was fit enough and scribbled in his scroll. The leaves were always in his hands or by his side during these final months but we didn't see anything of what was in them, except for the shapes – the forms and patterns that told us that whatever he was scribbling was different. Not that they were *poems* – but that they were *different*. The words started almost halfway in and didn't stretch to the other side of the page. They were carved into neat blocks that formed a separate design for each sheet; and, although he appeared to write and scribble and score and sketch over the lines again and again and again, he always managed to leave an enormous amount of fresh air and space around them.

'For the Botchers, see,' he said twisting awkwardly on his numerous pillows 'to find a blank space' between his wounds. 'Never get them too hemmed in.'

He kept jabbing at the lines with his pencil, studying them, scoring out, starting again, over and over. Nothing was ever *quite* right. He seemed only to *substitute* words and never added a page to enlarge the bundle. Stabbing at the empty areas around the edges of the page with the pummelled point of his 2B he told us: 'Must give them breathing space.'

He kept mumbling to himself, as if testing the words for their feel and sound, like voicing his roughs: scratch, scratch; or selecting his notes: plink, plonk.

'Always leave them plenty of room to get away.'

We were never in any doubt that what lay hidden within his precious papers was his alone. Whatever he'd seen of 'battles and Botchers, winners and losers, heroes and dodgers', whatever Great Secret he'd become party to during his five years' absence, it snuggled within his curled up bundle.

'In the Beginning, God created the Heaven and the Earth ... and planted a garden eastward in Eden, and therein placed the creature he had cast – the Botcher.'

After he came home with his 'wounds and medals, map and scribbles', he explained Botchers to us in a familiar style.

'And the Lord God created all Botchers in the same image and made multitudes thereof to be Baby Botchers and but few to be King Botchers. And he blessed the King Botcher with one difference: one teeny-weeny flaw that he himself can never ever see – he doesn't know he's a Botcher too.'

'Botching's not that simple, you know,' he said, 'You can't expect to get it immediately.'

Each time he braced himself against the pillows to lift himself up and away from one of his wounds, the smile turned to a wince.

'Now King Botchers strive with all their might and with all their main to make Baby Botchers be what they're not, and they give them medals for trying. But they never learn that Baby Botchers can never be what they want them to be. And they can't either.'

We heard the bed creak as he moved laboriously to locate another spot – and my brother rerolled the *Adventure* very tight. And we heard the sigh as he pinpointed another spot with precision – and my sister focused hard on a Flanders escape route. And we imagined each wound as an actual hole in his body being pressed down and squashed out of shape as it took his weight – and I pushed down harder into King George's head.

Each time he retold a tale it seemed to gain 'another cubit in stature' and gradually, like a newer testament, to acquire a sort of biblical reverence of its own. We watched him concentrate on the scroll as if he were actually reading from the text and finding more and more words and ways in which to tell it each time. But although he scribbled in and scored out again and again the words couldn't have been written there as he only ever wrote in the middle of the page and never dared stray into the sacred margins.

'It's both an art *and* a craft, botching,' he said. 'Half inspiration, half hard graft.'

Each time he settled down we squeezed our eyes to hear the sigh as the previous hole popped back to form a neat covered-in circle again.

'Takes a lot of working out, botching. But the main thing to remember is that the Botcher needs his margins to hide in. And margins are like mistakes – *other* men's.'

And peering ever deeper into his scroll as if to see more and more of the story, he said: 'But verily I say unto you, never underestimate a Botcher. And never ever think you've rumbled him.'

GORDON BLUE

Somewhere in France, 1939

*And he spake unto them, saying: Ye shall not want,
neither shall ye fast, for I am come as a servant who shall
nourish you with the divine root and the beef of cans ...*

Two

When Gordon Blue reached the Maginot Line early in
October 1939 while the last leaves were still clinging
desperately, he knew he'd come home.

'That's it, lads! Just like my old man said. Maginot
Line to you, maybe, but End o' the Line to me.'

'What you on about, Blue? War's hardly started.'

'Finished for me, though. Not going any further.'

You could tell it was going to be a Botchers' war from
the start.

It wasn't much to look at, the Maginot Line. Wasn't
anything, in fact. Looked like a long line of concrete
clumps and barbed wire and ditches and dug-outs left
over from the Somme – more a set from *All Quiet on the
Western Front* with the French troops hanging about
slurping their coffee like extras around the catering
wagon, waiting for the '*Action!*'

And the way they glowered at us from behind their
frog sannies you could tell they were intent on fighting
in the same way all over again, starting from where
their dads left off in 1918.

It was going to be that kind of war.

For Blue it was the smell of garlic that did it – wafting
over from the open stoves of the French Army's
Cuisinery Corps. He knew then that he'd arrived.

'Ah, yes, that's it!' he gasped, stopping in his tracks

when we were still kilometres from our destination, and inhaling deeply. ' "The bouquet that beckons!" as my old dad used to say.'

'Bloody hell!' The rest of the platoon shuddered to a halt, caught their breath, and exploded. 'What the bleeding hell's that, Sarge, mustard gas?'

'It's the glorious garlic,' beamed Blue. 'The blessed root!'

As one man we coughed and spluttered, fumbling for handkerchiefs, sneezing, gasping and gobbing. All except Blue.

'Where's it coming from – them silos?'

'No,' said Blue, haughtily, 'from them sentries,' and pointing towards the blunt end of the Maginot Line, added poetically: 'Yonder, see, by the French settings.'

'Cor, prithee, which settings – the latrines?'

'No, it's the garlic that you divine – their divine root!'

'What they doing with it?'

'Eating it, I should think. Having their breakfast.'

'Streuth!'

'Or their Onzes. They don't have Elevenses in France, see. They have Onzes instead – with garlic.'

'Sorry, Sarge, mutiny or no mutiny, this far and no further. A fighting soldier's got a right to protect himself.'

And the entire detachment, with all its gear and tools, dropped by the roadside.

The Maginot Line was built by the French after the First World War. It wasn't likely to do much for modern warfare. But everybody *thought* it would. They were still thinking 'Lines' in those days of the phoney war. We might have had tanks and transport and aircraft and all the technical paraphernalia of the twentieth century at our disposal, but the *thinking* was still static – Lines, miles and miles of *Lines*. Although we once thought we spotted some mounted cavalry brandishing swords.

'Hallucinations,' said the Sarge. 'Lots of ghosts around these parts.'

Every time someone cried 'war!' you reached for your pick and shovel and dug deeper and deeper holes and covered them with wood and tarpaulin, and made parapets of sandbags to climb over if you ever felt like advancing. But most of the time you stayed below, sheltering like a sodden rabbit, and poked your gun through the slots in the bags or up through the roof, and kept firing away until you ran out of ammunition or it got dark. Even then you didn't have to stop, except that some chaps were over keen on their shut-eye and often selfishly insisted. Then, when a lull came, you sent a few others over the top to see how you'd done during the blasting bit, but as not many ever came back you never knew how you were getting on anyway. So there was nothing else to do but start firing off again. It went on like that and not a lot used to happen, except you lost a lot of blokes – literally *lost* them because you couldn't find them again – and the enemy did the same back to you and shells kept dropping down the holes you were sheltering in.

They had a name for that kind of war – 'attrition', after all the sneezing you did from the colds and flus you caught living down below in the damp for years on end. In keeping with contemporary thinking, we had been sent to help extend the Maginot Line because it had stopped at Belgium and there was nothing between the BEF and the Jerries all the way up to the Channel, except flatlands and Flanders. And our detachment found itself right next door to the French.

'The join's always the hardest bit, lads,' beamed the Sergeant. 'That's why they've sent *us*. Got to make a perfect splice, see. And remember, we're not just here to tie a few bits of old rope together – we're here to cement relations as well.'

'So what's it to be this morning, Sarge – tying or

cementing?'

'Get digging, Warburton.'

The wind kept veering between west and north west, wafting the garlic like a capricious damp cloud, teasing and flirting and threatening to stop dead suddenly and empty itself all over us as we recovered in the ditch.

We were still some way from the French lines – the join – and it looked as if we might be in for a spot of difficulty, mutiny even, because the smell wasn't going to ease off the nearer we got to our rendezvous. So the Sergeant went around his men, reassuring and comforting them – 'delivering his patter' – and trying to fortify them with helpful comments like 'They don't eat all day, chaps, not even here,' and 'The wind veers a lot in these parts, the met men tell me.'

'Maginot anything to do with imagination, Blue, cos if …'

'Nothing at all. It's the French *mange genoux*, actually.'

'What's that, then?'

'*Mange genoux – mange*, eat, and *genoux*, legs. Frogs' legs. Well, knees actually. But near enough.'

'Where d'you learn all that stuff, Blue?'

'I was brought up on it.'

'Stone the bleedin' crows! Where?'

'In the Mile End Road.'

'Blimey, which end?'

'None. The Middle. At La Cuiller Grassieuse.'

'The what!'

'Me Dad's restaurant – The Greasy Spoon, to you.'

The Maginot was the brainchild of a real Botcher. Only a Botcher could have dreamed it up in the first place. And only a supreme Botcher could have thought it was worth anything in 1939. But only the supremest Botcher could have thought of going ahead and extending it further and deeper. Yet that's how it was when we arrived. We were supposed to be there to help out the

French, but it was obvious we hadn't been able to come up with any better idea ourselves.

Blue was right when he said he recognised the place. They might have built the actual Maginot Line long after the First World War, but the scene must have looked exactly as his dad had described it to him from 1918. And the only bloke who got any satisfaction out of seeing the prehistoric heap was Blue, but then he was there for more creative reasons.

Blue had worked with his dad in bacon sanny caffs since leaving school at fourteen. 'Well, ten actually.' *Officially* it was fourteen.

'Just didn't bother turning up after my tenth birthday. Not much point. Nobody minded or noticed. None of us lot were going anywhere anyway – not if your old man runs a bacon sanny caff and you have the music of the Mile End Road in your north and south.'

'Not if you call it The Greasy Spoon.'

'No, it wasn't that, and it wasn't no gammon or bacon greasy spoon either. Very up-market, it was. Or tried to be.'

The caff was only one in a long line of *'Mange Anews'* – a French-style chain his dad tried painstakingly to establish in the Twenties, about the time the French were trying to establish their own Maginot chain. Old Man Blue had derived his inspiration from four formative years in France from 1914 to 1918 – covering the battlefields and absorbing 'all things French and garlic'. And when he came home after the war with his kit bag and his garlic squeezer he vowed to spread the garlic gospel to the heathen of Hackney and points east. 'Could have stayed on,' he said, 'but I had a mission, see. I'd seen all these men who'd been brought up on bad food with not so much as a sniff of the divine root between them struggling through four years of war. I had to try to change all that. So I came home to preach the good news the only way I could.'

By the time Old Blue reached the Mile End Road he'd done Whitechapel, Bethnal Green, the Isle of Dogs, Wapping, Cable Street, Hackney, Holloway and Holburn – and Elmer's End.

Old Blue wasn't much appreciated wherever he went.

'This is where the Old Man said,' Blue declared, recognising the spot as if he'd been coming here every summer holiday.

'Hardly a sight to remember, is it?'

'A sight for sore eyes for me. Wish me dad could see it.'

Once again the pungent cloud menaced.

'Cor. That's rough, that is.'

'The Mile End Road all over again,' said Blue happily. 'Back to my divine roots, this is.'

'You call that divine!'

'Fruit of the vine, wine. Fruit of the divine, aye … ye.'

'Aye … ye?'

'Garlic to you.'

Garlic apart, if garlic can ever be apart, Blue's dad gave touches of the French spirit to all his caffs. He draped the tables with red and white checked cloths and decorated them with candles fixed in blue, aladdin-type tin dishes.

He laced the bacon, beans, sausages and egg with garlic, and even sprinkled it on the toast. He baked baguettes and croissants you were supposed to break with your hands but never provided plates to catch the crumbs in. The result was that they littered the tables and dishes and tea mugs and morning papers and dungaree laps like showering confetti. And he tried to wean his clientele off mugs of char on to coffee served in petite cups with handles you could barely poke a finger through.

He took his wife to see the Maginot Line when it was being built in the Twenties. He wanted to show her the source of his conversion and his subsequent dogged persistence in promoting the blessed root. 'Besides,' he said, 'the Old Girl needed a break. I mean, life for a wife in bacon sannies soon takes its toll, and life for a wife in garlic bacon sannies can be a right stinker.'

He won her over, and young Blue was conceived on that romantic trip. The inspiration was passed on, the succession guaranteed.

Blue set up his stove close to the end of the Maginot Line and got stuck in to his 'cuisine fit for a modern army'. All he had to work on was bacon, eggs, sausages, beans, bully beef, tomatoes and toast. However, undaunted, he responded to his dad's inspiration and set out to make army rations creative – to 'cordon it', he said, and the name stuck – Gordon Blue. And also like his dad, he garnished everything with garlic and threw in the odd wild mushroom when he felt like going 'out on a whim'.

'The Maginot may not show much imagination but my bacon sannies will,' he claimed. And he devised special names for his special dishes:

BREAKFAST PLAIN

BREAKFAST DEBONAIR

and a selection of lesser items:

The BEF	Bacon, Egg and Fries
The SAM	Sausage and Mash
The BOT	Beans on Toast
The BUB	Bully Beef
The BEST	Bacon, egg, sausage and toast
The TOM	Toast on *Marie est Malade*: 'good for colds'

The BUS	Bully Solitaire
The GESTE	Garlic egg, sausage, tomato exquise
The BEAU	
GESTE	Ditto de luxe

'You know Blue, them sannies are something else. Given a whole new meaning to Roll Call.'

'My pleasure.'

If only for a short space, Old Blue created a stir in each neighbourhood, brought to it a breath of different if not exactly fresh air, and each time gave himself and his family a regular buzz from 'a new commencement', as he put it. 'And if you can give yourself a new commencement two or three times a year, you got yourself something to live for, haven't you?'

With that spirit and determination he persevered in his desperate mission to civilise the British working man's mornings and set up caffs with names like The Dainty Assiette, The Chic Spoon, The Eiffel Brigade, The Lolly Bergères and, supremely, La Cuiller Grassieuse, the celebrated Greasy Spoon of the Mile End Road, often known locally as Blues.

'The only bacon sanny joint in all England with red and white checked tablecloths and garlic on the toast.'

He never lasted too long in any one place. Couldn't. The novelty just wouldn't last. The Blues always had to move on. 'I think the crumbs got to them myself.'

'One breakfast, Blue.'

'Plain or debonair?'

'What's the difference?'

'Well, the Plain is the straight bacon, eggs, sausage, tomato and beans, with fried bread and mash. And a double mug of sweet tea.'

'Sounds fine to me.'

'Coming up.'

'So, what's the debonair, then?'

'One lightly done egg, one rasher without the rind, and a slice of wafer thin toast. With a thimbleful of coffee.'

'Blimey, who eats that on mornings like this?'

'The debonair is for the … eh … more delicate, or very *early* palate. For those coming off nightwatch and unable to stomach too rich a dish. In my dad's caff he called it the Nox Nosh.'

'Oh, I see, *debonair*, like smart?'

'No, not smart. It's the very early repast taken after a long night without nosh. The French for very early is *de bonne heure*, which becomes debonair.'

'Still sounds a bit posh to me.'

'No, not posh. The Posh breakfast is something else again – that's the Poached On Sweet Ham one. Strictly for Officers – *and* above the rank of Captain. Them with scrambled eggs on their caps.'

'In garlic, of course.'

'The *French* officers, yes.'

'Don't half get complicated, do it?'

'Well, a true chef is no slouch.'

'Hmm. Well, every man to his own trade.'

'Cordon Bleu Cuisine is hardly a *trade*, mate. An art or a calling, perhaps. Definitely not a trade.'

'Well, I'll have the Fry-ups debonair, Blue.'

The smell of Blue's bacon and eggs and garlic was not lost on the French at the north end of the Maginot Line where they left off and we took over. For some reason we seemed to have a lot more food than they had at this stage of the war, and as Blue was involved in a permanent fry-up, trying to convert the stubborn BEF to the joys of *haute cuisine*, the aromas kept curling over the no-man's-land between, arousing pangs in the French nostrils and preying on the passions of the permanently hungry troops.

Soon stray French 'Tommeeees' began to wander over

and hang around Blue's field kitchen.

'*B'njour.*'

'Sure. Help yourself.'

'Onlee *morceau* …'

'Only more so … course.'

'… *peut être*?'

'Na, right out of them, I'm afraid. Do you some nice beans, though. Or mushy peas?'

'Well,' said the Sarge, 'it was old Napoleon who said an army marches on its stomach, but I bet he never thought of bacon sannies.'

The garlic crusade soon began to upset Blue's British customers. As the winter wore on so the novelty wore off, as it had done with his dad's customers, and the visionary Blue was forced to go the same road as Old Blue – 'stodge street'. Went quite morose, did Blue, and sank into such a slough of despair he was almost tempted to give up the war entirely: 'Feel like jacking it all in, Sarge. Just packing up and heading off back home.'

'Ah, don't do that, Blue, not yet!' the Sarge encouraged him. 'You can't expect a whole army to change the habits of a life's crime, not just like that. Gotta give them time.'

'Gave my old dad a lifetime. Look where it got him!'

The French, on the other hand, were easily wooed and won over, not only because they were always hungry, but because they could sympathise with the struggle Blue was having to stay creative in a hostile environment. More and more stray French soldiers kept wandering around, nostrils in the air, like hunting hounds on the scent, admiring what he was doing, under the pretence of cementing relations, or even tying them, but always benefiting from a bacon sanny or two to sustain them on their long trek back to their concrete line a hundred yards away.

Blue took to nipping over to cook for them as well. Strictly against all the rules, of course, but it kept him and the Frogs happy and relations between the two sides more than amicable. And he began to dream of being won over, literally of moving in with the Frogs and getting to know some of their secrets, maybe even getting a secondment or transfer or even … well. But, although they were so overwhelmed by his visits and fry-ups *de matin et de tout le jour*, they didn't seem the slightest bit interested in teaching him anything, not so long as the clouds of grease and garlic continued to envelop and enchant them.

Blue had to wait for his King to come and deliver him.

Things were getting a bit bogged down by the winter of '39 – not a lot happening except the odd skirmish or probe by a Jerry patrol wandering over and lobbing in a spare grenade. Now with Christmas around the corner and no hope of getting home, far less the war being over by then (despite assurances to the contrary by our leaders), they had to think up some morale booster to keep 'our Boys' going. And they hit on the King himself. He would come all the way from Buck Pal and wander amongst his troops like great kings were wont to do in plays whether they wanted to or not.

Of course, as soon as the announcement was made the lines had to be inspected to make sure everything would be in order and fit for a king – scrubbed and polished and painted and spruced up even if it *was* France and open country and soggy and dark and mid December. And of course the King would be accompanied by lots of French top brass.

'The Royal Party may need to be fed, Sergeant,' said the Adjutant, consulting the Suggested Itinerary.

'Sir!'

'Probably not, of course, but we ought to be prepared.'

'Sir!'

'Don't suppose they'll be carrying packed lunches, do you?'

'Doubt it, sir.'

'Then we'll have to see about rustling something up for them, shan't we?'

'Be a nice gesture, sir, yes.'

'So what have we got, then?'

'Not a lot, sir, to be honest.'

'Hmm. How about that famous Blue bloke of yours?'

'Old Blue don't speak much English, sir, far less French.'

'Speaks with his Aga, I hear. The only man in the British Army that can make his stove sing, they tell me.'

'Well, he does have a way with the old nosh, sir, but I …'

'Garlic on the brain, rumour has it. Well, that ought to please these frog chappies. Have a word with him, Sergeant, will you?'

'Sir!'

And so it came to pass that Gordon Blue was asked to lay on a meal for the visiting brass which had to be 'basically frog' if only to show the King how well his loyal soldiers were cementing and tying relations with their allies.

'Can you rustle up something special for the French geezers, Blue?' asked the Sarge. 'A touch of the old frog mange, eh?'

'Tried before with the limited resources at my disposal, Sarge, and that didn't get me very far.'

'Ah, but that was *our* lot, Blue. Them's real live frogs this time. Genuine Frog Brass.'

'Oh.'

'Who knows, now may be your big chance! Think up something *grande*, pull out some of these *arrêts*, Blue Boy, like you're always telling us your old dad used to do. And you never know what it might lead to.'

And, glimpsing something else beyond the task, Blue stirred from his morose blue mood for the first time in weeks.

'Do my best, Sarge.'

'Course you will. Nothing *over*elaborate, you realise, but something extra nevertheless.'

'Yes, Sarge.'

'I mean, no need to make a meal out of it.'

So Blue pulled out all the *arrêts* he could lay his hands on in his supplies of bully beef, bacon, sausages, eggs, tomatoes and beans and rustled up one of his *de luxe de bonne heure* type fries, only this time he did it for lunchtime.

He even prepared a menu proclaiming:

> *Oeufs Royaux*
> *Bacon Lebrun*
> *Gort Beans*
> *Bully Gamelin*

in recognition of the visiting brass.

'Specially done in their honour, Sarge.'

'They'll like that, Blue,' said the Sarge admiringly, 'even if it *is* on lined paper.'

Blue kicked the whole menu off with his *spécialité du chef:*

> *Le bacon drôle de guerre*

'What's that one, then, Blue?'

'Well, it's like a special bacon roll for this time of the war, see.'

'Nope. But it sounds good.'

George duly arrived on 4th December and did a quick whip around the fortifications, stopping to chat with blokes here and there, asking if they'd seen any good Jerries lately, inspecting the trench systems on our section of the Line, and taking a spin on the underground train for carrying men and ammo, and a quick shufti at no-man's land. Then he inspects us, all lined and cheering joyfully – 'put your bleeding backs into it, there!' – and stops to admire the Order of the Day we got hung up in Big Letters to welcome him:

On ne passe pas, on les aura

and below:

No one gets past here and no one nicks what's ours

'Quite a day out for the chap.'
'Like Clacton, yeah.'
'Nice one.'
Then, as the Suggested Itinerary stated:

Meet Blue and have Nosh

However, the Royal Party had in fact had a bit of pie up the road in some Frog pub and didn't really get the benefit of a true Blue garlic sanny. But, as often happens on these occasions, everyone *else* tucked in, including the attendant French officers. The whole effect was 'too ta fey electreek' and the official party 'too ta fey overwhelmed', so much so that the French officers, who had so far been shielded from Blue's efforts, thought he must have been *cordon bleu* trained and suggested he might like to come over to their lines and cook for them, for which 'exchange arrangements can be made'. Maybe even, hint, hint, 'a job *pour la guerre* if not *la vie.*'

But the Sergeant intervened:

'Nah, we got to be on our way, monsieurs,' he said, 'thanks all the same. We're moving out tomorrow at dawn, see, after the King gets clear.'

'Ah non, quel domage!'

'Well, if you ask me, I think it's a pity myself, but there you are.'

*

Back at the Company Commander's Office there's satisfaction too:

'Everyone delighted, sir.'

'Yes, I thought they got stuck in to the bacon sanny spirit, these chaps.'

'Definitely ong shong tay, sir.'

'Well, jolly good show, Sergeant.'

'Sir!'

'And regards to Blue.'

'Sir!'

That night after the King goes there's a celebration over in the French lines, and of course Blue is invited as the guest of honour, so off he goes with his French 'ameese' to join in and prepare the odd *spécialité* for them, thinking maybe he might swing it yet. Or even …

'Don't, Blue, you'll never get away with it.'

'They appreciate me, see.'

'If they miss you at roll call, you'll be a bleeding deserter!'

'More'n you lot do.'

'Remember, we're moving out in the morning, Blue,' shouts the Sarge, suspicious. 'You make sure you're back on time, or I'll have your garlic for garters!'

'Promise, Sarge.'

Of course at the celebrations, Blue is the Toast of the Line. And he's now sporting the Maginot Medal given to all those who have served there. 'Not quite a Cordon Bleu award but it's a start!' he declares proudly. 'And after all, it wasn't for soldiering or fighting, was it, but for cooking and slaving over a hot stove!'

Whether Blue intended to come back or not, no one knows. But he stuck in with his soul mates well into the night, and he was still there when the first rays of dawn were groping their way over no-man's-land, enough to help Jerry on one of his occasional probes, teasing rather than testing the Maginot Defences when they least expected it. Not much, just a brief skirmish, but enough time to lob in a couple of grenades including one that goes right down the chimney of the old Frog Aga Blue's doing a celebration garlic bacon sanny on.

'Well, it's what he would have wanted, isn't it? Smell of garlic in his nostrils, bonhomie in his heart, dream coming true, doing it all for his dad. Not a bad way to go, really.'

RIP VAN

Somewhere in France, May 1940

Yeah, tho' he had walked all his days through the valley of the chalet of death, at last the Great Call came for him to make swift speed and succour sick souls, and he didn't half put the old foot down …

Three

Rip Van gave up his job as an undertaker in Penge to come to France and help us out at Valenciennes.

'Dead chuffed, I was,' he said, 'when the posting came through.'

There was chaos in France in 1940, and particularly on this one gloomy Sunday in May, when we found ourselves outside a town called Valenciennes – 'a place of any old lace and iron'. We had retreated south through a dense forest and when we stopped to take the roll call we discovered we'd left a couple of chaps back at St Amand, a village on the north side. Partridge and Preston had been in a ditch giving us cover while we panicked to get the hell out of it with the horizon swarming with Jerries, and it was one of those botched jobs when the right hand never knows what the right hand is doing.

Rip said he'd spoken to them seconds before he scrambled aboard and took it that they'd got up and grabbed the last truck when we were all clear. He knew the spot, not far out of the forest on the outskirts of the village near a ditch by the river, and immediately offered to drive back and get them.

Nobody else seemed particularly fussed – sorry, maybe, but not exactly put out. But Rip was 'dead keen':

'Partridge and Preston,' he said, 'the perfect

protectors! We can't just abandon Two Pees on their tod like that!'

Rip volunteered for France from his reserved occupation as an undertaker – 'reserved only because me dad was getting past it' – because he wanted a breath of fresh air instead of being cooped up 'in all them morbid parlours and dark chapels of rest and damp churches with everyone always moping about and me always getting sodden under all them flowers.'

'I was getting so bloody miserable with life in the death business,' he said. 'Couldn't see an end to it.'

Rip Van – 'RIP as in death and VAN as in hearse' – had been in the 'trade of demise' since he was a nipper, and badly needed a break. 'It wasn't the job itself, I mean as *such*, it was the hours and them wet flowers.' People used to pop off at any old hour of the day or night – 'not that you could blame them, because we weren't living through such happy times, were we?' – and he had to be on standby more or less all the time. 'But the real trouble was that whenever anyone went all their relatives ever wanted was the same old miserable black routine.'

He had desperately wanted to liven things up a bit, 'put some more life into them wakes,' and throw in a few laughs. But tradition dies hard in the undertaking business and it got that 'the sadness was getting to me. I was getting bouts of depression and real weepy myself at funerals.' It was good for business and all that because the distraught mourners assumed Rip was grieving for their departed, but not a bit of it. He never gave a tosser. 'Just couldn't see a bit of light anywhere.'

Rip shook his head at the misery of the memory of it all, and the memory of the misery too, and drifted off into a few bars of his signature tune, a French number he'd picked up on his way across the Channel:

Je mourrai un Dimanche où j'aurai trop souffert
Alors tu reviendras, mais je serai parti …

which meant something like:

I shall die one Sunday when I have suffered too much
Then you will return but I will have gone …

Not that Rip knew the meaning, but he had been so impressed with the music he had tried to learn the French words and wasn't making too bad a job of it, even if he didn't understand them.

' "*Sombre Dimanche*" is its title,' he said, 'I know that much.' But he didn't know it meant 'miserable Sunday'.

That Sunday the Germans were all over the place as if the boil had burst. One minute we're all messing about trying to figure out how to get through another miserable Sunday and how to fit in all these new divisions they keep sending over and how we're going to feed and entertain them, and the next the Germans are swarming around us and screaming 'dump them in the bloody Channel, or we will!'

Suddenly everything was collapsing. Germans everywhere, clobbering the Dutch, hounding the Belgians out of Belgium, and flushing the French out of the Maginot Line, and it looked as if we'd be next on their visiting list.

They had crossed over into France ahead of us to the north and were coming round behind us to go for Cambria and St Quentin to the south. The rumour was that most of their Panzers had pressed on to Sedan, sweeping all things French before them, which was bad news for the French but for us, holed up outside the Forêt des Raismes at Valenciennes, it meant the only opposition at the moment might be stray probing units and the odd sniper picking his lone way through the woods. Bad enough because these odds and sods can be niggling bits of enemy, but at least there was no major force bearing down on us, so the panic to get back down through the forest had probably been misguided, but then everything was that spring – chaos and pandemonium was giving a new meaning to Sundays.

Sombre Dimanche …
Funny how Rip had chosen that song, not knowing what it meant:
Miserable Sunday …

> *les bras tout chargés de fleurs*
> *Je suis entré dans notre chambre le coeur las* …

> *My arms laden with flowers*
> *I entered your room with a heavy heart* …

because 'flowers was the very thing that got to me in the end.'

When all the ritual ceremony at church and graveside was over it was Rip's job to go around sorting out the flowers, unloading and unwrapping them, because most were in some sort of waterproof covering like cellophane. 'One thing they never skimped on was flowers. The box, yes, often, but never the flowers.' They used to arrive at the parlour in their van loads and there were always piles waiting in the church and a lot more up at the graveyard, so he never knew how many he was going to have to deal with 'until the last trump'.

The greatest obsession was that they had to look pristine fresh and the mourners ensured that by watering them right up until the last call, so that the flowers retained a lot of water in the packets and were always dripping when Rip unwrapped them. No one would be seen dead delivering unfresh flowers to a funeral and the ones waiting at the church and graveside were always being given last minute dowsings to keep up appearances. And it was all a part of the heavy ritual that they had to be laid out for inspection, so that the guests could file past and admire them and make muffled remarks about each other's contributions. Rip had to carry them in and out and lay them down for inspection and unwrap them and gather them up again and place them by the graveside. They were always soggy or plain wet and they dampened his sleeves and spirits more than any of the heavy wailing that went on. And the whole operation from 'primary parlour to terminal parting' meant that he was coming home after each booking soaked to the skin and in danger of 'catching my death of cold'.

Once he had been the life and soul of each funeral party but it got that he couldn't express his natural joy in the confines of that Penge parlour anymore so he started to look for another outlet. Then the War came.

'All in all it was a good reason to get out and kill two birds with one gravestone, so to speak.'

> Je suis resté tout seul et j'ai pleuré tout bas
> En écountant hurler la plainte des frimas …

he sang, like a swan song to his parlour:

> I was left all alone
> Crying softly,
> Listening to the room full of silent echoes …

When Rip suggested he make a mad dash back to collect the Two Pees the military instinct was to say good luck to them, they'd either bought it already or would be prisoners soon enough anyway, but it wasn't so mad as it sounded because there was a fair chance he would make it.

'Well,' said the Sergeant, gazing around his ragged, sweaty unit, and then up and around the skies as if the attitude of the scurrying clouds might give him some clue to Jerry's progress, 'might have to forget it.' Then, indicating the road out of the forest, he added: 'Getting more cluttered and clogged by the metre with them refugees, and now all them bleeding French wandering around without aim nor discipline. Huh.'

'Never driven in an emergency in my life before, Sarge,' said Rip, who was desperate to prove himself, 'cos there's never an emergency at a funeral, see, because by then it's all over, but I could do that trip in an hour or so.'

'With all clutter! Doubt it.'

'Just try me, Sarge!' Rip insisted, rubbing his hands eagerly.

'Anyway,' said the Sarge, consolingly, 'shouldn't worry about them Two Pees over much. They'll probably be alright if the Jerries get them. They know the rules, these bastards. That's what I hate about them. Don't know about them bleeding Nazis, mind, but this guy Rommel knows, being one of the old brigade.'

And he wandered off, mumbling about the transport scroungers of the world, to take stock of what was left for him to win the war with.

Thinking he might still be in with a chance, Rip sits himself down with a fag and his secret flask of port and has a quiet, contented sing to himself, because this is the open air adventure bit he'd come for, little suspecting that what he's singing is not *that* far away from the purgatory of Penge parlours:

> *Alors tu reviendras, mais je serai parti,*
> *Des cierges brûleront comme un ardent espoir*
>
> Then you will return but I shall be gone,
> Leaving candles burning in fervent hope …

There was no holding this new Major General Erwin Rommel with his 7th Panzers. Holland and Belgium apart, mere milestones on the way rather than obstacles, the French Army was more or less collapsing under his very gaze. And he hadn't even bothered to break into his boxes of reserves yet. His Panzer success at Sedan rocked the French to their garlic roots and they were withdrawing all over the place. The roads of Belgium and northern France were choking with their bewildered troops as well as armies of refugees. The only hope was that he might be so surprised by his success or the lack of opposition that he would make mistakes.

The main German attack was now expected to come at Menin but that was a bit north of us, and as Sedan was a bit south of us, our particular neck of the forest wasn't in any immediate danger.

The rumour was that *we* were planning a counter-attack against the Panzers and the SS *Totenkopf* motorized divisions near Arras, hoping to give Rommel a good run for his geld, but it all looked a bit too late and forlorn that *sombre Dimanche*.

Rip sat humming '*Sombre Dimanche*' to himself. 'Chance of a lifetime,' he said, anticipating his courageous dash through the forest. 'Especially with me being in death all my life.'

Rip came from a long line of undertakers. 'Born into the trade. It's in my bones, see. Our pedigree goes a long way back. My old dad says he can trace it through a thousand years of graveyards and that his old dad, who died at ninety-eight, had been a living witness to the family achievement.'

'I appreciate you've had a new lease of life or death since joining the army, Van,' the Sarge said shortly after he joined the unit and was still spreading his enthusiasm, 'but I'd welcome a bit more restraint, because it tends to affect some of my more sensitive charges. After all, we may not be fighting in a graveyard but there's always the *suspicion* – no more than that, mind – that there's one just around the next corner.'

'Understood, Sarge, no offence intended.'

'I should concentrate on that Jean Sablon voice of yours, if I were you. It's got the right lilt of the lament, if you ask me.'

But it's difficult to break old habits, and when we pulled up at Valenciennes the talk was all about the eerie effect of this new kraut whizz kid called Rommel. Nobody knew anything about him, of course, except the Sarge, who said he'd done his apprenticeship in the First War and therefore was pukka. But when the name was first mentioned, we all had this strange feeling as if it rang bells, echoing and warning, as if it had been around us all our days.

'Haunting us, like,' said Rip, putting his finger on it in his own way. 'Like you've got it in your bones. Like it's been engraved on your heart. The same feeling like when someone walks over your grave, except that kind of thing never usually affects me cos it's me what's usually doing the walking, see?'

'Think you should tone it down a bit now,' said the Sarge, who had wandered back. 'Some of the lads are not quite able to see it in your terms, see.' And, glancing at the grey skies, he added: 'Might be the heat, of course – or the bully beef.'

'I can't help it, Sarge,' said Rip. 'Swear. Over my dead body. Same in any trade. You get that the language of the business haunts you. Whoops! And you keep using expressions like deathtrap, and dead loss, and die-hard, and ghost of a chance, and old haunts and stiff upper lip, and grave warning – know what I mean?'

The Sarge paused for a moment, then said: 'Maybe you ought to get going, Van.'

Rip was on his feet in a flash.

'And fond remembrances to Partridge and Preston.'

Grabbing his 'decanter' of port and leaping into his little truck, Rip revs up as we're shouting our condolences:

'Stiff upper lip, mind!'

'Watch out for the Panzers. Rommel calls them his Ghost Division!'

*

The French Army's retreating from the Scheldt, cutting
through British and Belgian lines and causing chaos.
We're pulling back with the Belgians along a fifty-mile
front, and refugees are swarming like locusts, but Rip's
got his mission of a lifetime.

He's off, roaring back through the forest along the
road seething with troops, trucks, vans, cars, carts,
bicycles. And refugees: hapless, forlorn columns of the
discarded pitiful, looking like animated prints out of an
old schoolbook. Rip told Partridge he had a touch of
nostalgia on the way up because they looked exactly
like the miserable lot he'd escaped from in Penge. They
became his image of war: 'Pilgrims passing in the night
of history', he told Partridge on the way back, and was
dead chuffed with the notion.

All the way there and back he sang his mournful
French song, '*Sombre Dimanche*' – which he couldn't let
go of.

> *Et j'ai chanté des mots d'amour et de douleur.*
>
> *And I have sung words of love and sadness.*

'It just keeps on in my brain, drumming, insisting,
know what I mean?'

> *Je suis resté tout seul et j'ai pleuré tout bas …*
>
> *I am all alone and have cried softly …*

Actually '*Sombre Dimanche*' wasn't French but
Hungarian, and Gypsy at that. It had that plaintive,
vagabond wail sound of the eternally forgotten who live
on top of mountains, meditating on misery, which you
usually associate with distant peoples and certainly not
with what's fashionable down in Penge. That's
probably what got to Rip – the sheer otherworldliness of
it.

He kept repeating it – in French, or what might have
been French once, over and over, again and again, 'to

memorise it', he claimed, although it got on all our
wicks – 'like candles in your bleeding morgue, Rip' –
and that was the sole reason no one volunteered to go
back with him: 'not panic of the Panzers, mate, but
dread of the dirge.'

Je mourrai un Dimanche ou j'aurai trop souffert …

I shall die one Sunday when I have suffered too much …

'Do me a favour!'
And it was a Sunday too, which only added to the
pain. Whatever the state of war or peace, a Sunday is a
Sunday anywhere on earth and feels like it. So if you
put Sunday together with the '*Sombre Dimanche*' Sunday
and stick it in the middle of a falling France in May 1940
with Germans wandering all over the place and streams
of refugees wailing and moaning along the highways
and byways, you've got yourself a sombre Sunday
alright – drab, dreary, dull and desolate too. 'Gloomy'
was the English translation – solemn, sober, sad and
sorry too.
And the last thing you want to share it with is
someone who's into the miseries, even if he *does* think
the sounds are wonderful and doesn't know the
sentiments are straight out of the Book of Condolences.

Rip drove at breakneck speed, negotiating the traffic
and refugees, and reached the spot only to find that
Partridge was wounded and Preston gone – kaput – and
instead there's a German sniper lying beside them,
unconscious from Preston's bullets. And as Rip lifts
Partridge into the wagon, the German opens his eyes
and looks up at him, sorrowful like, and mumbles his
name over and over like he's reporting to the Sergeant –
'Pfeiffer, Pfeiffer, Pfeiffer'. So, being the sentimental
kind of Penge undertaker's nipper newt who's seen his
unfair share of grief in his time, Rip hasn't the heart to

leave the kraut behind in case he conks it before his own mob catch up. Besides, with Preston gone, the double act of the Two Pees is looking a bit diminished, and a Pfeiffer might fill the vacancy nicely, if not purely.

So Rip picks them both up and dumps them side by side in the truck like they used to do in his dad's special old Big Rolls – the old 'double decker' which was broad enough to do a double funeral (you could just squeeze two in and they'd done it a couple of times): 'So impressive that the streets of Penge paused while we came through, though probably more out of respect for the Rolls than the Dead.'

He didn't think the Two Pees would last the trip anyway but thought he'd have a go, since the double looked appropriate, linguistically and funereally. To keep them alive but quiet he gave the pair of them a double slug from his 'decanter' of port – admittedly a tea flask 'doubling for the duration, but you have to keep your standards up'.

' "Jack the Nipper", they used to call me,' he told Partridge to keep his spirits up, 'because as a youngster I had to nip round with the port and try to cheer them mourners up with a few jokes. In them days the undertaker's offspring did the pouring of the port and were known as "newts", see, on account of how we used to weave and wiggle in and out of the guests with our decanters. And of course we used to knock back a few ourselves as we nipped about during the celebrations, and that's what "pissed as a newt" means, straight up!'

He couldn't drive back fast because of his cargo and in any case he thought it better to hide himself in the column of refugees – and the only way to do that was to invite some aboard, which slowed him down even more, so that he was soon back to his funeral pace once again. It must have been the slowest drive he ever did and yet the only time he'd ever driven slow and been in a hurry.

And all the while he kept humming his sombre Sunday song.

'*Sombre Dimanche*' hit the right note for that Sunday or any Sunday: desperation, defeat, despair, wet – all the characteristics of any funeral parlour on Sunday in Penge. It actually revived Partridge because he recognised the tune! Turned out he'd picked it up in a café in Pompey while waiting for embarkation. Some sailors had been singing it, wherever they got it from, (but then you never asked sailors where they got anything from), and they had called it 'Gloomy Sunday' and 'Bloody Sunday' and 'Sodding Sunday' and various words to that effect and they sang it whenever they were four sheets to the wind, which was every noon and night. Partridge had had lots of opportunities to learn it and now the tune awoke him and convinced him to stay awake and overcome the temptation to let go and just drift as he had been doing when Rip turned up.

Je mourrai un Dimanche où j'aurai trop souffert …

I shall die one sad Sunday … Can't take no more of this pain …

And Rip picks up more refugees because, philanthropy apart, he thinks they'll do well as camouflage. So they climb on the canvas top and sit on the roof and cling to the sides and stand up on the flap boards and the bonnet too, clinging on and draping the truck with themselves and their bundles so you can't distinguish it from a farmer's hay cart.

Then – lo and behold! – not long after they get moving, this bloody kraut wakes up and starts singing '*Sombre Dimanche*' in German: '*Einsamer Sonntag*'!

Hielt in her Hand … einen duftenden Rosenstrauss

Holding in my hand … a bunch of roses

And *he* revives too! Comes round and finds the struggle to stay alive has a better chance if he just keeps at the singing because it takes his mind off the wounds and the bumpy ride.

Then the refugees pick up the tune and join in the singsong and in this way the wandering choir wends its way back to Valenciennes, through a long line of stray soldiers and demented refugees and dark wood, a twenty-kilometre chorus of '*Sombre Dimanche*', '*Gloomy Sunday*' and '*Einsamer Sonntag*'.

> *Erst da die Sterne verblichen*
>
> *And before the stars fade away*
>
> *Trat ich ins Haus …*
>
> *I wander back indoors …*

And they attract so much attention by singing to keep their spirits up that they start to pick up a few stray snipers as well, and three of the shots hit Rip so he drives even slower but sings even louder to keep the others in the back believing he's OK. 'Must have been the only time he had ever sung in a hearse before even if the song *was* a dreadful dirge':

> *Des cierges brûleront comme un ardent espoir …*
>
> *Candles burning bright as brightest hope …*
>
> *Du hast mir nur Kummer und Schmerz gebracht …*
>
> *You have brought me only pain and suffering …*

> *Sombre Dimanche … Sombre Dimanche … Sombre Dimanche …*

Rip had done well enough but his luck had to run out. As long as he was in the middle of the long line with wagons and bikes and loads of this and that and horses and the odd tractor, you wouldn't notice the little truck camouflaged in refugees. But, as Rip observed to

Partridge above the racket: 'the singing's a dead giveaway'.

During the final part of the journey one of the refugees crams up beside him and takes over the wheel, holding and guiding it while Rip works the throttle and pedals and keeps on singing and getting more and more drowsy by the metre, dozing off and keeping his feet working out of pure instinct. And that way, and to that chorus, they come right back into the ditch at Valenciennes from where he left off in the morning. But by then there's not much left of Rip apart from the voice.

When they arrive the refugee pulls on the brakes and Rip slumps forward like Jimmy Cagney in a gangster movie. Of course, all the women and kids leap out screaming and shouting cos they'd made it to safety, as they thought, and we forgot all about Rip for a spell until we got them calmed down and settled and lifted out Partridge and Pfeiffer who are still chanting 'Miserable Sunday' and '*Einsamer Sonntag*' like an old run-down double act of *The Two Pees*. Then we went back to find Rip.

'Well,' said the Sarge, studying him slumped over the wheel, 'he certainly kept up the family tradition to the end, didn't he? His old dad back in Penge will be doubly proud of him.'

FREAK PEAN

Dunkirk, June 1940

And at the time of their sorest trial, when the enemy hosts were upon them, there arose from amongst them a youth in shining pack gear, iron clad, ghostly pale and dapple-pimpled, whose hour had come …

Four

Freak Pean plodded slowly back up the beach at
Dunkirk with his eyes fixed on the wet sand and the
roars of the crowd ringing in his young ears, drowning
out the wrath of planes and gunfire.

'C'mon Peak! Attaboy Peak! Show 'em Peak! Good
old Peak!'

The cries from the boat thundered around his head
like the stands erupting at the Oval, if they could ever
permit such a breach of good form.

But when their hero tramped passed Long Off and
still showed no sign of turning, the Sarge got a bit edgy
and stretched up in the prow to bellow out over the
sodden dunes:

'That's far enough now, Pean! Chuck it, will you!'

But Freak was in his own world now.

'I'll have you in bloody jankers when we get back!'

There didn't seem much hope for the BEF or what was
left of it on the beaches that day. Not that we knew
much about the overall picture, of course, or anything at
all in fact, but we could see for ourselves. They never
tell blokes like us anything relevant at the best of times,
and with the shambles that littered the Dunkirk beaches
that June afternoon there wasn't a hope of getting any
plan or forecast from anyone. But what we did know,
because we'd been through it ourselves, was that Jerry
had hounded us across France for months, from as far

south as the Maginot Line and up through Belgium and
Flanders, until he'd hemmed us in on the Channel
coast, stuck on a beach only seventy miles from Dover
so we could almost see the cliffs, but with this nasty bit
of water to negotiate first.

Along to the west, Calais was still supposed to be 'in
our hands', as they say, so all we could do was hope
that von Runstedt might keep his armoured mob
occupied there instead and leave us time to get down to
the business of scratching around to find enough boats
and rafts and things to get us off and away.

The trouble is we're trying to hold a thirty-mile
stretch of coastline and get the blokes moved out at the
same time. They must have got a couple of hundred
thousand clear by the time we arrived and when we
looked out over the dune tops to see the hordes
swarming over the beaches as far as the eye could see
and a bit beyond, we reckoned there must have been as
many again still waiting to go.

'Looks like an awful lot of boats to find, Sarge.'

'And an awful lot for Old Gort to organise.'

'*And* the Navy.'

'Still,' said the corporal profoundly, surveying the
frenetic scene and applying his strategic mind to its
analysis, 'miracles do happen, you know.'

The following afternoon we're all jam-packed like
sardines in our little pleasure boat waiting for Freak and
the day-trip to start. It's wet. Well, drizzle really. The
kind of day you always land when it's your turn for the
Skylark.

'And you'll notice the ice-cream wallah's done a
bunk.'

'Can you blame him? Bit parky for June.'

Whatever Gort and Co are doing with their little maps
and pointers and not bothering to tell us about, we've
got a pretty clear idea what's happening at our end of

the beach. We're up to our necks in sleet and sand for a start. We've been there since the morning of the day before, hanging about, miserable as sin, waiting for a lift back home. Been a long trek along the beach too, so there's not a lot of laughs.

Then late in the afternoon a couple of boats are detailed for us. Small. Nothing elegant. 'One-class accommodation only, I'm afraid,' the Sarge apologises.

'I was going to say,' says a depressed gunner assessing his maritime prospects.

'It's more the principle, really,' agrees his mate.

So we debate a bit then decide to give it a whirl rather than wait for the sun and the luxury cruiser the Sarge's been promising us since Valenciennes.

'Well,' says the Sarge long-sufferingly, 'it doesn't look much like clearing up, if you ask me. Besides,' he says, heaving himself aboard, 'I hear old Alan Brooke's been chatting with our Corp. Says nothing short of a miracle's going to save us now.'

'Proper little miracle just getting us here, Sarge!'

'Creeping'll get you nowhere, Colthorpe. Just get your arse aboard if you're coming.'

So we clamber in but now we're stuck in the mud and sand and shingle near the water's edge and are going to need one helluva great heave to get us off the bed and moving at all.

'Well, what do you know,' says the Sarge, watching us struggle aboard while he directs operations from the sharp end.

And we all look towards the last man trying to squeeze in. Freak, of course. Has to be.

'C'mon, Pean,' shouts the Sarge, 'don't bother settling down. Out and heave, me lad!'

Stuck there huddled together and stranded in the sand and shingle, it doesn't look as if there's anything left in us to organise even one more thing for ourselves, but if Freak Pean *can* get his arse into gear then we just might have ourselves our own little miracle.

Pean was his name – Reginald Arthur Pean. R.A.P. for
short. 'Marked from birth,' he muttered. Reginald
Arthur's observations were always muttered, as if he
was never close by you when he spoke but always
somewhere over there. 'Taken the rap ever since I
arrived,' he mumbled. And he didn't mean in France.

But the R.A.P. had nothing to do with us. That was
nature's quirk – or his mum's. We made our own
assessment, and choice. We never used the name
anyone was christened with, the ones mums and dads
had struggled so desperately to give. You could tell a lot
about a bloke's old folks from the name they chose for
him. But you couldn't tell a lot about the man himself.
You had to watch and sum him up in your own way.
Everyone got a new name to relate him to us, not to
anonymous mums or dads. They were someone else's
past. No future in that.

So we called Pean 'Freak', after Freak Pean, on
account of he always took the biscuit as well as the rap.
'Freak' was a bit cheap, really, not much flair in the
choice. But then that was Freak, really, and the name
just seemed to fit. Pays to go with the obvious
sometimes.

He was a shy lad, maybe because he was so young.
Or looked it. Fish and chip complexion, runny nose,
acne. The kind of bloke who's always hanging about,
humphing, shuffling, and you never know what to do
with. The kind of bloke you always field at Long, *very*
Long, Off. Must have spent a lot of his school years
down there, brooding, waiting for his chance to bowl,
dreaming of a hat-trick, hoping for the call from his
captain. But the only time he ever got called up for
anything was for active service and even then he was
still the Long Off type, deep, distant and dour,
wondering when his turn would come, if ever.

'I had a sister like that,' said Con unhelpfully. 'She played the bassoon, only the school orchestra never chose pieces for the bassoon, so she spent all her time turning the pages for the pianist instead.'

Anyway, the Sarge has got himself installed up at the sharp end nearest Dover – 'someone's got to watch where we're going' – and he shouts out 'last man in gives the push off!' And the last man's got to be Freak on account of the time it takes him to climb in with all the gear he carries and will never let go of, more than the rest of us put together.

'Pean needs his gear,' the Sarge had defended him on many occasions. 'Comforts him. Not like the rest of you lot – thick, insensitive.'

And with all that gear on, it's going to take Freak even longer to climb out again. But Freak just shrugs as if it's no more than he expects anyway, and wrestles himself out, gear and all.

First thing he does once he's out is bend down and peer into the water to examine the boat underneath, rubbing his chin and pursing his lips like a plumber estimating the extent of a leak under the bath and the possibility of it being beyond anyone's capacity to repair, except maybe his. It looks real bad but he might just be able to manage it if he really pulls out all the stops – in a manner of speaking. By which time he thinks he's convinced you he's the only one to do it and save the situation.

Freak rises from his haunches and moves to the water's edge, only a few yards, and stops to assess the lie of the land or the truth of the sea from there. But not to come at us and deliver the big heave yet – just to look. He stares hard at us, plopping and flopping, stranded and helpless, until the Sarge gets slightly narked and shouts: 'Come on, man! It's a boat and we're stuck, see. So get a bloody move on!'

'We got to make it before closing time, Freak,' says the Corp., taking the sting off.

Freak brooded – and not just *at* Long Off, *about* it. Brooded about being down there in the first place, it being his natural station in the field and life. And he brooded about when the call might come to pull him back from his distant broodings to come up to the centre of things and take his turn to bowl – and perform.

'I'm thinking there's more to this cricket lark than first meets the eye,' said Signals, watching Freak practise in a field near Sedan one tea break. Freak used to practise with stones and lumps of hard clay, anything that would give him a bit of exercise, but mostly dummy hand grenades.

That observation set him off.

'Oh, yeah,' he lit up and left his brown study immediately. 'Got to get the bodyline right. Head steady. Eyes fixed. Line of approach worked out. Got to get distance estimated to the inch. Paced clear to the blade – grass that is, not bat. But that too.' His mutter suddenly faded away. 'And stump. And umpire's hat rim. Got to get them all in your picture, see!'

'I'm beginning …'

'They're all marks on the way, spots on the design.' Freak blossomed into eloquence. 'Everything's got to be taken into account, see, composed to fit them in precisely. Otherwise the whole perspective goes for a Burton and the composition screws up and you might as well be delivering the bloody milk!'

'Ah, I see …'

But we never assessed Freak's pace. When he practised in those French ditches and fields he seemed to be trying all sorts of variations from fast to medium to slow left hand over and round. And as he never got a chance to perform anyway and we never got a chance to select and assess, we settled for him being a reasonable all-rounder, although neither life nor Lord's had ever given him the chance to prove it.

And Freak was always prepared.

'Never catch old Freak off his guard.'

'Lot of the Boy Scout in him, I reckon.'

'Baden-Powell would be proud.'

And always immaculate. Carted the lot with him. Even on that beach when we couldn't get down to the boats fast enough and we were only too glad to drop the last stitch if it hindered us. But not Freak. He brought the lot.

Freak keeps staring at the bottom of the boat, appraising the bulk and the balance, then turning to stare back up the beach. And then back at us again, to-ing and fro-ing as if weighing us against some distant object that only he could see. He does this turning back and forward a number of times, squinting his eyes as if to get a sharper picture because there's precious little sun around. Then very carefully he takes off a bit of his enormous pack and sets it down a yard from the water's edge, squats down and lines it up between him and our boat, gives the pair a few knowledgeable squints, moves it once or twice an inch or two, satisfies himself it's in the right position, then sets off at a trot back up the beach, leaving even the Sarge speechless. But this time we hear that his usual quiet mutter has turned into a moan, as if he's grouching like hell and cursing his bleeding luck.

Very OOC that was – Out Of Character – for Freak. Not at all like the meek Freak we knew. He always acted as if he knew all along life was going to be like that – resigned, like. Never tried to stop it. Just walked straight into it every time, philosophical like. Except this time. Now it seems he's letting it all come out, as if he's been stoking it up since his first pimple. We could hear him fuming above the racket of guns and planes and bombs.

And we were struck dumb, not just because of the

plight we were in but because of the whole damned shambles – beach, battalion, boat, bombs, balls-up, botchers ... Struck dumb and numb.

We didn't know so much about each other in those early days. Our minds were not yet on the business of war. We didn't know much about what was going on, of course, and maybe didn't bother much either, because we had other things to think and worry about, like home and jobs. It was as if, despite the last six months and Jerry chasing us out of France and Belgium, the war hadn't really got started yet, or we hadn't got started into it. Not like Jerry: he was well into the swing of it by Dunkirk, while we seemed still to be busking it, giving it a whirl, not playing at it but not taking it too seriously either, not applying ourselves. We hadn't really tuned in to *any* war yet, let alone a long one.

We were still thinking civvy street. Still thinking home fires and wage packets and cricket scores. So anybody's strange behaviour didn't bother us too much because it wouldn't last long enough to affect us or have any impact on what we were supposed to be doing. Freaks were freaks and cranks cranks and botchers botchers wherever you went, nothing to do with war. Human nature might move in mysterious ways, but we knew that long before Dunkirk and never thought it had any particular application to war or in war, and we weren't in any frame of mind to bother about it because it didn't concern us. We still lived at home. The Freak Peans didn't offer much either. Quirksome, oddballs, cards, that sort of thing. But not much else. Their quaintness related elsewhere, to the places they still lived in and kept pretty anonymous and mum about.

That day out at Dunkirk was a kind of turning point. We'd be home soon, if Freak got his arse into gear, except that we weren't going *home*, only to another phase of this thing called war we'd become stuck with.

*

Freak's heaped up like an old carthorse, so it's a slow business. We look at each other anxious like because, with all that unnatural cursing and blinding, we figure something's not quite right. But we need Freak, or we need the push, so there's nothing for it but to sit tight and shiver. We're past praying after we've seen the Padre flat out in the next boat quivering like Christmas jelly.

Freak plods on and on, getting smaller and smaller in the distance despite his Great British Burden, and by the look of his great heaving body he's still fuming. We get more and more uneasy, but decide that maybe he's just getting himself worked up for the attack, as fast bowlers often do.

Then: 'Don't worry, lads,' says the Sarge unconvincingly. 'He won't let us down.'

Gives a funny feeling, that comment. All our anxieties cool. We're actually stuck there stranded in the middle of a war, desperate to get away, and yet we've become completely absorbed in the antics of this unknown guy we call Freak.

Nobody else thinks of getting out and shoving, not even the Sarge. It's Freak's job and we have to let him finish it. But as well as being concerned about our own plight we're now obsessed with how he's going to do it. As if the joke about Freak has moved.

There's not a lot else we can do about it except abandon Freak and volunteer someone else to get out and shove us off but, although Jerry's around and quite busy and time's getting on, it never occurs to us. But now it's occurring to us that it never occurs to us.

By now we're all getting edgy and just in case something's gone horribly wrong, the Sarge heaves himself up, almost capsizing us, and shouts out: 'C'mon, Pean, that's far enough. Try it from there!' And the rest of us get the idea and roar our encouragement: 'C'mon Freak, move your arse! It's bloody freezing down here!'

But Freak goes on and on as if he's bound for the pavilion. He keeps looking back as if to judge the distance and lie of the land like any good fast bowler, thinking, worrying, sticking a finger up to the breeze, fixing his eyes down on the beach at his feet, taking in the whole field, devising, or maybe just making sure we're still there and haven't nipped off when his back's been turned.

'What d'you know,' someone breathes for all of us. 'Finally gets his big chance, then blows it and walks back to the pavilion!'

'And after all them years waiting out in the wings.'

'Brooding down on the boundary.'

At last the Sarge stands up again, nearly tipping us into the drink this time, and bellows out: 'Pean! You're keeping us bloody waiting, man!' More appeal than anger in the tone. 'I could have you in bloody jankers when we get back, you know!'

That did it. Just as we're convinced Freak's taken the huff and the years have taken their toll and he's off to give himself up to Jerry and get it over and done with, all that waiting and hoping and fretting and brooding finished, he stops dead, right on the command 'jankers', and turns around. Miles away, he is.

We can see him peer down at us with his hands cupped around his eyes like a pair of binoculars.

'Measuring it up, Sarge.'

'The distance?'

'Yeah.'

'Or us.'

'Maybe he's doing a running commentary from the pavilion.'

Everything's gone dead quiet. Freak has abandoned us. We're stuck in the Dunkirk mud like a tortoise on its back. Even Jerry stops bombing to watch.

We're waiting for Freak to shout back something of his own – back to us, back to the Sarge, back to the world, about all those lonesome years being a nobody under the pimples and the acne at Long, *very* Long, Off. You could have heard a grenade-pin drop on that beach.

Then he lowers his hands from his eyes to his chin, pulls off his helmet and sets it down, measuring again. One last look at the whole scene and he turns and walks back another ten yards and swings around violently, and stands there stock-still.

Then, slowly, ever so slowly, he begins to swing his bowler's arm. Round and round it goes, very slow at first then quickening. Over his head and back it weaves, gathering speed in the gathering sea breeze like a windmill's sail. Then he bends forward, crouches, and digs his boots into the sand like an impatient racehorse dredging out his starting blocks. Then up he comes and sets off on his run.

We're still struck dumb. Can't believe anything now. He trots up to his helmet and then at the second he reaches it, his whole frame straightens up and changes its appearance as it launches itself forward into a run.

Unbelievable. This tiny plump figure in the distance carrying half the platoon's gear, pasty face glowing against the khaki, suddenly changes into another being, tall, powerful, athletic, all trace of his previous incarnation gone, coming thundering down towards us, gathering momentum with every stride.

He hasn't taken the huff. He hasn't deserted us. He's not on his way back to the pavilion. He's right here, or there, Great Scout that he is, coming pounding down to save us, determined to do his duty and keep his appointment with destiny.

He's got it all worked out down to the angle and the wind and the distance and the time, and he's moving on a curve from his starter mark so that he'll make the stern wicket at maximum speed and power.

'Larwood!' shouts Tarzan. 'Bodyline. That's what it is.

It's bloody Harold. I should know. I seen him enough at Trent Bridge.'

We knew then what those Aussie batsmen must have felt when they looked up from the crease and saw Larwood turn to start off on his run.

'Good Old Freak! Good Old Freak!' An almighty great roar of encouragement breaks the Dunkirk calm. 'Attaboy, Pean!' Like the stand erupting at the Oval.

And Freak charges on down into history, maybe not to a hat-trick, but sure as Larwood to a wicket with his first Test delivery. On and on he comes, hands crossed over as if clutching the precious leather to his guts, working up perfect steam, giving it his all. And careers straight into our arse-end. He's got enough padding on him to take the blow and give him the purchase and deliver us the most almighty heave out into the Channel that leaves all the other boats lined up alongside us standing and stranded and struggling with the ragged regiments of old England staring agog at this amazing performance. And the power of Freak's inspired heave means we're nearly half-way back to Blighty from his single match-winning delivery.

Course, old Freak himself goes arse over tit into the drink, doesn't he? And with all that bleeding equipment on, he hasn't got an earthly. Last we see of him as we career off to the old White Cliffs is his poor old sodden arse bobbing up and down in the Channel like a retired marker buoy.

MATT LOWE

Biscay, October 1940

And they went down to the seas in stout ships hewn of oak, and a wild tempest roared, and the oceans opened up and he beheld the three badge denizens lurking in the deep …

Five

'Chitties for brooms!' he screams at us. 'That's what he said: "Chitties for brooms!" '

And he leapt to his feet, wrenching his mad eyes away from us, and tore across the deck like a buffalo gone berserk. And the last we saw or heard of him was the seas arching over the stern and wiping away the figure into the mists of the Biscay, and engulfing the dying howl of 'Chitties for brooms! Chitties for brooms! Chitties for brooms!'

Gave me the creeps, the Navy did.

'Another breed,' said Matt. 'Another bleeding breed, mate. Mark my words.'

We're bound for the sea and the sun and the sand of the Med. Behind us there's Dunkirk and the Blitz and all that austerity stuff that's worse than war, and the winter setting in too. Glad to get away for a spell of unseasonal sunshine.

Thousands of men are sardine-packed into a luxury liner doubling as a troopship to Alexandria. Full pack: kitbag, uniform, helmet, groundsheet, gas mask, water bottle, rifle, 'and anything else that you think might come in handy in a wadi, lads.' They're jammed in so tight the commanders have to detail one squad to sail with a pukka Navy escort vessel instead. Us, of course.

'You'll be sharing with the Marines, lads,' says the Sarge. 'Fine bunch of men.' Which meant bad blood for two and a half days until the Biscay Blight strikes and then everyone's in it. 'Great little leveller, seasickness,' says a Marine airily. 'Rolling democracy,' says Matt warily.

He was right. First time we ever set eyes on proper sailors, we could tell. We could *feel*. 'Another breed, I tell you,' he said, shivering on the quay at Pompey, staring up at the line of matelots staring back down at us. 'Mark my words,' he said again, softly this time, very softly, through clenched teeth, as if his words might actually penetrate the dockyard din and reach the ears of the sailors above. 'Another bleeding breed, they are.'

'Move it along, there! Keep it moving!' The order rang out against the rigging of HMS *Victory* and twanged back down over the Solent as it passed the time while awaiting the next unsuspecting bunch of landlubbers. Matt shivered, keeping his eyes fixed on his boots, and whispered: 'I tell you, nothing good can come of this mix-up, mate. Fate. That's what it is, mate – Fate.'

Hanging over the guardrail, staring down at us lined up on the quay below, mists swirling about their beady eyes to collaborate with the slow clouds of tobacco smoke from their duty frees were the hearts of oak of old wives' tales and the jolly tars of new wives' fears. Even their fags had thick blue lines painted down the length of them to show they were Navy issue. Definitely Senior Service. Definitely another breed.

Two and a half days out from Southampton and it's a proper old Biscay brew-up. And when the Biscay Blight strikes, everyone suffers. Not just squaddies. Jacks and all. Hanging over the rails, squirming on the decks, heaving in the hammocks. Retching, coughing, spitting, choking, moaning, groaning. Offering up everything from breakfasts to prayers.

The roughest number, seasickness. Definitively democratic. Takes away the mind. A man'll do anything to get free. Talk about psychological warfare and brainwashing and scaring the arse off blokes with threats of rats and snakes and sacks and blindfolds and mock executions. Waste of time. Put any man in a boat and shake it about a bit and you've got a looney for life. Lick your boots to get away, he will. Admit anything. Sign anything. Confess anything. Free a man from seasickness and you've got yourself a slave for eternity.

Matt knew. He'd served in the Andrew* before the war: 'Seven years before the blast' – the blast of wind and the blast of man. The wrath of the waves against the jockeys who dare to ride them, and the wrath of the matelots against the landlubbers who dare to know the unknown.

And then Matt's dad died, leaving his mum with five kids, and he'd been released on compassionate grounds. 'The Authorities, that is,' he said, 'not the Navy. *They* never release anyone.'

His ship happened to be in dry dock for a refit at the time. 'Otherwise, I wouldn't have made it. If we'd been at sea, they'd have kept me there forever, gone spinning around the ocean into eternity rather than dock and give me up. Anything not to let you go. The Navy *never* lets you go, you know. Breed of their bleeding own.'

When the news came we were sailing with the true blue Navy, the Royal one, and not the wavy merchant type, Matt flipped.

'Troopship's packed to the gunwales, lads,' the Sarge announced. 'So the Navy's kindly offered to give some of us a lift instead.' And he cut off a dozen of us with one sweep of his arm – including Matt. That's when he broke.

'Not the *real* Andrew, Sarge?' he pleaded. 'We're not sailing with the *real* Navy, are we?'

'Yep, my boy. The Real Nelson. The True Trafalgar.

* Naval slang for the Royal Navy

That's us for the next month. Privileged lot, we are. Special guests of the Senior Service. Sticklers for ceremony and tradition, is the Navy. Got to watch your teas and queues. Proper line-ups for the char, they have. None of this ill-disciplined charging about you lot do. They do things their way in the Navy. Matter of fact, there *is* only one way – the Navy way.' Who in his right mind would dispute that now? Sarge points to the lurking Solent and the Channel beyond, patiently knitting away its empire of waves. 'Deviate and you're done. Expecting a lot from you lot, this trip. Ambassadors, that's what you'll be. Diplomats.'

Matt was ash-pale. 'Any chance of a swap, Sarge?' he tried.

'Swap? Swap!'

'Well, someone else might appreciate the experience, that's all. Someone who hasn't already known the privileges and pleasure of the Andrew, like I have.'

'Not a chance. You've been *volunteered*, Lowe, me boy. It's already in Company Orders. Can't change it now. 'Sides, I'm relying on you to keep the others informed, in line, on the straight and narrow. Because of your deep knowledge and insight into the weird and wonderful ways of His Majesty's most senior of Services you will be a great asset, a go-between, a sort of intrepid interpreter.'

Cried his eyes out, quietly, on his own, Matt did, as if his mum had gone and died too, but when he looked up at us we could see it wasn't grief on his face. It was horror – 'plain 'orrible 'orror'.

The Andrew gets you both ways. If you're seasick, you're done for. And if you're not, you're at the end of a broom or a brush, sweeping and scrubbing, washing and wiping, painting and polishing. Big thing in the Andrew – cleaning. Furbish and burnish everything they set eyes on. Brushes, mops, cloths, brooms, dusters – they carry much more of them than ammunition. If they chucked all their supplies of polish and brasso at the U-boats they'd have cleaned up the Atlantic in a fortnight. Course they wouldn't do that – wouldn't waste their precious polish on a bleeding U-boat.

'Proper Pilate Complex, the Navy has,' said Matt. 'Do anything, them matelots: plane the lino, shave the carpets, comb the cobwebs, hone the dust.'

But of course, Matt doesn't get Biscay Belly, does he, being a sea-bred urchin himself with the salt stinging his veins and the brine smarting his spine, so he gets detailed to clean instead. Don't matter we'd been scrubbing and rubbing since the Solent, spitting and polishing for forty-eight hours, and the whole ship as sensitive as raw flesh by now.

'You there,' barks the Jaunty – a sort of RSM with the gloves off – 'fetch some brooms, there! A.28 Starboard For'ard. And at the double! Diz-mizz!'

'Takes you over, it does. Like a religion. A cult. Gets under your skin, into your bones. A kind of magic. Not black, *blue.*'

Matt had fretted from the moment the order came to embark with the Marines, but when we marched round the corner of the quay at Pompey dockyard and came face to face with that towering battleship-grey hulk, it really hit him for the first time and he almost threw up on the spot.

'They're not the same as us, matelots, you know. Believe me. They come from somewhere else. Not born of women, like. Mermaids maybe, but definitely not women.'

It got to him long before the Biscay business.

When he was called up in '39, Matt was automatically drafted to the Navy but he knew they'd never forgive him for leaving the way he did in the first place. So he made a special plea for the Army on account of him having been too long ashore and having forgotten so much that he'd be bound to let the side or the ship down. Had to have a special tribunal to judge his case.

'There was a Jaunty and his three ABs at the back of the room, see. Put the fix on me, they did. Could feel it through the back of my neck. I tried the lot, including claiming I got seasick nowadays on account of an ear infection that had unbalanced me. Didn't count.

' "Nelson got seasick," they spat. "*He* mastered it."

'Then I claimed I couldn't swim anymore on account of losing the power in my legs when I fell through ice on a pond one winter.

' "We got boats," they sneered.

'In the end it was the MO that swung it, bless his stethoscope. Said I might do more harm than good, having been wounded so violently that first time when I had to sever the connection: "wrenched so untimely from the womb of the ocean when so young", was how he put it. What a line, eh! I loved and kept it. Clinched it, of course. They let me go. The Enquiry, that is, not the Navy. The Andrew just kept silent.

'When they ordered "Dismiss!", I saluted and turned to leave the room. But I had to pass the Jaunty and his Three Gondoliers. Them navy blue eyes are boring into my brain to this day.'

'Fetch the brooms. A.28 Starboard For'ard. At the double! Diz-mizz!'

Chinese to us. But not to Matt, who's still on his feet. And you don't question in the Navy. You run – anywhere – long's you're doubling, you're alright.

Matt goes straight for the nearest gangway – staircase – and down and down and down past piles of moaning, squirming corpses. Bedlam from top deck to bilges. Down and down until the next one's Davy Jones' locker, searching for colours – green starboard, red port

– only way you can tell if you're coming or going. And bodies pitching and groaning or scrubbing and polishing.

Ship's heaving and tossing something horrible. He staggers on through the cable locker at the sharp end of the ship and into the last curve in the hull. There's a tiny bend. Sort of edge-end of the ship. The overlap. The tucked in bit. The flap you turn over and stitch back in. Nothing beyond but surf. Then there's this shape like a door in the bulkhead.

The magnet was strong on the jetty that day. We tried not to look up at the rows of matelots staring silently down at us, but it pulled.

Matt struggled to keep his head and not look up to meet again the blues of eyes he'd last met at the Tribunal, and he turned away so they wouldn't notice him. 'They've noticed alright,' he whispered. 'They always notice.'

We saw the eyes too. And he was right. Another bleeding breed. Like Red Indians, drifting sinisterly on the far horizon up there, taking a cool shufti at the wagon train of pasty-faced greenhorns in the valley below. And tattoos running all up and down their arms and hands and poking out from underneath their beards, like war paint.

They came at us out of the mist like a ghost ship swaying inshore for a quiet look-see before dropping back into the Mystery again. Didn't seem to belong to anywhere. Except the Ocean, maybe. No strings. No dependents. No obligations. No allegiance. Except to themselves and their own far country somewhere back out there.

You could tell it in their eyes. Screwed tight after half a lifetime staring into the mists to sight the land they didn't want to see anyway. And blue green, they were, same as the water they sailed on, after spending the

other half of that lifetime peering down into it to
unravel its secret. But never finding anything, only their
own souls reflected back. Reckon that's what gave them
their detachment, their silence, and their peace. It was
peace alright – never heard a voice raised on board. As if
they were permanently stunned. As if all they'd ever
had reflected back was what we saw coming up that
gangway. That's one helluva life sentence.

As we humped up that creaking ladder, nausea
drifted towards us like a mist. No idea what they were
thinking, or putting out. Curiosity? Contempt? Pity?
Their expressions said nowt. And it wasn't the swaying,
the slurping of the water below, or the fear of what lay
ahead. It was something these geysers gave off. A cross
between Cherokee and Vulture. They *knew* something.
And we knew they'd never tell us even if they could
have found the words. Which they couldn't. We went
all squeamish – limp, collywobbled. Not just Matt.

And their bleeding cats! Dotted all over the gangways
and guardrails, all over the fittings and pipes, anywhere
there was a claw-hold – even on the matelots
themselves, arms, shoulders, necks, heads, and knees
as they leaned forward, arms on the upper railing and a
foot on the lower. Fixing us, rigid, silent, staring, as if
stuffed, but with their eyes narrowed like their mates'.
Their tails quivered around them, wrapped like
arrogant togas; detached as vultures, they were, biding
their time. And I swear some of *them* were smoking too.

Definitely another breed, the Andrew. The Last of the
Elizabethans. Who said that? Conrad, London? Well,
they should have. Maybe because when Old Queen
Bess died, they felt they'd lost a mum, and, like most
men, were so shattered they just couldn't ever face
coming home anymore.

The ship dips and on the split second between down
and up Matt lunges all he's got at what looks like a

handle and he's through, his face up against an inside wall. And stunned.

He has no idea where he's got to, except he does know it's the last wall before the Biscay and you don't have to be a three-badge AB to figure that out, because it's hammering outside with ginormous kerrumps like depth charges going off around a submarine.

He takes a few seconds to gain his balance again and finds he's in this room, or room-like space, only he's clinging onto the door handle, frightened to let go in case it's the last wall itself and he gets tossed into the drink. And all he hears and feels is the pitch and toss and thump and crump of the waves hammering and clawing at the wall outside as if desperate to get in because they too are trying to escape from another monster.

For the first time it dawns on Matt that he's been sent on a crazed errand and might never get back again, that this will be the justice of the Navy – he knew they'd get him in the end. But what could he have done? It was either the wrath of the waves down below or the wrath of the Jaunty on deck. Now he knows for sure he's going to end his days on a mad, unstoppable roller coaster and he screams out in horror and pleads for forgiveness to God and Davy Jones in whose locker he now finds himself and to anyone else mad enough to be within earshot. And he remembers the words from some hymn or service and he shouts out:

> *'Hear us when we cry to thee*
> *For those in peril on the sea!'*

There's a long pause save the thundering of the seas, which won't abate, then a lull; and he realises this is it: he's crossed over at last. And the voice of God itself comes to welcome him, and to soothe and calm his torn nerves: 'Do you mind!' it says. 'Do you *bloody* mind!'

The world or heaven is vertical now, as if hovering for a plunge like it did in the Biscay. It tips over the apex

onto the dive, hovers shuddering and the voice comes
again:

'Will you shut the bloody door! There's a dreadful
draught in here, you know.'

Matt grabs at the matching inside half of the door as
the ship of heaven begins its downward lunge, heaves it
shut, thrusts his whole weight and strength down hard
on the handle and – miracle! – the thing snaps tight.

And he plunges down with whatever vessel is going.

'That's better,' says the voice of God coolly. 'Don't
they teach you manners in your mob?' Matt shakes his
head to clear it and is immediately misunderstood. 'No?
Huh! Well, then, a spell in the old Andrew will do you a
world of good. Knock some politeness into you, for a
start.'

Heaven *would* be like that too, wouldn't it, thinks
Matt, disciplined and polished. How did he expect to
escape after all those years! Bull into Eternity, that had
to be his lot.

Now he's shivering, steadying himself on the wall,
more like a shop's counter, and behind it he glimpses
this vision. It's a haven, this heaven. Yeah, he thinks,
that's it, a heavenly haven. I'm here.

Proper oasis, it is. Drawing room. Suite. Executive.
Plush. Admirals, for the use of. Or Hollywood tycoons.
Oil paintings covering the walls, and drapes. Dimmed
lights. Bookshelves. Cabinets fixed on the bulkhead.
Standard lamp. Divan bed or chaise longue. Thick
patched quilt. Rich tapestry hangings. Potted plants.
And this enormous armchair – heavy, wall-armed,
densely cushioned, flowing covers in black and purple,
green dragon motifs straight from a Shanghai palace.
And sunk deep down into it is this godly geezer in navy
blue ensconced behind a book he's holding up in front
of his face. Over the top of the page, Matt can just see
the curve of a head top, bald as a coot save for three or
four strands pinned across like barbed wire, and bushy

eyebrows hovering over heavy lids. And hanging down below the book a great red beard. The seasickness must have got to Matt before he crossed over.

The shelves are covered in books: novels, histories, manuals; poetry, shanties, annals; chronicles, year-books, legends – all about the sea:

'It's also bloody rude to stare!'

Matt opens his mouth but nothing comes.

'Your mouth's open. Sure sign of bad breeding.'

The weird thing is nothing moves. It's all limbo. As if the second Matt clamped down hard on that handle he shut out the other world and entered this new one. As if the room or cabin or den or whatever the hell he's in is fixed on its own giro. Giro limbo. A haven and a paradise, a desert and a mirage, a miracle and a heaven, all in one.

'What you want, then – brooms?'

With a soft curse and a heavy sigh the apparition sets aside the book, heaves himself out of his plush depths, stands up and takes in Matt in one move. He's all of five foot five and almost round. Wearing proper Navy blues: bell bottoms, tight jacket, white shirt square across the neck, and left arm covered in red stripes and stitched badges.

He comes forward to the counter and takes a little book from underneath. Three by four inches. Brown paper cover. Yellow pages. Licks the lead of a pencil and says 'Name and number?'

Writes in a heavy, deliberate hand while Matt keeps staring. Sees the stare and stabs his left arm.

'Able Seaman Kipp Ling,' he announces. 'How many?'

Matt is wordless. Seven years in the Andrew brings back no memory of any such experience.

'Thirty five years service. Five badge.' Taps his arm.

Matt stares on.

'The Seven Seas,' the AB goes on. 'First World War. And now this. How many?'

'Eh, three.'

'Sir.'

'Eh?'

'Sir.'

'Sir.'

'Please.'

'Please.'

'Mind your manners.' He squints hard at Matt. '*You* should know better.'

'Sorry.'

'Sir.'

'Sir.'

'You're a guest.' Squints again. 'But you're more than a guest. You're special, you are, aren't you?'

'Dunno.'

'Sir.'

'Sir.'

'Ho, yes, you do!'

'Sir.'

'The Navy's guest.'

'Sir.'

'An honour.'

'Sir.'

'An honour *repeated*.'

'Sir.'

He turns the book, keeps a tight hold on it and points:

'Put it there!'

'Eh?'

'You know, your bleeding moniker!'

'Oh!'

And Matt writes in immaculate Force 8 copperplate. The AB turns back the book towards him, scrutinises the signature, tears off the slip, folds it neatly in four and hands it over.

'That's you, then. Now, bugger off!'

'Not like the other services, the Navy,' Matt gave us our first lecture on naval affairs and customs squeezed in between a mound of greatcoats and a snoring Marine. 'As a soldier, you're not loyal to the Army, you see. You're loyal to the regiment. And the RAF's too young to know about loyalties yet, heads still covered in clouds and Brylcreem. But the Navy's something else. You owe loyalty to your ship and your mess and mates and your King and your Country. But over and above all that you owe loyalty to the Navy.'

We tried to breathe between Marine socks and polish.

'Don't even stand to drink the loyal toast, you know. They say it's because in the old wooden days they'd have banged their heads on the bulwarks when they stood up. But that's the Navy for you. Reason away any custom and tradition, they will, and make it sound even more wonderful and awe-inspiring. But underneath it's about survival, not of man, mess or ship, but of the *Navy*. They don't stand to toast the King, see,' he changed to a whisper now, 'because they reckon they're bloody superior, that's why!'

Matt was whispering because, even if the Marines had this running rivalry with the Navy themselves, you couldn't trust them. The Navy was one thing. The Marines another. And the PBI* was something else. Not down the social scale, but *off* it.

'All them wonderful sayings and phrases and customs and traditions they have like "splicing the mainbrace" and "toeing the line" and "swinging the lead" and "son of a gun" and "keel hauled" and "four sheets to the wind" and "the bitter bit" and "walking the plank" and "port and starboard"; and customs like slinging your sword at waist high and seven creases in your bell bottoms, and bell bottoms for a start anyway, and saluting by touching the forelock with the hand turned down and in, shortest way up and back, all that bull directly opposite from everyone else, and piping

* Poor Bloody Infantry

aboard and bosun's whistles and tots of rum and grog
from old Vernon and hearts of oak. It's all in the name
of survival. Like the masons, only deeper, not so much a
Senior Service as a *Secret* Service cos they're preserving
something for themselves against everything and
everybody – their bleeding Navy.'

The day he walked away from his ship Matt was a
marked man.

After getting his signature, the Five Badger shrugs,
sighs, heaves, turns back to his chair, falls into it and the
leather gives a great whoo … ooossh as he lands. He
retrieves his book and reads aloud:

> *I was a child, and she was a child,*
> *In this kingdom by the sea;*
> *But we loved with a love that was more than love –*
> *I and my Annabel Lee.*

'Know that one?'
'No.'
'Sir.'
'No, sir.'
'Hmm.' He sneered and went on:

> *And so, all the night tide, I lie down by the side*
> *Of my darling – my darling – my life and my bride,*
> *In her sepulchre there by the sea,*
> *In her tomb by the sounding sea.*

'No?'
'No. Sir!'
'What was that you were reciting when you came in?'
'Don't know.'
'Sir.'
'Sir.'
'About those in peril. Where d'you learn that?'
'Forgotten. Sir. Must have been a reaction like
something jolted from my memory.'

'Hmm. But you must have known it – once.'

'Maybe. Dunno.'

'Sir.'

'Sir.'

'Hoh, yes, you did! You knew *everything* once.' And he reaches to the shelf for another book and opens it.

'Ever read the story about a manuscript found in a bottle?'

'No, sir.'

'Hoh, but you should, you know. It's all about the crew of a ghost ship, all old and moving in a dream, their clothes and instruments of another age, and one man is lost on board in a limbo of a greater limbo, lonely, desperate, doomed, haunted, hunted, horrified. In a ghost ship searching for its chronicler. Only then will it rest.'

He snaps the book tight and replaces it and says: 'You should try it sometime.' And he fixes Matt and snaps: 'Now get!' He settles back into his chair, picks up his first book and adds: 'And close the door quietly this time.'

Matt's still clutching the paper, waiting for his brooms. But Able Seaman Kipp Ling is already deep in his book again.

'But what about the brooms, sir?' Matt manages.

Mr Ling looks up again, this time in complete disdain. 'C.84. Port.'

'You mean, not here?' asks Matt, not grasping he's come all this way only to get a slip of paper.

'I said C.84. Port! At the double!'

Again Matt looks around at the Underwater Palace in disbelief. It registers. This time the apparition gets up very slowly and pulls himself up to his full height.

'Able Seaman Kipp Ling,' he announces himself afresh, heaving out his chest. 'Thirty-five years service. Five Badge.' Taps his arm. 'Seven Seas. And every port in the Universe.' Waves his arm.

Matt follows the movement that describes the world.

Again Kipp advances slowly, shoulders hunched, barrel chest swelling, and thrusts his red forest across the counter so Matt can feel the heat from the bristles.

'Able Seaman Kipp Ling,' he announces again. 'Five Badge.' Taps his arm. 'Thirty-five years. The Seven Seas. The First World War. And now this One.' He raises a stubby hand and points straight at Matt like the old Kitchener poster, Your Country Needs You. 'This is your war! Not mine!'

Then, with a mighty heave of a deep breath he pushes his chest over the counter after his beard. And in a terrible whisper that rises above the roar of the Diesels and the Biscay, he says:

'I issue chitties for brooms, mate. Not brooms. Chitties.' Deep breath. 'That's my number. And that's going to be my war. Chitties, see. Chitties for brooms. Now get!'

'Chitties for brooms. Chitties for brooms.' That's what Matt's muttering when he gets back to us: 'Chitties for brooms.' Over and over and over again. Shaking. Like he's gone.

' "Lost his bottle in a pool",' quotes some bright spark.

'I've seen him,' says Matt. 'The five badge AB in the anchor locker, issuing chitties for brooms. Not brooms, mark you. But chitties!'

Well, we knew no man's got *that* job, of course. Chitties for brooms! Rubbish. Must have been a mirage – the seasickness, but then Matt's got sea legs nobody else has. Or could it be some wilful deceit?

'Think they set him up? Tried to send him mad?'

'Maybe they spotted him from the guardrail. He told us they had, remember.'

And if they'd had any doubt after that, it went when things started stirring up and the Biscay began bellowing and braying for a bit of blood, and Matt was one of the few still standing. Showed he was the only one of the 'guests' with a pair of sea legs. I mean, anyone can have a good pair of sea legs, just as any sailor can get seasick. But when you've got a pair of sea legs that's not only solid as oak but can nip around in a heaving ship like a boisterous pup as well, then you're something real experienced and special. So the Jaunty had noticed and sent him below on this weird errand to gather brooms.

'Reckon it was all set up.'

Course Matt falls for it. No fear *he'll* not find his way alright, or that he'll keel over. They know. They know their own breed.

'Only the chitties for them! Do you hear me?' Matt's voice reaches a squeak now. 'Not the brooms, you understand. Only the chitties for them! I'm telling you! That's his number. Down there. *Way* down there. Next to Davy Jones. Right by the sharp end. I seen him. Reads poetry. Poetry and chitties. That's what he does. Got an extra badge. For long and faithful service to poetry and chitties!'

We're huddled underneath the lifeboats trying to hold him. Pale as a ghost, he is. Worse when he tells us about the story of the manuscript in a bottle. Eerie, that is.

Maybe *that* was the feeling we had on the jetty at Pompey. We knew there was something strange floating around us when we stood there. We put it down to the smell of the sea and ships. But maybe it was more than that. Maybe it was the smell of things past. Of retribution. Of promises unfulfilled. Maybe they were all fixing their bleary eyes on Matt. Not on us at all! Nothing general about it. It was all particular – Matt.

'They're *all* ghost ships,' he mumbled now. 'It wasn't just me mum.'

We tried to calm him but he was off in a world of his own, lying there leaning against the tarpaulin of a boat in a corner of the sea-swept deck open to the Biscay, but totally oblivious to it now, and neither the Jaunty nor the Navy anywhere to be seen.

'Nobody deserts the Andrew,' he goes on. 'That's treason, see. Worse than desecrating graves.' He thinks about it. 'Worse than a batsman not walking.'

'The great Andrew in the Sky. That's what I've seen – a glimpse into the great Andrew. Like seeing my next life, the one I could never escape from.'

The ship rolls, the sea pitches and tosses. The wind howls and Matt rambles on against the din: 'The denizen of the deep too ... the AB of ABs ... throned in his submarine Palace ... guardian of all things Senior Service, issuing judgment – and chitties for brooms!'

And he ups and offs, careering across the deck, screaming to the wind that can't hear or care or heed or read. The last we see of him is a great shower of Biscay engulfing the stern, rising up over the ship like a waterfall, hanging a moment before crashing down and hiding all beneath it. And this voice crying on the wind: 'Chitties for brooms! Chitties for brooms!'

INTERLUDE 1

Six

My heart was a desert
You planted a seed

My mother made a Christmas out of every Thursday –
because the packet of Botcher letters arrived each week
like a present from Santa Claus.

At that time we were supposed to be living in times of
great 'uncertainty and trial' and in constant need of our
'spirits uplifting', so she devised a series of Occasions,
highlights with which to probe our darkness, and she
chose Thursday for the main event of the week – the
Reading of the letters and the Gramophone Hour.

And this is the flower,
This hour
Of sweet fulfilment

'Now then, children. Time to round you up.'

She issued the first call to order at a quarter to five,
fifteen minutes after we'd started to hang around the
table.

'Now then, children, settle down.'

She issued the second command at five o'clock, after
we'd been sitting rigid with expectancy for another
fifteen minutes, gazing at the packet in the centre of the
table like desperate dogs staring at their bowls but not
daring to move until the command: 'Now!'

Can it be the trees
That fill the breeze
With rare and magic perfume?

By the time our father embarked for the desert, after the long drag of 'Girl Guide camps' in England, 'frogmires' in France, 'day trips from Dunkirk' and 'desert training in the gardens of Kent', we had settled in for a long siege. The pattern was set and we had to find our place in it.

Letters arrived regularly because our father was obviously determined to achieve at least *some*thing each day – 'like shaving'. But because he had to eat so much to keep his strength up to cope with the Boche and the Botchers – 'got a lot on my plate at the moment' – he didn't always have enough time, so some of his letters were rather short. He decided to save them up and send them once a week instead.

As he was establishing a shape to his war, so we responded by giving it a shape too. Whenever his letters arrived we saved them up and gave them a context – the Thursday Readings.

They arrived in batches, with an air of bumper Christmas annuals, collections of the best of the year's goodies, which my mother emphasised by placing the packet in the centre of the tea table before we were summoned in for the Occasion. She could just as well have stuffed them in a stocking.

O, no, it isn't perfume,
It's love in bloom

The evening opened like a Mass with the solemn celebration of Special Tea at Five and flowed on naturally into the Gloria of the Gramophone Hour between six and seven.

Is it all a dream
A joy supreme
that came to us in the gloom?

We had inherited boxes of thick, black, heavy gramophone records from my mother's parents because their dog had died. His picture stood out on the hard cardboard packets – a little white terrier with his head cocked, listening, with the same speechless curiosity and wonder as we did to the fantastic sounds coming down that long funnel: Fritz Kreisler's violin, Bing Crosby's groan, Harry James' trumpet, Richard Tauber's pain: '*Humoreske*' to 'Love in Bloom', 'Stardust' to '*Dein ist mein ganzes Herz!*' But when the little dog 'went in the night', our grandparents couldn't take the pain of listening to his favourite songs anymore so they passed his collection on to us.

You know it isn't a dream
It's love in bloom

Each of us had a personal favourite which had to be played at least once during the Thursday session:

So, wie die Blume welkt
Wenn sie nicht küsst
Der Sonnenschein.

My sister's favourite was Richard Tauber singing '*Dein ist mein ganzes Herz!*'. She listened with head bowed in the same reverent and humble posture she assumed for studying the maps which she composed on the backs of brown paper bags.

Dein ist mein schönstes Lied

seeming to catch in his voice the same summons to the end of the rainbow.

weil es allein
aus der Liebe erblüht.

Sweet fulfilment.

> *O, list thee, pretty maiden*
> *while I tell thee in a trice*
> *just who I am, what I do, and how I live.*

My brother always claimed he liked so many he
couldn't plead any particular favourite. Crosby,
Fitzgerald, Kreisler, Caruso, Hutch, Hylton – it was all
the same to him:

> *I am ... only a poet!*
> *But my employment, writing,*
> *Is that a living?*
> *Hardly!*

Yet somehow we always managed to have 'Your tiny
hand is frozen' at least once during the hour although
no one ever requested it. And the *Wizard* always got a
special twist when Heddle Nash strained at the bit
about the poet and dreams:

> *So inspire me with passion*
> *In dreams and fond illusions*
> *And castles in the air!*

Sweet fulfilment.

> *Ma n'atu sole*
> *chhiu bello, ohi ne*

My mother's favourite was Caruso singing the
Neapolitan serenade '*O Sole Mio*'. She listened upright
in her chair, as if sitting to attention, her eyes closed.
Her eyelids screwed up more tightly on certain phrases
as if she couldn't quite catch the words, and as Caruso
seemed to be singing from the far side of some river it
was understandable and probably difficult for him too:

> *'o sole mio*
> *st nfronte a te!*

Sweet fulfilment.

> *My heart was a desert*
> *you planted a seed*

Mine was Crosby's 'Love in Bloom'.

> *And this is the flower,*
> *This hour*
> *Of sweet fulfilment*

Especially the 'Sweet fulfilment' line.

It didn't have any 'meaning' for me because I couldn't understand the words – 'he just likes the sound, see.' But it did things to me that nobody else knew about. And of course it was the 'Botchers' Song'.

Caruso, Fats Waller; Artie Shaw, Heddle Nash; Chevalier and Sablon; Fitzgerald and Ellington. From these sessions of sweet fulfilment, quite meaningless lines began to flow through us like the swaying rhythm of a carousel, guiding the way we moved and thought and what we thought about.

No one ever said Caruso sang in Italian. No one ever said Tauber sang in German – *other* languages, let alone the languages of the enemy. And no one ever translated anything. No one even suggested that the words of Crosby and Nash, and Tauber and Caruso, that vibrated and flowed through and around us, were different. Different to what? They weren't words; they were *sounds – notes –* things we felt and absorbed, and not just with the ear. They entered, moved within, and *moved* us, like the drumming of the sun and the nudging of the sea.

Sweet fulfilment.

After the Gloria of the Gramophone Hour the Mass lifted up and away into the Reading from the sacred *Book of Botchers*:

Dearly Beloved:

Nothing was said between Caruso's final phrase –
'*alto bene*' – and the first words of the letter. Page One of
the *Botcher* was the next line of Caruso.

> *And lo, it came to pass that a certain Botcher …*

Sometimes they sounded like the Bible, sometimes
like the *Wizard*. Sometimes like the wireless. Sometimes
like the postman, who had been at the Somme and
'could tell a tale or two'.

> *"'ere!', said the Commander in Chief when the shell
> dropped through the bivvy roof and chopped his Aga
> down the middle of the caviare, 'What d'you do that for,
> Adolf?'*

He had many ways of telling his Botchers' tales. But
they had only one sound: my mother's voice. Or
Caruso's.

> *And lo, on the road to the tabernacle at Cassino they met
> many pilgrims hurrying along the way they had newly
> trod. And when they enquired of them 'Prithee, wherefore
> hast thou come?' they answered with a brace of
> blasphemies which, being interpreted, urged them to
> begone …*

After each weekly READING we smoothed out the
creased pages of the letter and added them to the stack
which we kept in the glass bookcase beside the upright
gramophone in the living room at the rear which led to
the 'forlorn', a distant prospect of damp potatoes that
had once been a run of green but which was now being
dug for victory and was not restored to its original
incarnation until long after the war had ended, our father
had 'gone in the night', and austerity had passed over
like an obese rain cloud. We grew up staring out into that
drizzled wasteland believing 'our lawn' to be the same as

'forlorn'. The sounds, and the prospect, were indivisible.

> *Now it came to pass in the dunes of Cyrenaica, during the time of a great famine of men, they beat their Corporals into Captains and their Sergeants into Kings, and a right Botchers' paradise that turned out to be …*

For five years we watched the buoyant volume blossom in the bookcase like a tenacious aspidistra. To keep the pile in place and prevent the pages floating around in the breeze each time the door opened, we held them down with a ¼ pound grocer's brass weight which we used to keep the kitchen door open in summer and which now glistened like an ever-glowing lighthouse, climbing up proudly and ever more precariously inside the glass door, like mercury gloating in an anxious barometer. Appropriately enough it must have reached boiling point somewhere between Alamein and Tobruk, whereupon my mother started a second stack by its side which was getting edgily hot by Monte Cassino, but fortunately VE day arrived before it blew the roof off the bookcase.

The evening concluded with the bedside Benediction as we beseeched the Lamb of God to watch over the whole flock of Botchers, but 'especially our father and the better Boche ones'.

Our Father …

There was only one Father. We recited our prayers to Him every night, seven days a week for five years.

With chart in Heaven …

Nobody said the one in the photograph upstairs with Mother in her white dress and done-up bun was another person. Had my father come home occasionally I'd have had trouble with two Our Fathers. But he didn't. He stayed away, presumably at the War that was 'going on' in heavenly places like Monte Cassino.

>   *Hallo, Dad! Be Thy name …*

Whatever, we wrote to him regularly and waited for only one to return:

>   *Thy King down come …*

back to us:

>   *On Earth, as he sits in Heaven …*

Sweet fulfilment.

We didn't see the War. We *heard* it – the sounds of it. These sounds made the music of our rituals all through the War, although we'd no idea we were going 'all through' anything. They were simply the sounds we learned at our mother's knee, together with those of news readers, announcers, crooners, soldiers' boots, sergeants' lungs, tanks, engines, aircraft, sirens, all-clears.

When the day finally arrived for Our Father to come back from Heaven with his chart all our experience of him had been through his own Bumper Comic – *'out every Thursday'* – and what we had seen when praying to him every night.

We were waiting to see an enormous man in a funny hat and baggy trousers, waving a glittering cluster of rainbow balloons and jingling bells, coming down from heaven on a milky cloud, mounting the steps at one bound, entering the house to a special signature tune like Tommy Handley's, and coming to tell us more stories about the Heavenly Troupe of Botchers.

In fact, he arrived silently on a white stretcher that creaked loudly – 'a botched job, of course' – and everyone in the street was very quiet.

CON BRIO

Sidi Barrani, December 1940

And the silence of their wilderness was touched by sublime sounds, as of stars breaking through darkness, and all were consoled save the consoler ...

Seven

It should have been a half day, being a Wednesday, but the Sergeant said we'd got to take Sid from the Eyeties first.

'Guess what, lads,' he declared, long before breakfast or sun up. 'Got a proper treat for you today.'

The whole platoon froze, not a particularly common-place event in the African desert. But when the Sergeant pulls out his dulcet tones, anything climactic is possible.

'What's a *proper* treat, Sarge?'

We're rooted to the spot, waiting on his answer, the bacon and eggs still hanging around in the pan.

'Give you three guesses.' He tried to sound cheerful.

'Extra can of bully beef?' someone ventures, licking his knife.

'Nope.'

'A new fly swatter for the mess?' another examines his rusty fork.

'Nope. But getting warmer.'

'Long weekend at home for Christmas?' said the lance – '*free* lance, if you please, I do it my way' – indelicately emptying his Crown Derby slops in the virgin sand.

'Nope. But nearly.'

'Give up. What's it then?'

'We're taking Sid from the Eyeties today!'

'Aw. Saaa … rrge!' A concerted moan rumbles around the camp and drowns out the soothing notes of

'*Voi che sapete*'.

Taking Sid wasn't going to be a big deal anyway. We'd already done the hard bit a couple of days before out in the desert at the Eyeties' fortress Nibeiwa. That was Biggles stuff.

Spent two whole days moving forward under cover of darkness, thirty odd thousand men and tanks. Even used hurricane lamps to guide us through the rough patches. During the day we took the windscreens off the trucks so the sun wouldn't reflect on them and give the game away. The whole army lay doggo in the burning heat and moved only at night.

Did a sort of pincer movement by getting round to their western side while they had their guns facing east. Took them by surprise at breakfast when they were still digging into their coffee and rolls. Biggles would have been proud.

We're on something of a winning streak these days and a winning army doesn't rest on its streaks, so we'll be off soon enough. But we're feeling a bit blasé when the Sarge tries Sid on us because we know we can play hard to get. And Sid'll be easy after Nibeiwa. Eyeties have probably left anyway.

'C'mon, just one more heave, lads.'

Only six months after Dunkirk but we've heard this cajoling tone often enough already from the Sarge whenever he wants something extra out of us: 'Just one last push'. 'How about just one final final effort, eh?'

'A just man, our Sarge.'

We're in the 'proper' war now, not the 'phoney' kind, but it still has the Biggles touch. Everything's still explained in terms of sports and playing fields, maybe not of Eton or Eltham but definitely of England and Empire. So today we're at Twickenham and it's fifteen points each with three minutes to go and the scrum's on their twenty-five. Could just as well be on match point at Wimbledon or in the last over at Lords, but it's December. The temperature says summer but the calendar says Christmas.

'No, straight up,' the Sarge says slightly anxiously, sensing a touch of resistance on the desert air.

Except for Con. He's not interested anyway. He's crouched down under his groundsheet, which he's got pegged up like a sunshade at Ascot. Gone totally oblivious, he has, having just finished playing morning reveille on his flute and turned to charming us and whatever's inside his tent with '*Voi che Sapete*'.

'Looks exactly like one of them Indian snake charmers.'

'You can imagine the little blighter of a reptile twisting and turning underneath his canopy like a Cairo belly dancer.'

Only it wasn't a flute, not out here, not with the kind of gear we had to hump around. But it could have been a full flown flute or even a bona fide bassoon. Amazing what some of our lot lugged around with them. One chap brought his family Bible, a huge bound tome from early, *very* early Victorian times, with his family tree dating back to yonks before – lists of names, dates of birth, marriages, christenings, deaths, and signatures, all in grand copperplate. Another geezer fancied himself as a bird watcher – 'taking up ornithology when I get free of this mob' – and dragged around a stucco effigy of St Francis. Chirped to it every morning, he did, 'to remind me of home' – well, he did until after Tobruk, anyway. And another had a bronze sculpture of a frog geezer called Grellet complete with 'graven image of his immortal message' on the supporting plinth: 'I shall pass this way but once. Any good that I can do, or any kindness show to any fellow creature, let me do it now, for I shall not pass this way again.' Used to read it out loud whenever we were preparing to 'go in', but it was

such a long piece the Sarge got him to cut it down to the
bare 'I shall pass this way but once' – 'just so we can
move it along, mind, no offence'. Used to mutter it all
the time like a Catholic kid doing the Hail Marys. The
Frog Philosopher, we called him. Didn't last too long.

So maybe it wouldn't have been so surprising if Con
had brought his flute with him.

There's another stumbling block. It's early on in
December and we're right in the middle of our
Christmas planning, so any surprise job the Sarge turns
up with at this time isn't likely to go down well at all.
Even the mosquitoes sound depressed.

'Look, lads,' the Sarge pleads, knowing he might
have chanced his arm once too often this time. 'Tell you
what. I'll make it up to you in Tobruk. Benghazi at the
latest. Honest.' And delicately sensing we're not
amused, adds: 'Besides, you might be through by
lunchtime. Not really a big job, is it?'

He seems positively jovial now, but we're still not
impressed. 'I mean, a fearless fighting foe like you ...'
Amazing what one crumbling desert fort can do for
morale.

'Got dreams of grandeur now, our Sarge has.'

Well, taking Sidi Barrani from the Eyeties may be
simple enough stuff, but as someone points out:

'Ah, but we mightn't get it done by lunchtime, Sarge,
and that means we're into Wednesday and a half day.'
Mutiny looms large.

'And Christmas nearly upon us.'

The Eyeties could be upset too.

'I mean, there's war and war, isn't there?'

'Can't let it muck about with basic institutions.'

'I mean, we don't mind helping you out, Sarge, but
it's the principle!'

A general rumble moves around the ranks, confirming a conspiracy of principles.

'You've got to state your rights even in war, you know.'

'Given up enough as it is.'

'Far from home. Permanent heat. Bully beef. Living cheek by jowl with men and mosquitoes you've never met before.'

'*And* never knowing where they've been!'

'There's a limit, you know.'

'Can't just let them go around mucking up our Wednesdays as well. I mean, that's exactly what war's about, isn't it? What we're here for! Defending our right to half days.'

Con Brio didn't have a flute. He had a recorder. And what he was charming under the shade of his groundsheet wasn't a snake but a music stand with a score. Did it for hours on end, at any time of day and often night, whenever he had a free moment. Had a whole repertoire 'from Purcell to Irving Berlin'. Made everything sound plaintive like one of those mouth organs they always have in Westerns, playing sad tunes like 'Shenandoah' and 'John Brown's Body'. Charmed us all the way across Egypt from the docks at Alex right up to the day we bumped into Tio Graziano, who must have heard of Con's flair and come rushing all the way down from Rome to welcome us.

'Well, they like their music, them Eyeties.'

Everytime we stopped, for a stretch or a puncture or a tea break or a night's kip, or just a wander around to admire the scenery, up went the awesome awning, out came the celebrated stand and score, and on went Con's resonant recorder.

'Does it have to be a Wednesday, Sarge?'

'Well,' he says, 'the way I look at it, there's not much you can do out here in any case, is there?' And he waves his baton over the miles of empty dunes that even the vultures seem to have abandoned. 'I mean, not a lot of

shops open around here, Wednesday or no
Wednesday.'

He had us there. Well – for a moment. We shuffled
and hung silent, not exactly lost for words – mislaid,
more – trying to get the right balance between justice
and reasonableness.

'When we going to do our Christmas wrapping then?
If we don't get it done and the cards sent off this week,
they won't get there in time, will they?'

'Some lovely bazaars in Sid,' he encouraged us,
sensing we might still do a deal. 'You'll be much better
off shopping there. Pick up some nice little bargains,
you will.'

Then the thin notes of *'Voi che sapete'* struggled over
the mutinous throng like a confirmation of our
complaint, soothing our resentment, or probably just
lamenting Wednesdays.

It had its effect. The shuffling started up again. We
were definitely weakening.

'Tell you what,' he adds quickly, banging his fists
together. 'Take Sid before lunch and you can have your
half day as well. Right?'

The notes of *'Voi che sapete'* floated gently into the lull,
soothingly yet pointedly, reminding.

Con played anything and everything for us but *'Voi
che sapete'* had become a kind of signature tune. He
played it at reveille in the morning and like a last post
every sundown. It was more than a regimental tune, it
was a highly personalised piece of music that *became* us,
and only us. Con charmed us and his hidden scores
with a hundred pieces so that we always had some soft
accompaniment to the heat and dust of the desert, but
when he played *'Voi che sapete'* he was talking only to
us, setting us apart from his entire musical repertoire,
reminding us we were special.

'What's it mean, Con?'

'What's what mean?'

'Voy Kay Zapetty?'

'Doesn't mean anything. It's music.'

'But you said it was an arreeyah and had words.'

'Aria.'

'Same thing. What's it mean?'

'Oh, the words, you mean.'

'Yeah. What's it saying? The words!'

'Well, the words don't mean so much. It's what the music says, isn't it?'

'Yeah, but it'd be nice to know.'

'Well, *voi che sapete* means … well, it's about you who have known about … love …'

'Oh!'

'Something like that.'

'Thought it sounded like Waltzing Matilda.'

'No.'

'Well, you learn something every day, Con.'

'That's hardly a bonus, Sarge, is it? We got a right to our half day anyway!'

'Tell you what, then. I'll throw another one in for you tomorrow. Thursday. How's that? Two half days in one week, *and* Saturday.'

'Well, it's not a bad deal – two half days in a row. Give us more time to shift our Christmas stuff. But it's not that simple in the Army. We can't just let them in charge think we're an easy touch.

'Then again we might not take Sid by the afternoon, Sarge, in which case that means we've still only got one half-day.'

The clear notes of '*Voi che sapete*' fill the lull.

Suddenly he disarms us. 'And two half-days next week as well? How's that?'

Well, it's not much of a sport bashing Eyeties, anyway, we figure, to console ourselves, knowing we've been caught with our shorts down, but it passes the time.

And he's right, of course, there might well be better bazaars in Sid for us to complete our Christmas shopping.

'OK Sarge,' the platoon gives a joint shrug: 'We'll give it a whirl.'

'Ah, bless you, bless the lot of you.' He brightens up. 'I tell you, you're lovely. All of you. You really are. I keep telling the CO in my reports and the missus in my letters home. And I was only saying to General O'Conner the other day: "I couldn't have wished for a finer bunch of warriors."'

'Forget it, Sarge. Any time.'

'No, really. I mean it.'

Anyway, the deal's done, we stretch out, flex the muscles, rub the sleep and sand out of the eyes and things, sort out a clean shirt and pants and a rifle or two, have a shave, and contemplate the sun coming up to the soothing notes of '*Voi che Sapete*'.

Con always sat outside his tent. Everybody else crouched inside, on account of the heat and sun and flies and sand. Or cold even – got quite chilly some evenings. But not Con. Oh, no! He had to have the shade for the scores of his blessed Mozart and Beethoven, Purcell or Berlin.

'Otherwise, they might frazzle up, see?' he said. We did.

Con could play everything by ear, but whenever possible he played by his score. 'Got to keep up the standards, you know,' he said. And if he could have had one of us inside that tiny tent turning the pages for him, he would have. 'Mustn't allow war to get in the way of standards.' And he never did, however torrid the heat the Egyptian desert threw up.

'Why not get your bonce inside for once, Con?' we often tried to convince him. 'Get yourself cremated out there, you will.'

But Con only ever shrugged, before stretching

forward to turn a page, wet his lips and get stuck in
again to *Eine Kleine* – another bedtime favourite – or
'Kay what's its number', as we called them.

'No,' he said once, just south of Wadi Begarr, where
we'd pulled up for elevenses and the water was boiling
before we got the caddies out, 'what's inside here's a lot
more important than me.'

The morning of Sidi Barrani, Con hadn't been
listening to the Sarge. Well, not just that morning. He
rarely did. Usually just kept on playing and waited for
us to pass on the information later.

'Well, this is my job, see.'

And it was true. Con's music was part of the unit, the
routine, the mood and the style. We wouldn't have
asked Con to stop playing any more than we could have
asked the Padre to stop praying. That's what they were
there for. So we always had to repeat everything for him
afterwards, because he never bothered to turn up to our
meetings and briefings.

That morning he'd been playing the unit tune as
usual – 'Con's regimental aria'. Now he was hard at
something else.

'Con!' we shout out. But he doesn't move a decibel.
Head's down, straining into the awning, studying the
next piece.

'We're taking Sid this morning. Get your arreeyah
into gear!'

Stops dead, he does, right in the middle of his scales
… Pulls his head out from under and gazes around.
Stunned. We'd got so used to his background
accompaniment to the mossies, the sudden silence
rings out like the crack of doom. This time we know
something's wrong and once again the whole unit
freezes into silence. The Sarge wanders over to his little
tent.

'What's up then, Con, me merry minstrel?'

Con pauses and wets his cracked lips, then stares up. 'But we can't go today, Sarge,' he whispers, aghast.

You could have heard a camel drop.

'But we been and done a deal, Con,' says the Sarge reassuringly. 'Me and the lads. You're all getting an extra half day.'

Con still stares up at him, the recorder mouthpiece hanging wet on his lips.

'And a couple more next week.'

'It's not that, Sarge,' he manages to say.

'Why not, old Brio, me lad?' says the Sarge, good-natured like, resisting slapping Con's back only at the last minute. Con didn't like having his back slapped. 'Something to do with his breathing.'

'It's Berlioz's birthday,' he said.

You could have heard another camel drop.

Give him his due, the Old Sarge knew when he'd met the proverbial Irresistible Force. He'd won the first round with us but he hadn't counted on any trouble from Con. This time we all looked for inspiration elsewhere. But the Sarge gathered himself quickly, stretched, shrugged and tried an appeasing laugh: 'Oh, well then, many happy returns!'

An hour later we're all spruced up in our Wednesday bests, toecaps shining and fresh short back and sides, ready for the Sid outing. But Con's still charming away on his recorder. Hasn't budged a semi-quaver.

'C'mon now, Con,' the Sarge goes over and tries again. 'There's a good lad. Last call for the donkey ride along the sands to Sid, eh?'

Con didn't even stop playing. Seemed to shake his head slightly but he might just have been wavering his notes about a bit.

'No, there was a distinct wobble in his warble,' said Shakes later. 'I marked it well.'

'C'mon, Con!' Sarge tries again. 'Don't matter if

you're not spruced up.'

'Can't, Sarge,' Con quivers.

'Aw, c'mon! Just come as you are. The Eyeties won't mind.'

'Sorry, Sarge,' Con quavers.

'Now don't make it difficult, Con,' the Sarge pleads. 'Where's your bloke from, then?'

Con manages to warble 'Pa … rr … rr … ris.'

'There you are, then. You can celebrate his birthday in Sid. Lots of lovely old Frog-type cafés *there*.'

We're all a bit puzzled by the name. Con's never mentioned Berlioz before. Although he never mentioned anyone unless you made a point of asking who wrote whatever piece he was playing, and *then* you had to drag it out. But we'd never heard a sniff of this geezer. So we figure he must be something special: 'Maybe even related.'

But Con just keeps on staring in at his hidden score, shakes his head and says: 'It's not that, Sarge.'

'What is it then, my nightingale?'

'Well …' There's a pause, then for the first time Con moves the recorder away from his lips. Keeps on staring at the score, mind, but stops vibrating.

'Come along, now,' says the Sarge. 'You can tell Uncle.'

'Well …' You could see Con was having a terrible struggle. 'Well … you see, Sarge, Hector really loved the Eyeties – more than he loved Harriet.'

You feel the sand dunes deflate until the whole desert lies whacked, waiting for a bumper bellows to pump it up into life again.

'Uh, *huh*,' was all the Sarge could muster.

'Travelled all over Italy serenading them on his guitar.'

'You don't say.'

'Yes.'

'Well, that was nice of him, Con.'

'Yes.'

Another long pause and the Sarge asks, softly: 'So?'

'So, you see,' says Con twisting, shrugging, shuffling, pondering, searching the sand for the verbal inspiration that had always eluded him. 'I couldn't go and bash them today now, could I? Not on Hector's birthday!'

It was the only speech we ever heard him make. Con only ever spoke in notes.

The Sarge considered for a while, gauging the might of the Irresistible Force. Then he clicked his teeth as if to say 'Well, I see what you mean,' stroked his moustache, pensive like, and tried once more:

'How old's Hector, then, Con?'

Con withdraws the mouthpiece, wets his lips and says: 'A hundred and thirty-seven.' Direct. Deadpan.

'Ah, well, there you are, then,' the Sarge shrugs. 'That's it. Not a lot you can do with an answer like that!' And he turns away.

So we left Con there with his birthday celebrations and spent the rest of the morning taking Sid.

Later on we're sitting having a cuppa in Sid's Greasy Spoon on Barrani's Main Boulevard when this truck roars out of the Piazza opposite with a couple of heavyweight MPs high up in the back and a cruiser-weight driver. Tears away in a cloud of sand and almost wipes out our view of the Avenue where most of the lads have gone off on their Christmas shopping spree. And as the storm settles we see our Sarge emerging through the dust and coming towards us. He's almost up to the verandah when he spots us reclining inside on the best window seats, and stops dead in his tracks, startled like, as if we're the last people on earth he expected to find there. Then, in one and the same movement, he turns away with a kind of tic of the shoulders, more of a shudder than a shrug, and marches off back down the Boulevard.

'Well,' says a voice, 'there's gratitude for you. You waste a perfectly good day off – or half of it – taking back Sid for him so he can ring up old Churchill and arrange his medal, and what does he do? Ignores us! Not so much as a tip of the old titfer* or a measly mercy bowcoo.'

'Yeah, and all that bull about making it up in Tobruk!'

'Bloody bad manners, that's what I say.'

'Reckon?'

'Breeding. That's what it is.'

'Or lack of it.'

'Right.'

'Can't take blokes like that anywhere, can you?'

'Wouldn't show him to my mum. Tell you that much.'

'Too right.'

'Bloody well take Tobruk himself, for all I care.'

'Right.'

'Makes you want to pack it all in and get off back home, doesn't it?'

'Right.'

Later still we're out for our early evening stroll when we see the same truck coming back again. Same two heavyweights on board and the cruiser driver. Don't exactly know why, but we sort of half expected Con to be with them. We'd forgotten all about him until then. I mean, we hadn't talked about the morning incident, and we hadn't seen the Sarge since that glimpse from the café an hour or so before, but you get a hunch about things. But the truck roars up and past and disappears in another cloud. Not a trace of Con. Neither man nor kit, recorder nor tent, stand nor score. Nothing. Not then. In fact, not ever.

Course, as well as being a fully accomplished musician,

* Tit for tat = hat

Con had become a fully qualified deserter – technically, that is. And a desert deserter, too. Some achievement, that is. I mean, where the hell do you desert to in a desert? We'd all thought about it at one time or another. But, better the camel you know and all that.

'Suppose we could have waited taking Sid until Thursday, you know.'

'Yeah, then Con *could* have had his half day as well.'

'A man has a right to his half days, even in war.'

'And if you want to celebrate somebody's birthday, it's up to you.'

'What we're here for.'

'Another pint?'

Usually you hear about things like that – jankers, cells, extra duties, demotion, that kind of thing. Some rumour, some word, some where. But not with Con. Not a word was heard, nor a funeral note, as they say.

Taking lollies from the Eyeties was never the same after Con Brio. Nor Christmas Shopping. Nor Wednesdays. Expect they still lull their goats to sleep down in the wadies to '*Voi che sapete*'.

HORACE COPE

Libya, June 1941

*And behold there came a person wise in the stars, telling
of fates and fortunes, and things of tomorrow, until he
fell upon alien believers and got his vicars in a twist . . .*

Eight

When Gunner Reginald Cope requested permission to publish his astrological predictions in Daily Orders a few days before the start of Operation Battleaxe, the Sergeant agreed, provided he named himself 'Horace' – 'to keep it light, see' – and admitted responsibility – 'diminished, maybe, but responsibility nevertheless.'

'Course, Sarge,' said Cope, 'I'm not proud. Or ashamed. And if it needs your little joke to get me noticed, fine by me.'

'Difficult war, this, Horace,' mused the Sergeant.

Life hadn't been quite the same in North Africa since Rommel arrived on the 12th of February and started playing hell with all our predictions. Until then it had been a touch embarrassing, with us winning battle after battle against the Italians, 'sweeping all before us', and taking so many prisoners we didn't have enough spare men to look after them or places to store them in or bully beef to feed them on. By January we were already clear of Egypt and well on into Libya and racing along the coast to the port of Tobruk which the Aussies 'grabbed in style', with the Italians simply packing it in as we moved on.

A month later it's Benghazi's turn and we're looking forward to Tripoli and Tunis, all inspiring names with a touch of the poetry in them as befits our Commander in

Chief, a highbrow sort of chap who leads his troops with a baton in one hand and a book of poems in the other. Not that we saw much of Wavell, of course, or any of the stuff he read or wrote, but it sounded a good Biggles prank and was just the kind of thing that rubs off and makes everyone feel real chuffed – especially as the Italians were offering little opposition and the North African campaign was good as over anyway.

But Rommel changed all that.

'I could have told you,' said Cope. 'It's all in the stars.'

'You see, Cope,' said the Sarge, slightly conscience-stricken, 'I'm going out on a rim myself, you know, right on the edge, taking a big gamble.'

'It's not a gamble, Sarge!' Reginald protested. 'I'm a force for positive good!'

'Well, anything to calm the lads' nerves,' said the Sarge. 'The new Padre doesn't like this mumbo jumbo sort of thing, but I just might be able to square it with the Company Commander, provided you don't give the lads the impression you're divinely inspired. Right?'

'OK, Sarge, I'll just stick to the astrological facts. But they'll get the impression themselves, you know, cos it's true.'

'Well,' sighed the Sergeant, long-sufferingly, 'maybe it's the heat.'

Our regular Padre had gone back to Cairo for rest and recuperation. He'd been at it for a long time – advising and encouraging, blessing and burying.

'*And* writing thousands of letters, don't forget,' said the Adjutant. 'Not just praying, you know. Fourteen per cent of these chappies can't even write home. The Padre does it for them.'

He'd been with us a long time. He'd got used to the foibles and fads of men at war. Needed a break. 'Lot of noise in war,' said the Sergeant. 'Gets on a man's nerves. Our Padre's a sensitive soul. Not like you lot.'

'Chaucer's poor priest,' said our poetic C-in-C on a visit one day.

'Like a mum, dad, wife and brother all in one,' said our pragmatic Adjutant, balancing.

'A Padre's work, like a policeman's,' said our patient Sarge, 'is never done.'

'Well,' said Reginald, 'there's a time and place for Padres. Usually after.'

'You're on the cusp, Cuthbertson,' Cope's voice resounded from inside his canvas-covered truck. 'Not too strong on hope these days, I'd say. But the vulnerable must be ever vigilant, you know. So watch it.'

Cope claimed he composed horoscopes because the only thing a man is interested in anyway is his own body and so his own life and death. And the only thing he really reads into the stars is his own destiny.

'Stars, that's me,' he said. 'Horoscopes. A man needs something greater than himself to look up to. None of this wishy-washy peering down into tea cups.'

But his form of adult encouragement wasn't necessarily the tonic needed during the run-up to an attack, even if the going *was* all in your favour. And when the Sergeant tentatively suggested that some of his predictions did sound slightly on the harsher side, Cope said:

'Well, they'll believe it if it's good and fight against it if it's not. Perverse, man is, and that's what I respond to.'

However, as Rommel grew more powerful in the desert by the day and Operation Battleaxe to relieve Tobruk drew nearer by the hour and more men queued up outside Cope's Consultation Canvas like supporters at a Cup Final – 'giving the new Padre a good run for his money'. Horace did try to tone it down a bit, but 'without tampering with the truth, understand?'

'Course.'

'Well, I shouldn't be *too* depressed, Cuthbertson,' Horace softened. 'If you ask me, this whole bleeding war's on the cusp now.'

And studying the lines of anxious warriors outside Cope's Canvas, the Sarge reflected: 'Quite an occasion, this war, you know. Unpredictable too. But then that's part of its charm, really.'

There hadn't been any job for Horace Cope during that early easy run along the coast of North Africa against the Italians.

'Perfectly understandable,' he conceded in the days when he was still Reginald. 'Blokes only get into stars and palms and tea leaves and crystal balls and things when the going's rough and they're on edge. But never when things are all wine and brandy.' Probably why we never noticed him much before.

But the day Hitler hit on his best idea of the war and sent the schoolmaster's son to the desert to see what he could do to prop up the Eyeties and stop the rot was the day Horace came into his own.

'Came into my ken like a comet, did Erwin. None of this drifting lark with Rommel.'

Tobruk had been under siege since April. The dusty, sand-blown seaport of Libya was the only viable harbour along the North African coast for 1,500 miles between Alexandria in Egypt and Sfax in Tunisia.

Rommel desperately needed its docks to get supplies in for his own forces, who were now severely stretched because of their breakneck successes, and his Luftwaffe had been giving the Aussie garrison hell. Twenty-one raids on one night alone between dusk and dawn. Four months of bombardment had to be enough.

So they set up Operation Battleaxe and Reginald became Horace.

*

'You see, since the arrival of Rommel, Sarge, and his run of successes, I been getting a lot more enquiries . . .'

'I understand, Cope, all the same . . .'

'And now with this Battleaxe lark in the offing . . .'

'Yes, it's bound to up the anxiety . . .'

'I mean, business is booming, you could say . . .'

'I know, it's a trying time . . .'

'So, with so many enquiries, I thought if I can do a general one in Daily Orders each morning it would help ease the pressure a bit on all of us.'

'Well, yes, but with that new Padre you haven't a hope, Cope.'

The Battleaxe offensive is Wavell's big card to try to break through to Tobruk and relieve the poor bloody Aussies because this *wunderkind*'s taken the stage and cut them off out there on their own with only the seaside free, and not much help, unless you control the Med, which we never seem able to do for any length of time. 'Like playing leg spin.'

'Not a lot going right these days,' said the Sarge.

'Who would have thought it could all turn upside down in a few weeks?' said the Corp.

'Well, it was in his stars from the start,' said Cope, opening up his flaps to air his tent and views. 'I remember it well. February 6th, a Thursday, when it actually took effect – when he *arrived* that is, slap bang in the middle of Aquarius. Been in powerful conjunction with Neptune for some time. That's what did it. Old Adolf had neglected the desert for too long, see. Left it all to Musso, while he got on with Europe. Then we go careering along, knocking aside everything in front of us, and it comes as a sudden shock to the Upper Kraut system when he gets the news, see. That's the Neptune bit.

'I think Adolf must have been rummaging around in his mind the previous weekend. Gone off to get away from it all, I should imagine. My considered reckoning would be Sunday the second. More than likely when he was having a quiet zizz after the roast boar. It was then the idea would have come to him, because it was another perfect conjunction.

'See, if you look at the night-sky chart for that month, you'll see that in Taurus, Aldebaran, The Bull's Eye, is smack bang in the middle of it. Like a great glistening blob bursting through the panoply of the heavens. I can just see old Adolf leaping to his feet shouting "I've got it! Send Erwin!"'

'Hmm. Very romantic, Cope.'

'It must have come at him like a shooting star,' said Horace, punching his fist in the air, 'bursting through "like stabs of light into the chaos of darkness".'

'Sounds just like a line out of one of the C-in-C's books.'

'"That'll do the trick," he shouts. "Why the Himmel didn't I think of that before?"'

'But don't get carried away. We'll need all the transport we can get.'

'It's the idea, see,' shouts Horace. 'The idea doesn't just *dawn*, you know – sneak up soft and cunning and creep-like, like kowtowing to the Corp. It comes whack-bang straight through the centre of the sky like a white charger in a circus coming crashing through the big hoop. Whoomph! "Send Erwin!"'

'Give me one good reason to give to the CO,' said the Sarge.

'It takes their minds off things.'

'Shouldn't they be *on*?' says the Sarge.

'Well, you'd think so but it don't work that way in real life.'

'*Real* life?'

'Yeah.'

'Isn't *this* real enough?'

'Not really.'

'So what's not really real about it, then?'

'Well, war's a bit of a contrived business, isn't it?'

'Never thought of it that way before.'

'Artificial like. You see, you got to look at them blokes as if they're still in civvy street. War's like an extra. It don't change the basic Botcher. And that's what I go for – the basic bloke and his basic stars. Stars don't change because of wars.'

'Hmm. Above all that, I suppose.'

'Right.'

'Well, every man to his own trade, as I always say.'

Sure enough, when Rommel took over we never knew what hit us. Talk about a commander with a baton and a poetry book. What this one had was bang up to date. Drove around in an open-top staff car right in the middle of his troops, so his men could see him. Or he's up in an aircraft leaning down and waving them on.

'I mean, that's *style*,' said Reginald, pre-Horace. 'Not to take anything away from old Cyclops Wavell, mind.'

He was right. Poetry *was* a mite intimidating, a touch above the rest of us, a smidge too formidable for the chaps down in the dune, a bit too Biggles.

'I mean, poetry and blooms and flowers fading and all that. Well, that's alright for afters, but not much prop in a crisis. For Cenotaphs, that is, not wadies.'

But Erwin was pure Hollywood. The wagon train's surrounded but the Cavalry's coming. Sound the charge, bugler! Ta-ta-ta-ta-ta-ta! Zoomph! Straight in. No messing. That was Rommel. Tea leaves, coffee grains, beer slops, crystal balls, whatever he used, it worked.

'Anyway, now that we're up against it,' said Cope, 'our chaps are going to need a bit of a leg-up, Sarge, and I'm your man.'

Now the next task is to take Tobruk – or rather relieve it – so Cope pressed his case.

'Them Aussies been stuck out there on their own for months with nothing but Aussies to talk to. Must be hell for them, Sarge.'

'Pity you can't send them some of your precious scopes, Cope. They got their own paper over there. *The Tobruk Truth*. Sounds just right for your stuff.'

'Think we could wire it through?'

'Na. Jerry might crack the code and then he'd know all our inner secrets, wouldn't he?'

'Well, them Aussies could be in one hell of a state without their stars, Sarge.'

'They'll cope, Cope.'

The Padre's replacement was a different breed of vicar altogether, more of a bishop type.

'What's the difference, Sarge?'

'Well, our bloke's like a lieutenant. This one's more of a major, with a mitre.' And the name stuck – Major Mitre.

Most of Major Mitre's experience was in Admin. And he had assumed most of Admin's characteristics, plus the jargon, poise, attitude, and demeanour of the serving officer – remote, smooth, smart, officious, all-knowing, self-satisfied.

'Funny they give them commissions, Sarge.'

'How's that, Felgate?'

'Well, they're more a sort of *sarge*, really, aren't they?'

'Well, there's officers and officers, Felgate. Now run along and polish your Bren, will you?'

Nevertheless, Major Mitre carried the authority of God and King and occasionally got them confused, as most of his own countrymen did. He was still the guardian of Established Religion and all its practices and operated to the word or the letter of his own Book – a sort of personal variation on the theme of King's Regulations and Army Instructions – 'KR and AI', as it was known. In Major Mitre's world 'KR and AI' became 'GR and JI' – God's Regulations and Jesus' Instructions.

The Sergeant 'squared' it with the Company Commander, who was preoccupied with other forms of stars and sightings and alignments and predictions, poring over a bundle of tatty maps where the lines were as vague as anything Cope struggled to interpret.

'Hope he has less trouble figuring out the mysterious ways of Orion than we have with those of Rommel,' he said flinging a pair of dividers like a dart at a tattered chart clinging indecisively to the 'wall'.

'Sir.'

'Oh, alright then, Sergeant, let him go ahead. But remember – it's *Horace!*'

'Sir.'

'I don't want any Memos from the Almighty. Got enough on my plate,' he added, still staring cheerlessly at his charts and smacking his head with his baton.

'That's alright, sir, I've told him it's a bit of a lark, as it were. Nothing serious.'

'Nevertheless, keep a sharp eye on both of them, Sergeant. You never can tell with these airy-fairy types.'

'Sir.'

'A wary eye's what's wanted.'

'Sir.'

'For the airy fairy.'

'Sir.'

'Got it? Wary for the airy fairy, eh?'

'I got it, sir. A wary eye, sir.'

'Right.'

Back at the covered wagon:

'CO says OK, Cope, but the moniker's Horace. Can't make it official like. Not like one of them war artists. None of this scribbling your roughs and nipping back home to polish them. You're staying right here with the rest of us.'

'Fair enough, Sarge.'

'And I'm keeping a wary eye on you.'

'Oh,' says Cope, slightly crestfallen.

'Well,' said the Sergeant, 'you never can tell with you airy-fairy types.'

So it came to pass that Horace – né Reginald – Cope set about compiling his daily horoscope charts and publishing them as an Appendix to Daily Orders. Nothing elaborate. Usually no more than one-liners:

Sagittarius: What makes you desirable is your looks, not your philanthropy. Stay clear of false mirrors until after dusk.

Libra: One of nature's most impetuous idiosyncratics, you always take great pains to shield your enigmatic identity. Come on down and muck in more.

Taurus: You would give the Earth, the Moon and the Stars to others. Before you do today, calculate what's left.

The Company was soon flocking to read Horace's forecasts, crowding around the flimsy sheets tacked up on a board outside the Company 'office' or whatever temporary accommodation the CO could find for himself. Even breakfast and mail began to take second place to the predictions.

Some memorised the day's offering, others scribbled on scraps of paper and went off poring over them, mumbling and debating, sharing and arguing, totally absorbed, all concentration focused in the Daily Offerings.

And those who wanted more, inspired or simply confused, made personal appointments with Horace for the evenings, so that there was an even greater sense of activity and buzz and preoccupation, and yet peace, around the unit. Battleaxe and Rommel seemed very far away.

'Certainly got them concentrating, Sergeant,' said the

CO, dangling his compasses. 'Wouldn't think that hardened lot could be taken in with such rubbish, would you?'

'A ploy, sir,' said the Sergeant, 'a very palpable ploy.'

'Pardon?'

'Oh, just something I picked up from the C-in-C's poetry book, sir.'

'Oh. Virgo, are you?'

'No, Fenchurch,' Cope's deep drone seemed to vibrate the canvas, 'can't say I can see any configuration of the firmament that would give you better odds than that.' He squinted up at the heavens through his powerful binoculars, but only as a gesture, because he did all his prognostications from his charts. 'Especially as Orion's been a bit shaky recently, ever since she came under the bellicose influence of Mars.'

Horace produced his forecasts for Daily Orders but continued to conduct personal surveys and give private consultations under the canvas of a truck which had the air of a promenade palmist's booth and, like a palmist, he composed horoscopes at once sombre, sincere and sensible.

'Now's the time to stop thinking so hard, Sheldon. Pressure in your solar house should make the options and alternatives that much simpler. I'd turn my mind to a more mundane hobby, if I were you, like gardening.'

Major Mitre was less convinced, however. By early June, as the queues for Cope got longer and the excitement rose, Battleaxe seemed to recede into the background, the name of Rommel to pass from everyone's lips, and the Padre to be completely forgotten.

'Rommel, Wavell and God would seem to have lost their sweetness on the desert air,' said the CO, browsing through one of the C-in-C's books he had left behind.

The Major was feeling confoundedly inadequate. When he took over, he had expected there to be 'some temporary local opposition, yes', but had accepted the Sergeant's 'bit of a lark' assessment. Now he wasn't so sure. As he snuck a glimpse at some of Horace's elaborate astrological designs that decorated the Daily Orders Appendix, he couldn't suppress the impression that the local was expanding to the universal. Bad enough taking second place to Rommel, but third place to Cope was something else.

'I understand there are – how shall I put it? – disquieting rumours, Sergeant.'

'It's a tense time, Padre.'

'Quite. And that's just the point.'

'Sir?'

'I mean, far be it from me to question the discipline and morale of our unit. I am, so to speak, but a passing pilgrim.'

'Sir.'

'A wandering witness, if you will.'

'Of course, Padre. Anytime.'

'But I am becoming aware of disquieting voices abroad.'

'Oh, bad news from home, sir? Sorry about . . .'

'No, no. Abroad *here*, Sergeant. Around the dunes and your flock.'

'Oh, how's that, then, Padre?'

'Report has it – Daily Orders apart – that certain souls in our care are seeking solace solely in the stars.'

'Oh, you mean *Cope*, sir?'

'I speak no names, Sergeant. But methinks it would be a mite unwise should anyone contemplate encouraging such an altogether primitive and unacceptable preoccupation.'

The Sergeant reported to Horace one evening in early June.

'He's worried about taking second place to Rommel, I should think.'

'Well, he should be, Sarge. I was just looking at what I had written when the Fox arrived way back in February.'

'You mean, you did a prediction for him then?'

'Well, a strange star had entered our settled firmament, hadn't it? And it was about to upset the even tenor of our desert ways!'

'Oh.'

'The question was, what manner of man was this who had suddenly swum into our ken?'

'Swum?'

'It's our language.'

'Ah.'

'Now, a horoscope is like a *view*, see – of a person at a particular hour – namely, his birth.'

'Fascinating.'

'And that lays down the kind of personality you have for the rest of your natural. And when you do a prediction at any one time it's a bit like an end-of-term report, see?'

'Ah, hah.'

'Well, now, born November 15th. That makes Rommel a Scorpio for a start.'

'Well, that would figure, the way he's been stinging us.'

'Very much so. And it means he's decisive, able, and got good judgement. He's got this penetrating eye that can see the meaning of things. A very highly developed sense of power and a striving for self-improvement, but his downfall can be brought about by turning the sting in his personality at the wrong people at the wrong time.'

'Very penetrating mind, yours, Cope.'

'So, at the start, I wrote: "Should do well once he settles in. Potential good. Determined to fulfil promise invested in him." '

'Just like a headmaster's report.'

'And very appropriate too, him being a schoolmaster's son.'

'And his interim report?'

' "Should go on to bigger and better things." '

'Hmm.'

'I'd say at the moment he's well on the way to fulfilment, Sarge. In fact,' he said, throwing open his canvas flaps for business, 'I should say – *peaking*.'

'Oh, I shouldn't worry, sir. Cope's bit in Daily Orders is no more than a bit of a lark to keep the lads' spirits up.'

'But they appear to be seeking *personal* consultations, Sergeant.'

'Harmless, I should say, sir. And not at all threatening to your position. Shouldn't queer your pitch.'

'It isn't my pitch or position, Sergeant. And far be it from me to pull rank . . .'

'Perish the thought, Padre.'

'At the same time, I *am* a commissioned officer.'

'Absolutely, sir.'

'And I have to advise, shall we say, *counsel*, perhaps, that any continuation of such practices would constitute an infringement of our regulations on these matters – Established Church and all that – and would probably not be taken kindly to – nay, *frowned* upon even – in high places.'

And the Padre looked upwards lazily but tellingly as if his gaze had just happened to wander there, but whether in the direction of Heaven or just the galaxy, the Sergeant was not well enough positioned to judge.

'But, of course, sir. I'll see to it.'

And back at the wagon:

'Watch it, Horace.'

It was certainly true from the moment Rommel arrived we had our work cut out. We had had it too good for too long. The Eyeties had given us a false sense of our own military might. Good for morale, but not for survival, and not when the tide turns. Wars don't get won that way. And the blokes up top should have noticed. They should have known the quicker you move, the longer your supply lines get. And they should have known Hitler would move in if he thought the Italians were so hopeless. Maybe he didn't much care for the North Africa campaign but he cared about oil and the Middle East and India. Adolf was no slouch. He wasn't going to sit around and watch it all happen. And taking men off to mess about in Greece and leave us right run-down was a real Botcher's decision.

And when Hitler appointed Rommel he picked the best. When he got the big stuff through he'd turn on the real heavy generalship. Meanwhile, what he couldn't do with Panzers he'd do with panache.

'It's because of Rommel, Padre. Cope has been so accurate, they figure he knows something.'

'I think we should have a word with him.'

So the Sergeant reported back:

'Padre wants a word with you, Cope.'

And Horace stepped forward.

'So, what do you predict for Battleaxe, then, Cope?' Being basically a military man, Major Mitre tried an outflanking movement.

Being basically a religious man, Horace met him straight on. 'I do blokes, not battles, Padre.'

'Ah, yes, you depict destinies.'

'No, sir, I predict problems.'

'And how, pray?'

'By being basically a Taurus, like you.'

'A Taurus! How do you know I'm a Taurus?'

'Well, you are, aren't you? Concerned with the hopeless cases, like me – or they're concerned with us.'

'Well, yes, of course, but …'

'Typical Taurus characteristic.'

'But nothing whatsoever to do with my birth sign, for heaven's sake.'

'Well, they all say that. But I know the signs – interested in unstable souls and wobbly spirits and all that. Go on, when's your birthday, then?'

'That's entirely irrelevant.'

'Maybe to you. But it's gotta be somewhere between April 22nd and May 21st anyway. And in my book that means being attracted by the more hopeless flotsam of mankind.'

'This is pure mumbo jumbo, Cope.'

'Well, you got your Book and I got mine, Padre. But it don't make much difference.'

'Hmm.' Major Mike shrugged and ran a finger inside his dog collar to air his chest before sitting down. 'And how,' he breathed, twitching to shuffle the air around, 'how do *you* deal with a man's problems, pray?'

'Oh, no, I don't do that. I give them something to think about instead. Lines to work on. And they apply them to themselves.'

'You mean, they don't take your stuff literally?'

'Oh no, no one can. You only take what you read into it. I give them a starting point and it follows on, forces each one to think up ways and means that will make his horoscope act in the best possible manner for him. I might give him an apparently dreadful one, like say: "the end of the day brings sunset in more ways than one." Now, on the face of it, that would seem to spell curtains. But as no man truly believes in his own end, you see, being a survivor at heart – the instinct to survive being man's greatest, as you well know, sir – he sets about reading into it the most positive interpretation he can. Because the one thing he isn't going to accept is his own death, so he enters into a struggle to make it impossible for his HC to predict it.'

'I see, helps his horoscope along, you mean?'

'In a way. Like a parable. It's what you read into it

that counts, isn't it?'

'To an extent . . . ye . . . es.'

'I mean, you've heard the one about the widow's mite and the prodigal son, haven't you, Padre . . .?'

'Well . . .'

'You got to keep them firmly on the ground too, you see. They got a job to do. It can't be all stars, no more than it can be all Jesus.'

'Hmmm.'

'I mean, life in the desert's not all a bed of wine and Moses, is it, Padre?'

Being basically a military man, Major Mike tried a quick outflanking manoeuvre: 'Would you do one for me?'

'Oh, I wouldn't want to do yours, Padre.'

'Why not?'

'Because you'd be testing *me*, not you.'

'Meaning?'

'Meaning, what you need to do with horoscopes is take them in and make them private. You'd be trying to catch *me* out.'

Major Mitre assessed his tactics again and switched smartly on to another move.

'Are you charging for this stuff, Cope?'

'Only a token.'

'How much?'

'It varies. I leave it up to them. Whatever they can afford, in kind mostly – a sock, a packet of fags, that sort of thing.'

'Is this justified?'

'You get paid, Padre.'

'It's not at all the same, Cope! And it's downright immoral to profit from other men's feelings.'

'Blimey, pot calling the kettle black, isn't it?'

'That could actually be deemed offensive, Cope.'

'Who's the Deemer then?'

'Deemer?'

'Well, if there's a *Re*-deemer, who's the bleeding Deemer that done all the deeming in the first place?'

'This is totally irrelevant and absurd.'

'Not to me, it isn't Padre. You pass the plate around. Only difference is you get a special place to do it in. I only got my canvas.'

The following forty-eight hours proved chaotic. Battleaxe was heating up. No one knew the precise hour of attack yet, or no one was saying, but the frenzy continued. Reinforcements kept pouring in. Dust and sand lifted off and hovered protectively over the units as they scrambled and struggled to get their kits organised and their machines and guns and transport and assorted bellicose gear into position and order. If Rommel didn't have inside dope on what Wavell's mob was up to, there was enough outside to be had for the mere monitoring.

Rommel wouldn't have needed an exceptional focal length of binoculars to detect and decipher the pattern of puffs kicking up from the desert floor – desperate dust clouds and sand halos rising like Indian smoke signals on the horizon down near the Egypt-Libya border, as the Allies prepared for the Great Secret Attack. Designs in dust rose like balloons on the skyline to wobble and wave and daub silhouette shapes on the blue backcloth, as the legions of lesser Wavells wheeled their trucks and tanks and armoured cars and sundry weapons into place and marched to and fro, and to again, to make doubly-trebly sure they'd got everything packed and ready and hadn't left unturned a dash of dust or a smidgen of sand.

All over the West Egyptian and the East Libyan desert from the Halfaya Pass to the Hafid Ridge, from Sidi Suleiman to Sidi Azeiz, the puffs erupted and hung like palls, then faded only to inflate again as if rows of children were festively skipping along the horizon line, blowing up balloons and tossing them aloft, and blowing them up again as soon as they showed signs of flagging or flaking, helping them to keep bobbing and the good ship *Battleaxe* to keep afloat, glorious in its joyfulness.

'Got a nipper of his own, has Erwin,' said the Sergeant. 'He'll be taking snaps to send home.'

But the outstanding contribution to Rommel's horizon gazing was the antics of Cope and Major Mitre. In their own ways they were struggling for dominion, or rather the Padre was – Horace didn't have to bother. The queues to Cope's Consultation Canvas lengthened by the minute, and with them the dust clouds billowed into the heavens as the Allied Armies kicked their heels, their impatient boots pounding the sand with edginess and anxiety, so that this one spot of sandy turmoil stood out above all the other minor signs of military tumult swirling around them. And in the midst of all this great Cope turmoil and lesser Wavell tumult sang the still small voice of the Padre's forlorn oasis, his modest if imperial temporary quarters a place of hallowed calm sheltering amid the storms about him. It was as if the good Lord himself – or even the CO – had granted him this blessed plot, this hushed garden west of Eden, in which he at least might enjoy the peace that passes all understanding, except that the peace hadn't passed Major Mitre's understanding at all because he knew hellishly well that it was the dark devilish Horace who had contrived the tranquillity.

If Rommel had had any particular desire to eliminate the religious support of those distant clamouring legions, he could easily have identified the C of E's consecrated corner of North Africa, the one *without* the merest puff of dust, the one free from even *one* balloon of sand, the one haven of rest and repose, the one oasis of serenity in the whole wide world of the Western Desert – because there, nothing, literally *nothing*, was taking place.

But more significantly, the CO didn't much like it, not because he was feeling sorry for Major Mitre, but because he knew he couldn't afford these tell-tale pockets of non-activity. *'Dead give-way,'* he mused to himself by his window, pondering the coming Great Secret Attack and jabbing his compasses into his perforated palm. *'All Rommel has to do is blast what's on either side. And that's us!'*

'Can't have that!' He pulled himself together suddenly and rapped out loud to the Adjutant and Sergeant. 'Between them, that star chappie and the sin Major are giving the damned game away!' He stabbed his palm. 'Best get shot of the pair of them.'

'Shot, sir?' asked the Adjutant. 'As in gun, you mean, or bolt?'

'Now, don't you come the bloody pedant with me, Cumbershawe! There's enough bloody intellectuals around this desert to last me a wartime.'

'Sorry, sir.'

'I mean, I ask you. Generals with their heads buried in Ovids, Padres with their minds wrapped up in rank, and Privates with their feet covered in Capricorns – what's a simple CO like me expected to fight a bloody war with?'

'Quite, sir.'

The Sergeant and the Adjutant could tell the CO was upset the way he kept alternately stabbing his palm and the wall map with his compasses.

'The heat?' the Sergeant asked the Adjutant, silently.

'More like . . .' and the Adjutant tapped his head with his baton, lightly.

'Highly civilised generals, indeed!' The CO pressed on. 'Educated wallahs, bah! Scholars, my eye! Classroom fodder, more like. Should have stayed on at school, if you ask me. At the last O Group meeting at GHQ, I asked what our chaps might expect to find around Tobruk and do you know the bloody answer I get? "Well," he says, "for a start, the remains of the temples of Ammon and the fountain of the Sun!" '

The CO stomped back to the window and gazed out at the storm of dusty activity around Cope's truck and the oasis of tranquillity around the Padre's den. The Adjutant and the Sergeant dutifully edged over behind him to follow his gaze.

'How's the Bishop taking it anyway, Sergeant?'

'Quietly, sir.'

'Nose out of joint, eh?'

'*Askew*, sir, yes.'

'Hmm.' The CO continued his look-out.

'That damned constellation wallah seems to have worked some kind of miracle.'

'Yes, sir,' agreed the Adjutant. 'It would seem that way.'

'Well,' the CO shrugged resignedly, 'two thousand years, you know. It's not as if they haven't had their chance, is it?'

The awesome silence of Christianity's missed chance floated through the room. Then the CO turned quietly and scrutinised his wall chart. 'Pity the Mitre blighter's been recalled to GHQ, isn't it?' The Adjutant and the Sergeant looked at each other. 'Still,' the CO went on, eyeing a point south-east of Tobruk, 'with a driver like cosmic Cope, they ought to make it alright.' And with that he drove his compasses into Sidi Azeiz.

Horace slung Major Mitre's bags into the boot of the CO's Sunbeam. 'Well,' the CO had said, 'I shan't be needing it for a few days and it's all we've got left, 'sides, it could do with a de-coke. Gasket's gone too, I shouldn't be surprised. They mightn't even make it.'

All around the Sunbeam the puffs kept rising as the frenzy persevered, and men and trucks steered around and past without so much as a brake or a glance. Once Cope's Canvas had come down, the war was back to its old familiar routine, normal hostilities were resumed, excitement was in the air again, and minds were buoyantly focused elsewhere. 'Maybe they're *on* something at last,' said the Sergeant.

When the Padre was told about the signal summoning him back to GHQ, he asked if it had to be Cope. And when Horace heard about the signal, *he* asked if it had to be Cope too. The Adjutant said it rather looked that way, didn't it? And the Sergeant said that's the way it is, anyway.

'Well,' roared Horace as a tank rolled by and more churned-up sand landed in the open boot. 'Maybe they're better off without us.'

They paused one on each side of the Sunbeam to watch the clouds lift from the earth as yet more armour and men wandered off in the general direction of Tobruk.

'Well,' said the Padre with a touch of Mitre haughtiness, 'if they think the stars will guide them, then yes, I expect they *can* work it out for themselves.'

Cope scooped another handful of sand off the Padre's morocco-bound valise and chucked it futilely into the air for another passing tank to throw back.

'Oh, they can teach themselves alright, Padre. But they can never be bothered until they're in trouble, see? Like undertaking.' Cope eyed the Major over the roof. 'I mean, *you* could do it yourself, couldn't you? Not a lot to it really, digging a hole.'

The Sergeant said, agitated: 'You got your directions now, Cope?'

'I expect you think,' the Padre retorted laughing, 'that if Jesus were around today he'd be writing horoscopes too.'

'Your directions, Cope,' the Sergeant intervened again, anxious to keep the war containable. 'Clear about them, are you?'

'Certainly, Padre, 'cos they're all parables, anyway, like I said.'

'Well, good luck, sir,' said the Adjutant, swinging the passenger's door pointedly.

'And presumably *you* could be him, Cope.' Major Mitre bowed down and squeezed in as if he had ended the exchange.

'Naw,' Horace shouted over the din, blowing the dust from the ridges before slamming the boot shut. 'Not me.'

'Oh, I don't know,' called the Major, adjusting his skirts. 'Second Coming and all that. The two thousand years are nearly up. You never know.'

'Naw. Not me, Padre,' said Horace, coming around to the driver's door and pausing to shake more sand from his shirt and shorts.

'Got everything now, Cope?' asked the Sergeant.

'How can you be so sure?' asked the Padre.

'Well, for a start,' said Horace, easing himself in and kicking sand off his boots. 'I don't believe in all this muck, see. Neither yours *nor* mine.'

The Adjutant slammed the Padre's door and stood back, saluting, and calling eagerly: 'Safe journey, sir!'

'You don't believe it!'

'Naw, too cynical, me.'

'I'd get clear of this lot smartly, Cope,' shouted the Sergeant, 'and stop as soon as the bloody dust has settled and take a bearing, just in case.'

'You mean, it's all a con trick?' The Major sounded genuinely horrified.

Horace adjusted his seat and switched on. The Sunbeam cleared its throat of sand.

'God speed, sir!' bawled the Adjutant, jovially.

'Course,' said Horace, turning to stare at his passenger for the first time. '*You* know that!' And pointing through the windscreen at the dark sandstorm ahead which spelt Battleaxe, he added: 'Just look at that lot out there, off to get their brains blown out while we sit back and watch them go, feeling smug because we've given them some inner secret.'

'Double back behind them carriers, Cope!' the Sergeant shouted above the revving. 'Then hard left and head on down. Couple of miles, then stop and take stock!'

'See you in Blighty, sir!' the Adjutant called out cheerily. 'If not Berlin!'

'We're not Tauruses for nothing, Padre.' Horace revved up and peered out through the windscreen with eyes clenched like a Spitfire pilot before take-off, wiping his hand across the window as if waving away the chocks.

'Of course,' said the Padre, regaining some composure for a second, 'caring for unstable souls and wobbly spirits, the flotsam of mankind, wasn't it?' And he smiled back benignly to the faithful Adjutant, signalling him a modest cross as he rapidly disintegrated into dust.

'No, not *that*,' said Horace, engaging gear for Halfaya, revving and letting out the clutch so heartlessly that the Sunbeam churned its brutal way ahead to swerve past a tank coming across its bows. 'But because we're both full of bull, Padre. *That's* why!'

The Sunbeam turned right and roared off in the general direction of Libya, passing the CO's office in a thundercloud, so that the Old Man at the window blinked and stabbed himself with his compasses as the Adjutant and Sergeant came bursting in to report that Cope and the Padre looked to have gone in the wrong direction.

'Oh, I don't know,' said the CO, still staring into his beloved Battleaxe cloud and jabbing his bleeding palm. 'I don't know.' Then turning to scrutinise his wall map pitted like a dartboard, he threw his compasses at Tobruk and added: 'Wherever you go these days, you're bound to bump into Rommel some time or another.'

TARZAN STRIPES

Benghazi, Wednesday, 24 December 1941

And the women and children fretted awaiting news of their beloved ones. And lo, a stalwart Mercury arose and sent greetings to all who were sore afflicted, and was so smitten in mind he greeted the Lord of the afflictors too ...

Nine

'Say!' this voice cries out in the wilderness, 'How d'you spell Rommel?'

December 24th. Silent Night. Holy Night. The world's waiting. We're waiting. And the Sarge is waiting … when up pipes the voice of this zealous herald, kneeling on his pink knees in the sand with his shirt over his head to cover his writing pad and his tiny torch glowing with a kindly light on the Christmas cards he's writing underneath – and wrestling with the last of the cardinal mysteries: how to spell the name of the Supreme Kraut Commander?

Not Jesus or Herod or Bethlehem or Nazareth, not Judea or Israel or Galilee or Capernaum, not Pharisee or Sadducee or Zacharias or Caesar Augustus, not even Kaspar, Melchior or Balthazar – but the name of the one who had come to establish dominion over desert, dune, wadi, camel and rat – Rommel!

'Spirit of Christmas upon you then, Corp?' asks the Sarge.

'Well,' says the prophet of philanthropy, 'you can never tell. Might be a nice enough bloke when you get to know him. 'Sides, must be somebody's son.'

Six weeks into Operation Crusader and everyone's a bit jaded, Christmas or no Christmas.

Tobruk's been relieved – or the Aussies inside have – and now it's supposed to be downhill all the way to

Tripoli and the end of the desert campaign. But it never works out like that. Benghazi's up ahead for a start. Not much opposition left, they say, but after a long slog across the desert we're running a bit short of supplies and support as well. Not surprising. You can't just charge all over a wilderness like this, even if Rommel's Afrika Korps *is* on the run at last, and expect the food and ammo to keep flowing free.

Auchinleck knew it from the start. Wouldn't lift an Enfield or a Bren until he had all the supplies he reckoned we needed. Started off with about 700 tanks and 700 aircraft, double Rommel's in each case, but didn't budge a tank track until he got them. Put Churchill's back up, he did – Winnie was desperate to get a move on and tell the world we were winning. But the Auk wasn't playing with flags on a map in Piccadilly, and we'd had our lot by the time we pulled up at Benghazi.

'You've got to get it right,' said Tarzan, groping under his shirt tent and getting no response from the battle-worn warriors of the wilderness. 'I mean, there's always more than one way to spell a name, isn't there? – like Freddy with a weye or a nigh ee and John with an aitch or a nought.'

'True,' said a voice from the dunes, 'I seen some blokes putting two ells on Churchill and sticking an aitch on 'itler.'

'There you are, then.'

Corporal Tarzan Stripes worried about people. We called him Stripes on account of his rank and Tarzan on account of him always calling us his Apes.

'That's what you lot are – bleeding apes! Every time you're asked something you just sit there scratching, picking your noses, and blinking away as if you'd never heard the King's bleeding English before. Should be behind bars, you should. And let out when we need you.'

But Tarzan thought about people a lot. 'You got to take

everybody very personal indeed,' he claimed. Everybody else kept their heads down and got on with it, but not Corporal 'Arold – 'as in 'astings' – not Corporal Tarzan.

When they gave him his first stripe at Sidi Rezegh, he said proudly: 'On the first rung of power, see,' and when he got another a couple of weeks later after we lost three corps in one skirmish with the Fox at Wadi Bahra, there was no holding him.

'Watch it, Sarge,' he warned. 'You could be next.'

Rommel might have been on the run but it wasn't plain sailing, although one literate general was supposed to have said it was more like sea warfare, with our tanks 'appearing and disappearing like ships in a fog' so that no one ever knew where the real formations were. But Rommel was no slouch, and time and again, with less than half the power at his elbow than we had, he gave us a right run for it – even cut the link between Tobruk and the New Zealanders when he must have had fewer men up front than we had minding the shop.

'Ever wonder what it would be like with the Old Fox on our side, Sarge?'

'He'd worry the eggs out of chickens like you for a start.'

Not surprising that someone wanted to send him a Christmas card.

Under the glowing shirt Tarzan's torch wobbled impatiently.

'Go on, then, you smart lot,' came the voice of muffled despair. 'You an' all your fancy exams and civvy degrees and all that. How d'you spell it?'

'Don't matter, Corp, it'll get there.'

'How d'you know?'

'He'll be expecting it.'

The torchlight flickered irritatedly. 'Not the bleeding point, is it?'

'What if there are two Rommels spelt exactly the same, Corp?' Another tired mumble from the dune.

'What, *two* Field Marshals?'

'Forget it.'

The torchlight fluttered again.

'You're thick, you are, the lot of you. You don't understand you just gotta get it right. Don't matter who the recipient is.'

'Nor the bloke what gets it, neether.'

'Right.' The flicker calmed down. ' 'Sides, blokes get touchy about their names.'

'Krauts don't care, Corp. They like to think they're all sons of Adolf anyway.'

'Not Erwin's fault he was born on the wrong side of the Eden blanket.'

'Deliver it myself, if I were you.'

The Auk's caution paid off. He knew the course and what had to be done, but even with all the support he had waited so doggedly for we were still dried out by the time we reached Benghazi.

Maybe they delayed us going in to make it easier. The rumour got about that some units had taken it already but they held our mob there on Christmas Eve, kidding us it was all going to be down to us. Proper little morale booster. They did that to units sometimes, if they'd had a real roughing up – delayed the final attack and sent them in late to give them an easier run. Like a bonus or a Christmas present.

'Maybe it's our turn now.'

''Bout time.'

'Maybe Benghazi's our Christmas stocking.'

'Maybe it was all over yesterday and they were setting up the big surprise for us.'

'Ha! Ha! Desert Fool! Never mind, come on in and have a drink. And a Merry Christmas to all our invaders!'

The wilderness gets you like that. The Western Desert gave a whole new meaning to Christ's forty days.

Very proud of his stripes, was Tarzan. Took his promotion and responsibility real serious. Not power crazy. 'You take on power as a responsibility, not a licence.' Used to write home to blokes' mums when they got done. The blokes, that is.

And he was obsessed with 'getting it right'. When he sat down in the evenings to write home to unknown wives and dads he made a meal out of getting the names correct to the minutest detail of rank, name, number, middle names, apostrophes, small cs or big cs in mac, or even none at all. Not a specially literary sort of chap – not too many letters after his name – so it was always a bit of a struggle for him, which only emphasised the effort and determination.

'Not particularly fluent of pen, our Corp, is he?'

'Not nimble of nib, you mean?'

'Nor quick of quill.'

In fact, it was a terrible pain for Tarzan 'to put pen to parchment', and when he did he used it like a navvy wielding a pick, chewing down most of the shaft while pondering the spelling. 'You got to admire him.'

'Load of old codswallop,' said Wool, watching Tarzan at his laborious task and himself sweating in his balaclava. Wool had a problem about *Comforts* that tended to set him on edge at times.

'Well, if it makes 'em feel better,' said Tarzan.

'Rum old honesty, yours. You never knew any of them well enough to write about them anyway.'

'Not the point. 'Sides. Doesn't do no harm. And you got to make sure you get the name dead right, if you see what I mean.'

We don't know much about the state of Benghazi, but we do know it's a rum place to be parked outside on

Christmas Eve. And we're all determined to remember better ones. Not for sentimental reasons, but because it's an order.

We always got time to 'focus in, lads', before going into action. 'Get your mind sharpened,' the Sarge would say. 'No distractions. Hone it right down to the heart of the matter.' That came after his own lecture, the one about the hail and the hearty, the ache and the anarchy, and about being all on our own once the attack's started and out of his orbit once we've gone through the 'veil of fire'. But that was another story.

This is a Christmas attack, so there has to be some variation.

'Try focusing on some better Chrissies, lads,' he says, tuning us in then asking for a few examples of more uproarious Nativities to get us in the mood.

It's not one of his best ideas but we come up with a midnight tea and sticky bun party with the Sally Ann in Salford; there's someone playing the voice of God at a sister's Girl Guide Nativity Play in Monyash; there's a moving hearthside vigil with red candles and peat fires burning up a Kilburn attic; there's someone posing for an artist girlfriend to do him in 'seasonal oils' in Cleethorpes; and a Joseph in the *Wandering Jew* at the Golders Green Women's Institute. All short, terse one-liners, not a lot of laughs or dramatic tension:

'Can't give much away in the desert.'

'Keep your past to yourself, I always say.' Difficult to break the habit even at Christmas. But the one-liners were good enough for starters. Didn't warm us up, but started tuning us in.

So now all we need's a sign, a signal, a show of some description. A star will do. Even a shell. But all we get is this sudden, staccato shout that keeps interrupting our peace and concentration:

'C'mon! Anyone! Rommel! How's it go?'

*

'Would you bother if you didn't have them stripes?'

'Course,' says Tarzan. 'I know we all use nicknames, *our* names, but mums and dads don't. They want to know the guy we buried was their own Jim, Joe or George, not someone else's Norm, Nick or Larry. Got to be meticulous. They've stopped being Freak or Con see, them was only temporary names. When they go through the great veil and pass on they go back to their previous incarnation, see, and pick up their old moniker again. Maybe they've moved out of our mortal ken, but they're really only passing through anyway, like us all.'

Tarzan couldn't write particularly well but he could always explain what he meant.

'Well, it's a comfort for the rest of us to know we'll always be in safe hands, Corp. – even unto the uttermost ends of the sand.'

'Oh, smart lot, aren't we? What your folks gonna think when *your* turn comes and they get a letter offering 'heartfelt condolences' for the loss of some other jerk, telling them what a great comrade-up-in-arms some other Charlie was, and they can hold their heads high on Armistice Day and look with pride on the great service and sacrifice some other git made for his Monarch and Motherland, and they can lay their wreaths and wear their poppies for someone else instead of you? How's *your* old Mum gonna feel?'

'That's why it don't pay to write, Corp.'

It was not often that Tarzan lost his cool, but that riled him. Took certain matters very personal.

'I know you lot think rank's only for the snobs,' he shouts back. 'Too damned grand, *you* are.' Brandishing his quill. 'Oh, I know all about *your* breed. Met a lot of you back home on the factory floor. Think cos a bloke's got some stripes he's getting too big for his boots and all that. Well, it's you's the snobs. "Oh, no," you say, "war's not *my* problem. Didn't ask it to break out, did we, no more than we asked to get born." So leave it to

the rest of us to take all the decisions for you. Why don't
you drop your rifle, then, and go get yourselves a
bucket and spade?'

'Got a mossie in his titfer, old Tarzan.'

'Well, maybe it's the heat.'

An hour earlier the Wise Men came through – Captain,
Staff Sergeant and Scribe; baton, map board and bumf –
to keep our spirits up and 'lend' us some encouragement: 'Right, now, men. You've done a damned
good job and we want you to know that the CO and the
whole Nation are extremely proud of you indeed. Been
an absolute pig of a slog, for all of us. But we know we
can call on you for just one last heave to push Benghazi
over into the bloody drink once and for all and before
breakfast.'

Then they slope off back again to cosier climes,
pretending they've got more important things to do, but
they're only too bloody keen to get out and leave us the
dirty work, with Sarge the Shepherd watching his
flocks by night all seated on the ground – well, all
crouching and cowering and complaining on the sand,
at any rate, certainly not up on the starry-lit hillside
dune rejoicing like the Chrissie cards claim. No, we're
all down below silently swearing and steaming in our
stinking sand holes. Should have been cool, relaxing
after the heat of the day, but Crusader had chosen some
rough weather, dull, wet, overcast, all the way, kind of
weather you never associate with desert:

'More like a Test at Old Trafford.'

'Huh. Rain never stops play here.'

'Rommel should have appealed against the light
instead of throwing away all them wickets.'

'Krauts were never any good on a turner.'

We should have spotted something a few days back
around Derna. Tarzan was digging in a few of the lads

after a skirmish we'd had with some stray units of the Afrika Korps. Covered them up temporarily – shallow grave stuff, until the Vulture Volunteers arrive to take over and do a proper job or ship them out so the rest of us can get on with the next botch.

Not really Tarzan's job. 'Corporal in charge' of the Graves Party when detailed but not expected to share in the digging.

'Well, I'm not proud. Always done it before. Couple of stripes don't change a man.'

'Another couple of letters for tonight, Corp, eh?'

'You're not *elevated* to corporal, you know. You're … *emphasised.*'

'Well, always something to do in the long summer evenings, isn't it?'

'Never lose the common or garden touch,' he says, digging away.

'Keeps you off the dunes, don't it?'

Pays no attention. Digs on.

'Relaxing after all that digging.'

Shovel in hand, sweat pouring down his spare ribs, back arched and fuming, he turns.

'How do you bleeding know it won't do no good,' he steams, 'any better than me?'

'True.'

'Well, then!' he shouts, stretching up from the hole in his desert rags like a violated vulture preening itself, blood and sand smeared all over, and a crazed light in his eyes as he folds up the corpse neat as a woman folding the ironing, struggling to tuck in the ends and the sleeves flopping all over him.

'You know, you just might have something there, Corp.'

'How do *you* bleeding know? *What* do you bleeding know?' And he picks up another Botcher, arms drooping around him like a soft ventriloquist's doll. Glazed. Gone.

'Must be the heat.'
We should have known.

Anyway, it's Christmas, and we're minding our own
Nowell business, quietly abiding ourselves in the wadi
fields, watched over by our very own Good Shepherd,
and keeping a sharp look-out for a star or any other
bright thing that might come hovering over where we
lay. And not one of your common or garden, oasis or
wadi, balmy desert evenings. This is a proper genuine,
Bedouin Christmas Eve.

'Might not be many of them left,' says a long-
suffering voice. 'Count your lucky stars.'

'Damp stockings hanging on the parapet.'

'Father Fritzmas arriving on his Sledge Hammer.'

'Slay-balls in the bag.'

'Who would ask for more?'

'Well, we got the sand, the camels, and the silent
night,' says an angel. 'If we can't get home for
Christmas, might as well enjoy it near to where it all
happened in the first place.'

Someone tries a few bars of 'Once in royal David's
city', then 'deep and crisp and even', then 'I saw three
ships a sailing', so we're soon feeling sorry for the folks
back home who've never been further than the Church
Hall for *their* Nativity Night.

We're settling into the mood, tensing up, knowing
he'll be here any moment now, heads down and mouths
tight shut. The mossies are still up, keen to see in
Christmas too, waiting for the promised rebirth of the
world – praying for omens, signs, sheep, stars, flocks,
shepherds, moonlight, wise men, the lot – and then up
pipes this angelic voice again, announcing: 'I'm serious.
How d'you spell Rommel?'

Not exactly a blinding flash of angel light, the behold
bit with the glory of the Lord shining round about. Not
exactly a loud hosannah 'proclaiming glad tidings of

great joy', but it *was* an enlightenment of a kind, definitely a sign of sorts. But more human than divine, like Joseph asking the Innkeeper: 'any chance of a nightcap before we turn in, Boss?', or: 'Any idea where we might pick up a bit of holly this time of night, young man?'

We wait. Not a dickie bird. No one thinks of telling him. Don't think he really wants to know.

A long time passes. We can hear Tarzan scraping and scribbling under his shirt tent, sighing and nibbling and shaking his pen, grunting and struggling as he tries and tests Rommel from all angles.

'That's it, then,' he declares, switching off his torch and leaving us staring at a kind of mystical glow. 'They're all done except Rommel's. No thanks to you lot.' And he ups and starts wandering about the dunes, to clear his head or work off the bile.

'Off to post them in Ghazi then, Corp?'

'Got any other suggestions?'

'Hand delivery?'

'When I get the name right, I might. But not until I do. Gotta be dead right, if you know what I mean.'

'We know.'

He wanders off around the unit looking for someone to help. But the peace doesn't last. He's soon back again, shouting:

'Looks as if nobody in the whole bleeding Eighth Army knows.'

'You could try the Ninth, Corp.'

'One last time. How d'you spell Rommel?'

And suddenly there was with the Corporal a multitude of the earthly host, beseeching the peace and goodwill of the Lord, and crying: 'For Christ's sake, 'Arold angel, nark it, will you!'

That did it.

'Well,' he stands defiant. 'I got glad tidings for you

lot. I'm not wearing them stripes because I covet them, you know, like what certain unscrupulous blokes do with their neighbours' wives, looking upon them with great greed and unseemly desire. Oh, no! I wear them to remind me to take some things seriously, and that includes burying blokes decently cos they deserve it and writing home to their next of skins as well as their mums and dads cos they deserve it too, and always spelling their bleeding names right!'

And with a jerk and a flourish he brushes the sand from his shorts, shakes it off his shirt, straightens his collar and titfer, and offs into the desert night with his little white card in his hand.

'Where you off to, Corporal?'

But he doesn't answer or look back.

'Taken the huff, Sarge.'

'Like Captain Oates.'

'Must be something we said.'

'Or didn't.'

'One way to get it over and done with.'

Next morning we're all spread out, heads down, hopping and flopping, fumbling and stumbling, knees bruised by the falls in the sand and tongues parched by eating the stuff. None of that old 'hold the thin red line' stuff. That's all Biggles. Proper anarchy nowadays. Common man's war, see, real common. Every man for himself. Any direction and 'the devil take the signpost'.

Not surprising you get split up. God only knows how we ever got anywhere, but then He always does. Him and the Sarge.

No sign of Tarzan, of course. Out there, soon's someone walks off, forget it. Not like back home. Back home everyone's always asking where you've been, what kept you, what you've been up to anyway … But not in the desert. Where a chap goes is his own business. Can't afford to fret or linger.

Suddenly we're standing right up on Jerry's lines and he's gone! Vanished. Scampered. Vamoosed. Not a dropped Iron Cross or an abandoned Swastika. Just like we figured. Others had got in before us. Desert's deserted to the horizon, as far as the eye can see and the vulture squint.

But suddenly there's Tarzan, all on his own at our feet, lying right up close to Jerry's lines, as if tossed back when they scarpered. Riddled and frazzled like perforated toast, still clutching his little white card.

Course the war stops. Always does on these occasions. *The Botcher's Hush*, we called it. The Sergeant bends down and takes the little white card from Tarzan's hand, gentle like, undoing his tight fingers one by one, like taking a dummy from a sleeping child. Then he stands up slowly as if the war has truly ended and we've all the time in the world now, reads the card and makes to tuck it into his pocket.

'What's it say, Sarge?' someone ventures.

A second before he turns.

'What you think?'

'Merry Christmas, Rommel?'

'Seasonal Greetings, Erwin?'

He holds the card a moment.

'Something like that.'

'Spelt it right, then, did he?'

'Got it in the end, then?'

The Sarge shrugs.

'Expect he spelt it with a bloody "i" instead of an "e"?'

'Yeah, shot him for bad spelling, then.'

'Not much help you lot turned out to be,' says the Sarge – nailing us to the sand. 'Couldn't even help the poor sod with his spelling,' he said. 'That's gratitude for you, after all he done for you, digging you in, tucking you up, writing home to your mums.'

He waves the card. 'Christmas too.'

Then pocketing the white indictment, he adds:
'Silent night, holy night – my arse!'

DAI FOX

Mersa Matruh, June 1942

And there was in their midst a stranger from another land whose people were sore oppressed by a race born out of wedlock. And he listened to their counsels and watched them at work so that in the days to come his promise might be fulfilled to blow up the illegitimate lot of them . . .

Ten

The *Desert* Fox might have taken Mersa Matruh much earlier had it not been for *Dai* Fox.

'Now only a hundred miles to Alexandria,' Rommel wrote home to his missus.

'Now only a hundred yards from Destiny,' Dai wrote home to his.

Rommel was on a winning streak during the summer of '42.

'No holding him now, lads. Got the grit between his teeth.'

The Afrika Korps entered Tobruk on the 21st of June, only a couple of weeks after we thought we had them cornered. One minute they're stranded in the Cauldron near Gazala, taking everything we can throw at them – from aircraft above and Crusaders below – pulverised and paralysed and pinned down in a desert pit that wasn't called the Cauldron by chance. Then – wham! – Rommel ups and breaks free from his blistering straitjacket and starts chasing us across the Libyan desert and we're scarpering down the road to Egypt and Alamein and Alexandria again – 'and Aldershot, if there's a boat'. Said he'd been playing a waiting game in that furnace – 'until the British used up their strength in the process'. And we did. Simple. But then the Fox was.

And then right in the middle of his onslaught, the crafty sod does it again – skids to a halt, whips around smartly and nips back to nick Tobruk.

'Wonder what he did that for,' said Dai, waiting at Mersa.

Dai Fox brought three books with him to war: one on Explosives, one on the Rights of Man, and one on Guy Fawkes.

As a regular soldier he was an expert on mining and explosives; as an ex-miner he was an expert on mining, explosives and the Rights of Man; and as a genetic patriot he was determined to pull all that accumulated expertise and experience together when he got back home and blow up the Houses of Parliament – 'the source of all our trials and tribulations'.

'Everyone thinks I should keep quiet about it. But I'm only a Taff, see, a deformed little miner from the valleys. Can't be taken seriously cos I don't *mean* anything. So I can speak very, very freely and you all think I'm a card and there's no substance in what I say. Little do you know I'm *all* substance.'

Dai bought his first book on explosives when he was holidaying at Llandudno as a young lad in his teens: *A Handbook of Modern Explosives* by M. Eissler, published in London in 1896.

He had already been three years down the pit by then – 'being all of fifteen' – and when he spotted the cracked tome in an old bookshop he pestered his dad until he was allowed to spend his holiday money on it. 'Not that I could read and understand it, mind, but it gave me a funny feeling of, well, *history*. Like it made my job important somehow, established, dignified like – made it a *profession*. When I carried it around with me it was like having credentials for my work. So that my job down there wasn't just all muck and dirt but one that needed skill and training and expertise that others would recognise.'

Dai Fox would succeed where Guy Fawkes had failed.

*

We only had ourselves to blame for losing Tobruk in the first place. We'd driven the blighters so far west the previous year, we'd gone a bit sloppy and let things slide. Allowed it to get run down. Imagine neglecting the defences of your main port of supply!

But no one expected Rommel to go back for it anyway, not even Ritchie or The Auk, far less Dai. Once the Fox had made that astonishing break-out from the Cauldron, he seemed hellbent on bypassing it altogether and getting through to Egypt and Cairo before we had time to think what the hell had hit us. And it was the obvious thing to do – leave Tobruk to mop up later and keep on hitting us while we were still in a state of shock and, like he'd figured, had used up most of our strength.

But there we were, dithering about at Mersa Matruh, trying to decide whether to put up some kind of stand there, and if so with what, when he about turns and goes back to collect Tobruk. Turns up at dawn while they're still having their breakfast and reading the weather forecast in the *Tobruk Truth*, and it's all over by early afternoon.

Dai was deep in one of his three books when the news came that Rommel had turned back. Went ashen pale, he did.

'What on earth – or heaven – made him do that?' he whispered.

'Maybe he forgot something.'

'But he doesn't need Tobruk yet.'

'Needs supplies, though. And wants his rear clear.'

'But it *is* clear. *He* knows that.'

'Well, maybe it's the heat,' said the Sarge. 'It gets to the best of us.'

'No,' Dai reflected, 'it's a deeper heat than that,'

pointing to the sun, 'much deeper.'
  'Been reading those spooky books again, Dai?'

'Biggest blow since Singapore,' said Types the clerk,
'Taken 35,000 of our chaps and God knows how many
tanks and supplies as well.' Types always got sneak
previews of reports that were withheld from us in case
they made us fret.
  'As if we're a bunch of bloody schoolkids!' said Toff,
sometime Cable Street cutter, sitting cross-legged in the
sand. 'Which we are, of course, otherwise we wouldn't
be here, would we? Only kids could have fallen for this
sand lark.'
  'I just don't believe it,' whispered Dai.

We never saw many regular soldiers, guys who'd joined
the Army as a career – apart from the Sarge. They were a
breed on their own the rest of us never really understood. Most of us could not grasp how anyone in his right
mind would do this sort of thing for a living. But there
were the odd ones, mostly specialists of some sort in
things like supplies or logistics or weapons or tanks. Dai
Fox was one, a regular soldier who joined up from the
valleys of Wales in 1935, not because he had got fed up
with mining, the coal kind, but because he wanted to
learn a lot more about mining, the explosive kind.
  'I didn't join this army to defend freedom, you know,'
he said. 'I haven't *had* mine yet. I joined to learn *how*.
  'Down the pits when I was eleven, I was, with me dad
and two brothers and three uncles and four cousins.
Same pit, same shift, for fifteen years. Proper family
affair it was. Relations on top too: in-laws in the winding
house, cousins in the baths, and sisters and aunts
scattered all over the offices and canteen. So much a
one-family affair, I used to wonder that we didn't own it.
But we didn't. The bleeding English owned it.'
  'Not me,' said the Sarge, defensively.

'No,' said Dai, archly, 'but your kind.'

'Hmm.'

However much Dai brooded over it – and he did, a lot – Rommel's decision to go back had given us a breathing space. But Dai started brooding even more than usual.

'Morose, Sarge.'

'Moreso.'

'Moreso morose, you mean?'

'More than that.'

Of course, Rommel was bound to turn again and resume hounding us out of Libya. But we might need to hold him up at Mersa Matruh until we could regroup in Egypt. The rendezvous was planned at some railhead there called Alamein. Straight out of a Hollywood Western.

'Did you say Alamo, Sarge?'

'No, Ala-*main*, Feathers! Got your seat booked?'

But there were few laughs for Dai.

'I only joined your bleeding Army to learn how to handle *real* high explosives, see, and find out about the way your minds work. And just as I'm getting somewhere this bleeding war comes along and mucks up all my plans.'

Rommel's return to Tobruk was another turning point for him.

'And now this,' he said, helplessly.

'He's only nipped back for supplies, Dai.'

'No, it's more than that. Exposed the fatal flaw, he has.'

'Besides, it'll give us a breathing space.'

'It's writ, see,' said Dai gloomily.

'Writ, Dai! *Written*, you mean?'

'No, writ.'

'Oh, as in Holy?'

'In a way. Guy knew it. Tom knew it. I know it. And Erwin has sensed it. He'll not win now.'

'Well, that's why they call him the old Fox, Dai. Did exactly what you wouldn't expect.'

'No, it's something else. *He* didn't decide that.'

Dai's moroseness apart, we had other problems. The rumble was – ie Types told us – that Ritchie wanted to draw a line at Mersa and make a stand but the Auk was all for waiting and making it at this Alamein place. But they couldn't make up their minds and we had to hang about at Mersa waiting for them to sort it out. The problem for us on the ground was deciding what the hell we were going to do if Ritchie won the argument and we had to defend the place.

If Rommel had done the decent thing and left Tobruk until later, the generals wouldn't have had their strategy problem and would have remained friends; we wouldn't have had our tactical problem, and would have gone on with the rest back to Alamein. And Dai wouldn't have had his moral problem: to do his duty by the army he didn't want to serve in anyway.

'Complicated business, war,' said the Sarge. 'Especially the people in it.'

When we reached Mersa Dai looked around and said: 'I know this place. Done my apprenticeship here.'

'That's right, Dai, November 1940, when we were all young and Rommel was still doing his square-bashing.'

'H'landestine operations,' mused Dai.

'What's that?'

'H'landestine operations.'

'Rings a bell.'

We had been at Mersa before. Some of us. Not long after we first landed in the desert, when we were still fighting Eyeties. We had set up our first big counter-offensive at Mersa, and from there launched our dash along the coastline to take Sidi Barrani.

One of our tactics then was to go out on expeditions

along the route of the proposed attack and dig holes and dump supplies so that we could pick them up when we advanced – like having filling stations and pull-up cafés along the A1, except we needed more than petrol and bacon sannies.

We were led by regulars and specialists like Dai because they were supposed to know better how to dig holes and plant things, especially Dai, because he'd been digging holes since 1805, or rather, his ancestors had. We operated at night and stayed out during the day, hiding and getting some shut-eye under camouflaged netting until nightfall, so we called these little trips our 'clandestine operations'. We buried our goodies along a seventy-five-mile stretch of no-man's-land westwards from Mersa Matruh and when we launched our counter-offensive the plan worked like a treat.

But when we reached Mersa on the run from Rommel in June '42 we thought we were only passing through, so there was almost a sentimental tone to the reminiscence.

'Oh, clandestine operations! Yeah, now I remember.'

'That's what I said,' said Dai, 'h'landestine operations.'

'And doing your apprenticeship! Course! It all comes back. Bit of a Biggles job, wasn't it?'

'Well, it *was* then. But it worked.'

'Like a dream.'

'Did it right under the nose of Graziani too.'

'Different times, of course,' Dai said significantly. 'Different names.'

The second book Dai brought with him was *The Rights of Man*. This one had been purchased on a holiday in Bangor.

'They named our pit Trafalgar. That was the first insult – there were plenty more to come. Our ancestors dug it in 1805 and all their sons and grandsons and nephews and nieces and cousins and in-laws have been mining it ever since. We were young and grew old in that pit for nigh on a hundred and fifty years. Small wonder everyone thought we owned it. But we didn't, and that's why I'm here. We knew something was wrong. We were stuck. But we didn't know how to get *un*-stuck.

'Then one day on my holiday I come across this book by Tom Paine in an antique bookshop in Bangor, and I read about man's inalienable rights and it all became clear. Everything fell into place, everything all the other books, including the Bible, were missing.

'Tom was an Englishman who went to America to help the Colonies get their independence. "It's the only way," he said. "Has to come some time or another and can only be more difficult the longer it takes." '

And holding up the thin, brown volume, Dai gestured around him to the Desert and all of us mucking about with our gear and trucks and rifles, then added: 'He also said: "These are times that try men's souls".'

'C'mon, Dai, get that explosive mind of yours going, we got to think up something extra this time.'

We were still hanging about at Mersa when the news came that Rommel had gone back, so everyone stopped to take stock. Or rather *we* did. The rest were pressing on to Alamein, but we had to wait for the brass to reach a decision – to go with them, latish, or hold here and wait for Rommel to come on as he soon would. Pretty bleak outlook either way. There wasn't much to defend at Mersa, or to defend it with, so we all wanted to keep going – and the Auk did too. But Ritchie was stubborn.

Until they decided, the Sarge thought he might as well chuck the problem at us rather than wait for the brass to find the answer – 'Keeps your minds out of mischief' – because the real question was: 'If we stay here, what do we do?' And as the expert in explosives Dai was as good a bet as any for a good idea. Except that Dai's mind was elsewhere.

Dai's third and most important book was *The Gunpowder Treason*.

'It's all in here,' he said, not just at Mersa Matruh. 'I found this book about Guy Fawkes in an antique bookshop in Aberystwyth where we'd gone for our holidays, and I thought now I can work out why he failed and how he could have done it better and how come he wanted to do it anyway.'

The Gunpowder Treason by Bishop Barlow of Lincoln, published in 1679, was another volume that gave authority to the history and dignity of Dai. It was a reprint of the original papers on the plot and the trial, called the *True and Perfect Relation of the Whole Proceedings against the late most Barbarous Traitors* (1606).

'It says in here,' – Dai read aloud to us whenever the mail was delayed and we needed something to occupy us during the long, dark evenings in the dunes – 'it says that Guy was "a man of great piety, an enemy of broils and disputes, and remarkable for his punctual attendance upon religious observances".' We all nodded wisely at Sidi Biranni. 'And it says he was "a zealous adherent of the Old Roman faith".' We went along with that too at Derna. 'And it says that when he was caught he made "no secret of his intentions", and carried himself without any "feare or perturbation".'

'Sounds quite a bloke,' said the Sarge.

'Yes, but they killed him,' said Dai, then mumbled: '*Per gradus ad ima*.'

'Eh?'

'Before they killed him they tortured him – *per gradus ad ima*.'

'What's that mean?'

'Don't really know. You have to imagine it. But I'll get

the right meaning yet. It's something to do with doing "it" to a man gradually, until he's no more. When I discovered that I understood I was up against men who could do unspeakable things to another made in the same image of God. And, like Guy, I realised that all you can do is blow them up.'

'C'mon, Dai! Guy tried to blow *them* up, didn't he?'

'Guy said he did it because "dangerous diseases require a desperate remedy".'

'Dai!' says the Sarge, 'You got it. Clandestine operations!'

Dai hardly blinked.

'Those dumps! What we did last time. Remember?'

'I remember h'landestine operations, Sarge, yes,' said Dai quietly.

'If we could find these places and get into them again we could stack up a few explosives to welcome Erwin with.'

'You serious, Sarge?'

'Course.'

'After all this time?'

'Maybe.'

'That's not a long shot, Sarge. That's infinity.'

It seemed a longer shot than that, but not a bad idea, provided these dumps still existed, because there certainly wasn't going to be any time to dig new ones, and provided we could get it over and done with in one operation – h'landestine, of course.

'Course,' says the Sarge, 'only certain blokes knew where they were and most of them aren't with us anymore, are they?'

'No, Sarge.'

Going back to these dumps or similar and filling them with explosives and booby traps and mines mightn't hold Rommel but it might delay him. And we'd have to do it in the dark again so we'd need to be spot-on accurate. If it was worth a go, it would be a pretty desperate go.

'What d'you say?' said the Sarge.

'Didn't say anything,' said Dai.

'Could we find them again, do you think?'

'They can't possibly exist anymore.'

'Hmm. Didn't make any maps of them, did we?'

'*We*, Sarge?'

'Well, you lot, then.'

'Dunno.'

'Anyway, moles like you are supposed to have them imprinted on your minds, aren't they?'

'*Some* things.'

'Thought you miner chappies never needed maps of the tunnels underground. You got them ingrained in your soul, they tell me, because you can always lose a map but never a soul.'

'I dunno,' said Dai thoughtfully – Dai said everything thoughtfully – 'I seen a lot of lads lose them underground, Sarge.'

Types appeared and read us another of his sneak previews. The Eyeties had got so goddamned pleased with themselves, or rather with Rommel, because he was the one doing all the work, that they were planning to land a couple of aircraft along at Derna airport – one carrying *Il Duce*, Mussolini himself, draped in medals and plumes, and the other carrying a white Arab charger for him to ride on at the head of his victorious army when they entered Cairo.

'Well, now, with confidence like that, the Eyeties obviously know something we don't, or *have* something we don't.'

'Of course they do,' said Dai. 'Rommel.'

'So what do you say, then, Dai? Worth a go?'

'Edward the Eighth came to visit us once,' said Dai,

coming out of his reverie, 'when he was Prince of
Bloody Wales. Proper laugh that was.'

The Sarge shrugged and sighed.

'They had this lavatory for him, see, specially built for
the one visit. Didn't last no more than half an hour, *and*
he only peed once. After that it was reserved for special
people like the owner's daughter.'

We stretched and yawned.

'But the thing that really took me was his skin, all
smooth and silkish, not just not lined or furrowed or
darkened like ours. More than that. Like as if it was a
different *material*.'

The Sarge stretched and yawned and we shrugged
and sighed.

'Then I saw that you English make your own gods,
see. You keep them and preserve them and feed them
special food and present them like prize dogs and
pigeons for us to worship. But you don't worship them
yourselves. You control them and chop their heads off if
they get a bit uppity. You can't afford to believe in real
gods.'

We all waited together.

'Now Guy worshipped real gods, see. And that's why
they killed him.'

We kept thinking we could hear Rommel starting up in
the distance. Banging doors and starting engines. And
shouting. But he couldn't possibly have left yet.

'A touch of the jitters, Wordsworth?'

'Could be the heat, Sarge.'

We should have been in Alamein by now, not
mucking about trying to remember from a couple of
years back things like hidden dumps in the no-man's
land near Mersa. Botchers playing Biggles. But Dai
wasn't bothered about rummaging through his
memory. All he could come up with was: 'Uncanny.'

In fact, if Ritchie didn't relent and pull us out before

Erwin arrived, the only real hope was that Erwin would
stay in Tobruk and enjoy a well-deserved piss-up after
all the success he'd been having. But that was weak
thinking. *We* might have done that, but not the Fox.
He'd either come back and go straight through us on to
Alamein before they got themselves unpacked there, or
leave *us* out in the cold at Mersa with the same
abandoned feeling the Aussies must have had at
Tobruk.

'The tide's turning,' Dai said dreamily.

'It's turned, mate. And we'll soon be washed out with
it if we don't come up with something.'

'Against us.'

'You can say that again.'

'No no, not us. *Us*.'

'He's flipped, Sarge.'

'Must be the heat.'

In the distance we thought we could hear more
shouting and banging of doors and revving up of
engines. And now there were other engines, heavier,
like tanks, and sharper, like aircraft. Maybe it was our
blokes at Alamein. Maybe.

The Sarge knew Dai was the only one who had a map
of these places in his mind's eye – or soul, and was
obviously wondering how to convince him and jog his
memory, even if it was only a kind of exercise to pass
the time while the Auk and Ritchie had it out. But Dai
was beyond dumps and maps, debating something else
– how it happened, how it had turned out this way.

'Well, maybe it's a daft idea anyway,' the Sergeant
suddenly announced. 'You're right. How can we
possibly find them after all this time?'

'Funny, isn't it?' said Dai as if to himself, standing up
and stamping the sand from his boots and buckling on
his gear. 'I mean,' he said, distantly, 'I join the British
Army to get the proper training so I can go back and

blow up their Parliament, which no one else has tried since poor old Guy because no one's done enough homework. And now I've done my homework, *this* happens.' And he flings his arms around at the mess and the military and the sand and the shambles. '*That*'s the irony.'

'The what?'

'*Iron*-ay. The hard bit.'

'Oh.'

'Five years and just getting into the swing of things, as the hangman said – getting the hang of it, see!' – and Dai smiled uniquely at Mersa. 'When along comes this bloody silly war and holds me up. And now at the precise moment of destiny my friend Rommel stops and goes back for Tobruk. That's a fatal flaw, that is!'

'Think you should be telling us all this, Dai? Someone might be listening.'

'Don't make no difference to me whether I go now or tomorrow, do it? No point in telling a drowning man to keep quiet about not being able to swim, is there?'

'Anyway, forget it, Dai,' says the Sarge, 'you don't have to do it. It's a bloody daft idea. I was only trying to keep everyone on his toes.'

'Course I have to bloody do it!' Dai shouted.

It was as if Rommel had fired off a warning shot. We stopped our stretching and yawning and fidgeting. Even the Sarge looked contrite.

'It's all decided, see! Erwin checked and went back. That's it. Everything else follows. You can't fight that. It's all in the hands of the gods, see – the ones *you* lot don't believe in.'

And with that he gathered up his bits and pieces and started tucking them into his kitbag, wrapping his three books carefully in his shirts and slotting them in.

'Stack the bleeding truck,' he ordered. 'I'll be off.'

Without a word or even a nod from the Sarge we stacked the light truck with anything we could find in the way of spare explosives and Dai walked off, still stuffing things into his bag. He climbed in and handed the Sarge two notes: 'One for you, one for the missus.' Then he switched on.

'Don't bother with your books, Dai,' the Sarge said, lamely, as if he had to think of something and hadn't the heart to say goodbye. 'We'll look after them.'

But Dai started the engine and revved up loudly and disdainfully.

'You won't need them,' the Sarge tried again, unhelpfully.

Dai eased it down an octave, waved the Sarge away and shouted: 'Oh, I'll need them. Besides, you wouldn't understand them. Over your head, they are.' And disappeared.

We hang around feebly for ten minutes then Types appears with a signal:

> *Rommel leaves Tobruk. Scarper.*
> *Auk overrules Ritchie. At the Double.*

The rumbling starts again. The Afrika Korps is on the move.

Long before midnight we've got ourselves together and are off down the road to Alamein. On the way the Sergeant opens his note:

> These are times that try men's souls – T. Paine
> Dangerous diseases require a desperate remedy –
> G. Fawkes
> *per gradus ad ima* – mind how you go – D. Fox

INTERLUDE 2

Eleven

'It's Monday and Strang the Terrible!'

We had our own brand of Botchers at home.

'It's Tuesday and the Wolf of Kabul!'

Except that, in my brother's comics, no one ever failed; in my father's, no one ever succeeded.

'It's Thursday and Cast Iron Bill!'

Each morning the cries rang out clearly and unfailingly from my brother's bed, like the reveille calls which the Sergeant always sang to the Botchers as he fetched their morning tea.

'It's Friday and Doctor Doom!'

My brother was a member of the Famous Five Secret Society which took its name from the *Famous Five* group of boys' comics which were published each week: the *Adventure* on Monday, the *Wizard* on Tuesday, the *Rover* on Thursday, the *Hotspur* on Friday, and the *Skipper* on Saturday. Wednesday was a rest day from the persistent onslaught of triumph and adventure.

'It's Tuesday and Morgyn the Mighty!'

The heroes in my brother's comics were the exact opposite of the Botchers in our father's. Men like the Black Sapper, Wilson and the Iron Teacher could never lose – their very names told us that, and we used to wonder if they'd got the name first and been forced into greatness, or if their greatness had thrust the names upon them.

On the other hand, men like Peak Frean and Con

Brio, Wool Sack and Rip Van could never win – their very names told us that. They had definitely been 'up against it from the start', and their names had made a profound contribution to their downfall.

'It's Monday and the Black Sapper!'

Botchers and Heroes complemented each other perfectly. Everything in our father's world was a mess-up, a cock-up, a foul-up, a hash, a bungle, a blunder or a botch – nothing could ever be adequate. But in my brother's everything was clean, wholesome, triumphant.

'It's Thursday and the Spadger!'

The very first casualty of World War II was the *Skipper*. One bright Saturday morning early in 1940, the news 'came through' that *S for Skipper* had 'failed to return'. However, 'undaunted by odds', and forever confident in their country's ability to 'turn the tide of world war' sooner or later and bring back normal basic necessities like the *Skipper*, the *Famous Five* proceeded as if one of their members wasn't missing after all, only temporarily 'seconded to other duties'.

'It's Friday and the Iron Teacher!'

I never had any reason to think one of our greatest weapons was missing anyway. For me there were five comics, and always had been – the *Adventure*, the *Wizard*, the *Rover*, the *Hotspur* – and the *Botcher*.

'I'm going out now,' my sister called to the world.

My sister lived somewhere in the Great OUT.

On behalf of the world, my mother replied: 'But you've only just come in!'

OUT was the world beyond our house – the Other Place, where wars were waged and my sister roamed.

'Where on earth have you been this time?'

'Out!'

'I can see that. You can't pick up muck like that in here!'

My sister lived in four basic conditions of OUT. She was either *going* OUT, *now* OUT, coming in from *having been* OUT, or had *just been* OUT.

'I'm going OUT now, but not for long.'

'Oh, for what then?'

The answer varied: 'For a walk.' 'For a chat.' 'For a spell.' 'For a change.' 'For a while.' 'For air.' And once, nobly, 'For ever.' But whatever form of OUTings she returned from, the result was always the same.

'Tell me, do you smear it on you? Or do you just lie down in the gutter and roll in it?'

Wherever she went she took with her one of the 'charts' that she was always drawing on frail, soft-brown paper bags, a colour that gave them the hint and tint of mystery – old, faded, wrinkled, dated, well-used, difficult-to-decipher documents stuffed into leather pouches, prised open under flickering lanterns, smoothed out by ancient nautical thumbs, secluded under creaking oak floorboards.

'What's the map for? You're only going to the corner shop.'

OUT played a large part in the 'war effort'. The Signal was always going OUT – to warn the enemy, rally the troops, inform the nation. The Message was usually going OUT – to tell England, teach Germany, remind the world. And the Word was invariably going OUT – the threat was here, the danger there, the challenge everywhere. Everything was going OUT – to our boys, our men, our troops, our allies and our enemies. Everyone and everything was always OUT, except me.

'Enough to drive you OUT of your mind, isn't it?'

I imagined OUT as an enormous field surrounding our house and forlorn. Hence the dirty bit. Three lots of people assembled there: 'our boys', 'grown-ups', and 'troops', all encamped in the mud, squatting, lying or sitting, waiting for the Message, Signal or Word to be sent OUT to them.

My sister was OUT there with them, splodging around from group to group with the aid of her charts, checking everyone was in the right place, sitting in the correct position, facing the correct way, wearing the correct uniform, and correctly replying to her in the correct voice, and all the time spattering her with mud as they heaved over and struggled to sit up straight and pay attention to her questions.

She was some kind of Lady with the Map who did her rounds regularly and painstakingly, keeping everyone's spirits up and ensuring they were calmly and correctly in place while waiting for the Message, Signal or Word that was being sent OUT. And lovingly sharing the dirt of the world with them.

'You can go OUT *after* the NEWS . . .'

The NEWS was our most faithful and regular visitor right through the war but I spent most of my first years *just* missing it.

'Remember, you have to be back and washed and tidied up and settled before the NEWS.'

Like any important guest, the NEWS had to be respected. Nothing but a clean shirt or blouse would do. But it was also appallingly elusive. I only ever heard it 'was coming through', or was 'through' or had just 'come through'. It never actually stopped long enough for me to catch a glimpse of it on its breathless journey.

'Remember, I'm not missing the NEWS because *you* come back late.'

But *adults* never missed it. They spent a lot of time with the NEWS, waiting for it, tuning in to it, getting it, listening to it, reading it, worrying about it, passing it on to others. Like Father Christmas, *they* always managed to see it and hear it, but I was never quick enough.

The NEWS was always about to happen, to attack and overwhelm us like a great wave of locusts. You could tell from the anxious looks on adult faces. But I was always looking the other way when it made its dash. And I was left with only the quivering voices and pallid faces of those who had heard it, watched it pass through and somehow withstood its terror – actually *witnessed* it burst in upon them, stagger past and drive on OUT through the back door to scurry away over our forlawn and shower the rest of the world with its storm and devastation.

The NEWS brought me out in a rash and drove me into a tither. I came through six years of war without ever once seeing it.

Another significant sound of our war – although he would have said *music* – was the song of Our Canary. As much as the cry of the gramophone and the call of the wireless, the bubble of the READINGS and the shriek of the COMICS, the warble of Our Canary accompanied us throughout all our days of 'uncertainty and trial'.

And not only did he stick with us throughout the War, he followed us throughout the house. As in later years we came to carry transistors from one room to another – kitchen, bedroom, bathroom, hall, living room, dining room, whatever – so we ferried him about and tuned into him whenever we needed company or music. He welcomed winter mornings in the bedroom, praised drab rations in the kitchen, warmed cold seasons in the bathroom, saluted chance visitors in the hall, greeted Caruso and Crosby in the evening, and accompanied the READINGS every Thursday. He spread his wings, his voice and his largesse all through the house and war. If my sister's world was the world of OUT, our Canary's was the world of IN.

He spent most of his nights in the bedroom I shared with my brother until our father came home and he was moved into the rear bedroom because 'Daddy loves to hear the birds sing'.

There was a magic in being first up every morning and taking his cover off. There was a magic in seeing him fetch his head out from under his wing and immediately blast into song as if surprised with his pants down and pretending he hadn't been caught in the act. And there was a perverse magic in whipping off the cover and whipping it back on again to trigger off his whistle, then cut him into dead silence again. He must have got very bored but he never failed us.

Each time we carried him to another room we made an expedition of the removal – 'a proper Pickford's'. There was never any question of simply getting it over and done with, a quick tearing off of the bandage instead of the slow torturing pull *we* could make of it – gingerly edging to the next location with the cage held like a fragile vase and accompanied by our mother's feeble attempts to keep his pekker up with a few wintry stabs at whistling. But all that ever came was that soft release of air from dying balloons, leaving the bird singularly underwhelmed.

When he was not energetically singing, which was seldom, he would wash off the sweat of each performance in his bowl and admire himself in the glass. But the true mirror image that excited him was that of the round silver head at the end of the long spindle arm reaching across the jet-black records on the gramophone. Precariously suspended, it danced up and down in the grooves on the pin-sharp edge of its needle, and precariously balancing on his perch the Canary imitated its movements, bobbing and swaying his body and circling and stretching his neck, clearly believing he was emulating its music – or perhaps simply encouraging the machine to emulate him.

Like the wailings of the sirens and the whistles of our mother, Crosby, Caruso and the Canary were seminal sounds of our war.

Another binding sound of that time came from the wireless on Thursday evenings, to take its place alongside Readings and Gramophone Hours and Sirens and Churchill speeches and Announcers' Newses.

ITMA and Tommy Handley entered the house at half-past eight and brought their own band of Botchers into our lives:

Colonel Chinstrap, Mona Lot, Signor So-so, Ali Oop, Frisby Dyke, Mrs Mopp . . .

They fitted in quite naturally with Caruso and Nash, Crosby and Tauber, Wapper Todd and the Wolf of Kabul, Freak Pean and Rip Van. You didn't have to understand them, anymore than you had to understand Churchill or Lord Haw Haw, Vera Lynn or Fats Waller; they were simply part of the sounds and the ritual. Everybody laughed and felt warm. So you did the same.

And 'It's That Man Again' distributed among us the music of more names and phrases.

I don't mind if I do, sir.

Whatever year Handley made his official appearance, whatever year he took over the 8.30 slot, for us he had been there from the beginning. The War was like that – one great chorus of sound and sounds. Chronology wasn't one of our words. Whenever we heard a name like Ally Main or Sally Erno, Sam Scram or Poppy Poo Pah, Strang the Terrible or Doctor Doom, Monte Cassino or Noblesse O'Bleech, we assumed it had always been there, lying dormant in the pages of the *Bumper Book of the Botchers*, waiting to be opened at any page or time. They didn't arrive or emerge at *particular* times; they were simply out there waiting to come in, and when they did we treated them as if we had always known them.

This is Fünf speaking.

'They're everywhere!' said my father on his sick-bed.

Don't forget the Diver, sir!

'And they keep coming!'

> *It's being so cheerful as keeps me going.*

'The Earth's overrun with them.'
Sweet fulfilment.

SEXTANT BLAKE

Alamein, November 1942

Fear not, for I shall guide you through the paths of perfidy and the wadies of venom and lead you far from shadier rills and suspect wells. And I shall light your way by the radiance of the stars and the brilliance of my homespun charts . . .

Twelve

'What's a shady rill look like, Padre?'

Trooper Sextant Blake set aside the Map of Heaven he was working on and stretched out contentedly on the gritty sands of Alamein.

'Oh,' said Padre Hadrian Felter, startled out of his studies on the zoology of the desert, 'a shady rill?'

'Yeah.'

'You mean, a *real* shady rill?'

'Got any other kind, Padre?'

'Eh, no . . .'

'Well, then, a real one'll do fine, thanks, Padre. Like you've got in your Bible.'

'Ah yes.'

'You know, the cool Siloam kind.'

'Somewhere near Alamein' we're relaxing under a full moon and a clear sky packed full of bright stars. As usual we're expecting to attack 'something special' at dawn, and it was customary on such occasions for the Sarge to encourage us to stay at home the night before, put our feet up and 'take it easy like, lads – you may have a long journey ahead of you tomorrow.'

But as the Big One at Alamein was supposed to be coming up soon we felt a bit peeved to be messing around before it really got going. 'Only some skirmishes, lads. Testing them, you know. Softening them up before the big crunch. Just the kind of exercise for idle intrepid warriors, like you.'

He always had to have us doing something. Never left us alone. Always organising some evening trip or daybreak outing – always surprising us with some intriguing '*mystery* tour'.

'In case you get bored, see. Can't have you fretting.'

'Do you mean,' said the troubling trooper, closing his eyes on Syrtis Major and furrowing his brow even further, 'there might be more than *one* kind of shady rill, Padre?'

'Oh, no,' said the Padre, flustered, 'I was merely confirming, so to speak, that you did mean *our* kind, Mr Blake.'

Trooper Blake's hobbies were maps, and religion.

Padre Felter's hobbies were zoology, and religion.

And Trooper Blake had decided he'd been far too busy with the war lately to think enough about the really important things in life. And Padre Felter had decided he'd been far too busy with what they were doing in the desert recently to think enough about the desert itself.

''Cos it would play hell with my topography if there are,' said Blake sternly, quite prepared to hold the Padre personally responsible for the numbers and types of shady rill to be found.

'No, no, Mister Blake, I was merely confirming, merely confirming.' Everyone was mister to the Padre. To his meek and all compassionate spirit, privates ranked with brigadiers – 'in *theory*, that is. I mean, *philosophically*.'

'Course.'

Monty's in charge now, with his dainty little titfer and his rabbity voice, whining away from the top of his tank about 'this far and no further'. This is another one of them 'last stands'. He's promised us the big battle.

We're not going further back than Alamein. So we're waiting. Everyone's in training – except us, of course. 'Always on the bleedin' move, we are.'

'Best form of training's the real thing,' said the Sarge. 'Besides, you gotta keep harassing them, otherwise you give them time to get trained and organised too. Remember, attack is the best form of attack. Keep 'em watching. Keep 'em wondering. Keep 'em worrying.'

Sextant Blake had come from the peace of East Broadstairs to the war in the Western Desert with numerous compasses in a wooden box and a navigator's sextant in a leather case. He continually checked, aligned, realigned, and boxed his compasses, took sightings with his sextant which he related to ordinary ordnance survey sheets, and distributed them amongst us with the solemnity of a vicar handing out the Eucharist.

In fact, maps were more his *obsession*, hence the Sextant title. He was in charge of maps for the section, the unit, the platoon, the company, and maybe even the regiment and the whole brigade. No one really knew. Sextant was self-appointed.

Padre Hadrian Felter, late curate of St Michael's, Stewe-on-Wold, was worried about what the war was doing to the world, and particularly to the frail habitat of the desert. That night he was deeply engrossed in *The Osteology of the Camel*, an article in an 1891 edition of the *Journal of Morphology* he'd picked up in Cairo on the way through.

'I mean,' said Sextant, not yet appeased, 'it could bear heavily on the structure of my artist's impression of the Eternal, couldn't it?'

'Yes, I do understand that, Mr Blake, but I assure you I was merely confirming, merely confirming.' And, accepting that his own meditations were over for the evening, Padre Felton carefully noted his place with the humblest of pencil marks in the chapter on *The Camel, Desert Gleanings*.

The Sergeant's obsession was wadies. He worried a lot about his wadies, particularly during these thousand and one Alamein nights of skirmishing by the light of the moon.

'No night on the Niles tonight, lads,' he would say cheerfully. 'No whooping it up in the wadies or painting the bazaars red. Just a relaxing evening together with our hobbies before turning in early, eh?'

It wasn't always wadies, but the Sarge called most ditches and depressions and clusters of dunes his wadies. Made him sound conversant with the locality, at ease in his surroundings. Didn't impress us much, but it all added to his colourful palette of patter.

Now that he'd tempted us away from the lure of the fleshpots, his quiet evening was fading fast once Trooper Blake and the Padre got going.

Sextant made his own maps, regularly disappearing on private recces into the desert to chart more and more acres of sand. With the precision of a draughtsman, he drew curves of deviation and variation, extra lines of eastings and northings, and twelve-figure map references of camel lines, goat trails and sand dunes that seldom lasted the night. But his greatest preoccupation since leaving Blighty was his very own Map of Heaven.

'Gotta get this picture sorted out in my mind, you see, Padre.'

'Yes, my son.'

Sextant spent his time drawing worldly maps for us and non-worldly ones for himself, and discussing with the Padre fundamental questions like:

> *What's Heaven really like, then, Padre?*

– not the general *idea* of Heaven, but the literal form

and structure of it.

'You see, if I can get a *proper* map of Heaven, Padre, I'll feel happier, more relaxed. Be able to know exactly where I'm going and won't be in any danger of getting lost when I arrive there, right?'

The Padre fingered his *Journal of Morphology* longingly but didn't open it. He was far too timid and polite to disturb the Trooper's train of thought that night.

Maybe Sextant was self-appointed, maybe it wasn't his job at all, maybe *no* one was in charge of maps, but Trooper Sextant Blake assumed he was. No one ever asked or queried, and neither did we, the Sarge or anyone else. But it was his obsession and as the Sarge never tired of saying 'A man has to have his own thing', and let him get on with it. The Sarge was happy to indulge any of his boys' whims just as long as it 'didn't do no one no harm.' *Indulgere et confirmare* was his motto – *indulge and encourage*. He'd cribbed it from another Padre in Rawalpindi.

So, with archaeological exactitude and reverence Sextant marked in items of garbage he found on his many private recces into the unknown desert, like the skulls of dead camels or discarded petrol cans. He calculated ranges and distances no one ever wanted to know of, and plotted routes and detours no one ever dreamed of taking. He delighted in scattering the desert voids with terms like *Hypot in Use Here* and *Beware Meridian Fading*, *Magnetic Insecurity* and *Fluctuation Feasible*, *Dead Reckoning* and *Live Confirmation*, *Triangulation Postulate* and, imperially, *Locus*.

Our job was to take out one of Jerry's key forward positions. He was supposed to be encamped in a vast wadi forward of his eastern sector that covered the route to his main positions. We had to try to pin him down and 'saturate him' before breakfast and then nip back again. All part of the glorious 'softening up' exercises in which the Sarge liked to believe we excelled, and all of course to make the coming big barrage better for the Monty in the Beret. 'Onion Monty' we called him. 'All he needs is a bike and a shoulder of onions.'

'Assessing the general position, then withdrawing again, that it, Sarge?'

'More or less.'

'In a manner of speaking, I mean.'

'You could put it that way, yes. Don't see why not.'

'I can see the headlines back home now: "Desert Intrepids probe Fox's Lairs". Big print.'

'That's imaginative, that is, Warberry.'

'And underneath: "Then scarpers".'

'What's boxing the compass mean, Sextant?' he asked, effecting his motto.

'Boxing, Sarge?'

'Yeah, boxing. Funny sort of term, in't it?'

'Well, boxing, you know, Sarge, s'like fencing or sparring. Fencing them in like to keep them from wandering all over the place. Deviating.'

'Ah.'

'Otherwise they'd get all undisciplined, like, and you'd never get a true reading, would you?'

'Hmm.'

The Sarge never questioned these things. Every man had a certain knowledge that was very private to him, and he always respected that. 'Never question another man's authority on what he knows,' he'd say. He was only ever superior about his own profession – soldiering.

'Ah', he said, 'so that's boxing, is it? Very well, then, every man to his own.'

The Sergeant hovered around the industrious pair, hoping they wouldn't get *too* absorbed in their hobbies because of the following morning's 'chores'.

Whatever *we* thought of the morning's mystery tour, this was the run-up to Alamein and he was getting a bit edgy. He manoeuvred closer to get a better look, knowing it wouldn't help him very much with his wadies. But he nodded knowingly down at Sextant's artwork as if expressing reverent admiration.

But it *was* a show in a way. The wadies were uppermost on the Sarge's mind.

'Where d'you think these secluded groves should go, Padre?' said Blake, squinting at his Divine Chart taking shape on the back of a large fold-out map of the sector. Tapping the page with the chewed end of a 6B, he said: 'And all them many Mansions, Padre. What are they anyway – the stately homes of Paradise?'

'Well,' said the Padre, 'I suppose that's as good a description as any.'

Sextant's Chart of Heaven – 'God's Map' – was a fabulous artist's impression of Heaven, complete with angelic symbols and cherubs, lines crisscrossing clouds and green pastures, and treasure island type observations on best army issue vellum. It paraded archangels and angels and all persuasions of heavenly host, floating about in flowing robes and luxuriant jewellery, their golden tresses brushing past clouds and sweeping the heavens and swirling off into the galaxies; mincing through Death's Valley, tripping along Paths of Righteousness, drifting in and out of swinging Pearly Gates, lying down in Green Pastures, relaxing in shady rills, bathing in quiet waters, sunbathing by cool pools, anointing themselves in oil, and packing up in the evenings to go off home to dwell in their many mansions.

Sextant had been composing his bumper Map of Paradise all the way from Aldershot and Alexandria. The map was carefully folded and moulded around his regulation clipboard, permanently fixed down with steel clips around the centrepiece – 'a proper piece of parchment like Long John Silver's'.

Blake worked away at his Sacred Chart every free second. He derived his information from star gazing, the Padre and his own fantasy. On top of the forty-eight-sectioned sheet he pinned the *Map of the Moment*, whatever piece of 'temporal cartography' was needed for the day. At every opportunity he squatted down, unclipped the top map, spread out the folded sections beneath and worked away at his masterpiece, the large segments flopping gently over the sides in the desert breeze.

'Obsessed with maps, I am, Padre,' Sextant announced to the night.

'So I've seen, my son.'

'Can't get enough of them.'

'No.'

'Tell you what, between you and me, like . . .'

'Now then, Troopah!' warned the Sarge, hovering nervously.

'. . . I'd rather have a bit of the old cartography than the other.'

'Troooo . . . pahh!'

'Right, Sarge.'

'Tell you what, Padre. Remember that old geezer in your Bible tied to the mast with all them birds singing their heads off at him . . .'

'Troopah Blake!'

'You mean, Ulysses, my son?'

'Yeah, that's him. You'll 'e says.'

'I don't think you mean the Bible, my son.'

'Course I do, Padre. Tied to the mast in the River Jordan, he was, when suddenly all them birds looking like Sphynxes come floating along from Egypt and start singing to him to get out and walk across the water so they can all have a good night out in the fleshpots of

Nazareth. *You* remember!'

'Eh, not quite like that, Mr Blake.'

'Then the waters parted and he was even more tempted to jump?'

'I think actually you are referring to the Sirens, Mr Blake . . .'

'Naw, not bleeding *sirens*, Padre. Not wailing minnies! *Love* birds they were. With real sexy voices.'

'Blake!'

'Right, Sarge. Proper touch of the Betty Garbos, they had.'

'Well, as you wish . . .'

'Well, what I was saying was, Yull got the crew to tie him to the mast so he couldn't get out and walk off with them birds to the denizens of evil, right?'

'Eh, ye . . . es.'

'Well, now, had I been Yull, they wouldn't have had any trouble tying *me* up.'

'Really?'

'Naw. I wouldn't even have *heard* them alluring voices. I'd have had me head buried in the maps, see. They could have tried any number on me – from the Old Groaner Crosby himself to the Andrews Sisters.' He paused to admire his work, then added: 'And even a few of their famous postcards as well.'

'Troopah!'

'I wouldn't have budged an inch,' said Blake. 'Not once I'd got the old head down in a map.'

'Bless you, my son.'

'Too bloody true, Padre.'

'Trooo . . . pah!'

In this way, and with that intensity, Sextant perfected his own special Chart of Heaven. But he always carried both maps with him: the Army Version, Plain, and the Hereafter Version, De luxe. 'In case one fails. The Army one, like as not.' Then he'd be 'ready for both worlds'.

The Sarge was impatient, and yet not impatient. He

had a job to do, or get done. But he also had an eye to keep on his brood. And Trooper Blake had recently become a trifle more intense as his masterpiece neared completion. Altogether more reflective, wordy too, and with a tendency to be more oblivious than usual to most things going on around him. He seemed to be living within the contours of his great opus.

'Spends his entire war looking after the meek and the weak, does our Sarge.'

'Shame, isn't it? He just never gets the time to enjoy it.'

'Reckon they've got dunes up there, as well, Padre?' asked Sextant, dabbing away in his own little world, sculpting celestial dunes. 'Dunes of Glory, eh? Like sunburnt clouds?'

'A delightful notion, Mr Blake.'

'Well, that's what life's all about, isn't it, Padre – maps? I mean, we're all trying to find out where we are and where we're going, aren't we?'

'How very true, my son.'

'Well, then.'

Sextant leant back to admire a particular flourish.

The Sarge hovered, worried we wouldn't get enough sleep. He looked down at the centre piece of Sextant's masterpiece, which faced uppermost like a title page when the chart was refolded. It was an elaborate drawing of two massive Pearly Gates done in charcoal black and edged with crayon gold.

'I suppose, Padre,' Sextant wondered aloud, still sculpting, 'Pearly Gates that size must need special hinges.'

'How about this shady rill, then, Padre? I'm nearly ready to fit them in.'

'Well, now,' said the Padre, finally abandoning his own profound preoccupations for the night. 'A shady rill . . . Eh . . . well, let's say it's a sort of . . . *cool*ish place where one can rest from the heat and toil of the day.'

'Sounds good enough to me,' said the Sarge, trying to get in on the act in the hope of breaking it up soon.

'For a tea break, like?' asked Sextant.

'When day is done, yes.'

'So what's a rill, *really*?' Sextant pressed on.

'Oh, a rill, really?'

'Yeah.'

'Well, really, a rill's really a kind of furrow, a sort of trench, a place you can drop into for shelter from the noonday sun when you're tilling the fields.'

'Uh, huh.'

'It's also a term in astronomy . . .'

'Oh, hoh!'

'Yes, it refers to one of those *furrow*-like impressions you can detect on the moon.'

'Ah, hah!' Sextant panned off Syrtis Major to seek the moon. 'So it *has* a direct heavenly connection, then?'

Following the tenacious trooper's gaze, the Padre agreed: 'Well, yes, in a way.'

'So, when the Bible talks about the shady rills we can look forward to being led by, it's more accurate than you think?'

'Well, to be truthful,' sighed the Padre, 'I think the prophets who wrote about them in their Psalms were thinking more of places near their beloved Jerusalem.'

'All the same,' pursued Sextant,' licking his 6B, 'all the same . . . sometimes people don't really know what they're thinking, do they?'

There was a long silence while the Sarge and the Padre searched for the moon.

'Shady rill,' Sextant savoured the words aloud. 'Shady rill.' Then he opened his eyes again and squinted professionally at Syrtis Major. 'I know what *shady* means, Padre, and I know what a *rill* is, or I *think* I do. But I've never put them together before.'

'No.'

'Sounds *poetic*, don't it?'

'Hmm. Yes, I expect it does,' said the Padre, '. . . come to think of it.'

'Then again,' said the determined trooper, 'that's what we got poets *for*, isn't it, to put words together you'd least expect. I mean, who'd have thought of putting shady with rill . . . eh?'

'Ah, yes,' agreed the Holy Man, quite resigned now not to getting back to his Camel contemplations that night. 'Who indeed!'

'Well, there you are then,' said Sextant, thrusting a coloured pencil towards the stars and compelling both the Sarge and the Padre to search for the track between the moon and Syrtis Major. 'Takes a lot of working out, that does, Padre. Separates the sheep from the goats, don't it? Or the Capricorn from the Aries.'

The trouble with wadies, or whatever else the Sarge had in mind, was that you could never really depend on them being where you expected. The map makers had done as reasonable a job as you could expect with millions of acres of sand, but you could hardly call the Western Desert *charted*.

But if anyone in the Western Desert knew about his wadies, Sextant Blake did. Sextant searched for the way and the truth in the map of the heavens like a 'sleuth of the stars' – which helped earn him his nickname too. But he also led us back and forward across the desert from Cairo to Tunis, through Alamein and Benghazi and Tripoli, and often enough more than once, through all the uncharted ditches and depressions that constituted wadies in the Sarge's world, and always with that tenacious religious side to him which he shared with the Padre, or thought he shared, because the Padre never objected, and never once hesitated to set aside his beloved books on camels and sand and the morphology of the desert rat, to debate the profounder issues of life with Trooper Sextant Blake.

The impatient Sarge hadn't any doubt about Sextant's role for the following morning, only about him taking up so much time airing most of his obsessions all at once. Usually he spread them about a bit. The Sarge badly wanted another O-Group for another rehearsal, plus he wanted us 'fit as fiddles for the morrow's foray'.

Still, he could depend on Sextant. Sextant had led us everywhere: 'Fear not,' he claimed, brandishing his own version of *L'Atlas archéologique du Nord de L'Afrique* published by the Ministry of Public Instruction (1895), 'for I shall lead you by quiet waters and pastures green.' And from his own annotated copies of various *recherches archéologiques* he prepared for us and the Sarge a way across the desert sands: trails, traces, tracks, ways, paths, routes, wadies, valleys, ditches, dunes, dried-up ravines and river-beds. Sometimes he got carried away: 'Behold, I am come to prepare ye a way – the way, the truth and the life,' but never lost. Spent all his time drawing temporal maps for us, a celestial one for himself and discussing religion with his self-appointed spiritual buddy, Padre Hadrian Felter.

'Got to get it all worked out before the end comes, haven't you, Padre?' said Sextant.

The Sarge stretched, stamped his feet, checked his watch and looked at the stars.

'What makes you so sure it's coming?' the Padre asked in case Sextant was worried about the morning.

'Coming to all of us, isn't it?'

'But not necessarily now.'

'Well, it'll be *now* when it comes, won't it?'

The Sarge skirted the figure sprawling in the sand with his artwork, ostensibly admiring yet obviously worrying very deeply about his wadies.

'Got to make my own map, Padre,' Sextant went on. 'No good relying on someone else's. Not in this unknown land.'

'No.'

'Nobody's been here before, see. Uncharted really. Bit like Heaven, eh?'

'Maybe.'

'What d'you think it's like up there, then, Padre? Lots of Green Pastures, eh? Shady rills? Cool Siloams?'

'Something like that, son.'

'That's what I mean. I know you can give me ideas but, no offence mind, you haven't really *been* there either, have you?'

'No, my son.'

'Well then. Best make your own's what I say.'

'Yes, my son.'

Sextant, like the Sarge, often seemed to be helping the Padre through his war.

Again the Sarge took a few paces forward and skirted the figure sprawling in the sand with his artwork. If you could never depend on wadies being where you expected them to be, you would never ever know if you'd got the right one. Sand had a habit of looking like sand wherever you were.

Again he edged closer to study the work in progress, but he was really testing how long it would be before a natural break in the trooper's labours would allow him to call for beddy-byes without hurting anyone's feelings. He certainly wasn't gleaning any information from Sextant's celestial design. Shady rills, maybe. Wayward wadies, no chance.

Knowing the Sergeant's problem and trying to suggest a conclusion to the evening's deliberations, the Padre sighed: 'Yes, I suppose you are right there, my son.'

But he only screwed it up again.

'And that's another thing, Padre,' Sextant spun round before the Sarge could get in, 'something I've been meaning to ask you for a long time: why do you always call everybody *son*?'

The Sarge winced and closed his eyes. Very patient was our Sarge, and especially patient with Sextant the night of the Alamein skirmish.

'Well,' said the Padre, stopping in the act of rising to go, 'you call me padre, don't you?'

'What's that got to do with it?'

'Well, padre means father, doesn't it?'

'What language is that, then?'

'Italian.'

'Eyetie! What's the point of that, then?'

'Well, because of Rome. Where the Pope lives. He's Head of the Roman Catholic Church.'

'What's that got to do with *us*?'

'Well, the term father is the name given to all priests.'

'Why's that, then?'

'Because we look after our children, our flock.'

'Like the Sarge, you mean?'

'In a way, yes.'

The Sarge shuffled in the moonlight.

'I can understand "shepherd" on account of all them lambs and all that but *father* beats me.'

'Well, father or padre was the father or leader of his flock. And the term was passed on to our church.'

'Why Eyetie?'

'Because Rome's where it all started.'

'Thought it was Jerusalem?'

'No, the *Church* started in Rome. And the Pope is Father of the Church. *Il Papa*. Means father in Italian too.'

'Not Latin?'

'No, in Latin it would be *pater*, as it was once. But the language of Italy is now Italian. So it's *papa* or . . .'

'Thought you said *padre*.'

'Well, actually the French . . .'

'No! That's *père*! I know that!'

'. . . but it amounts to the same.'

'Why French all of a sudden?'

'Because the Normans brought it over with them

when they came to England in 1066.'

'The Normans.'

'Yes, they were French.'

'*Normans*?'

'Yes. Norman means North Man.'

'*North* man! Blimey, France ain't exactly north, is it?'

'It is if you're in France.'

'What is?'

'Norway. It's northern Europe.'

'Norway?'

'Where the Normans came from. That's the real meaning of North Men.'

'Blimey!' Sextant turned exhausted on his back and gazed up again at the heavens. 'Gets bloody complicated, don't it? No wonder I need a bloody map! Soon lose your bearings in this lot. Up there *and* down here.'

On the edge of the dune the Sarge stood up decisively, flexed his shoulders in a layman's amen and added conclusively: 'Right then, lads!'

But it wasn't to be that night. Sextant's mind was in top gear. As he turned over in sheer frustration at the etymology of 'padre', all he could see was his beloved stars. And because of his only true obsession he was quickly distracted from the tortuous history of the Christian Church and the capricious growth of language.

'How about this one then, Padre?' Sextant shouted abruptly, leaping to his feet, pointing to the heavens and embarking on another theme. 'If the light from the stars takes millions of years to get to us, we can't know if it's gone out yet, can we?'

The Sarge groaned conspicuously. Sleep seemed very far away.

'Eh . . . no . . . o.'

'Cos the light that's coming off it right now, at this very second,' stabbing at the stars, blinking as if mesmerised by the commotion they were causing, 'won't be here for another million years, will it?'

Up there above him floated the source of all Sextant's curiosity: the firmament, the cosmos, the galaxies; the planets, the solar system, the stars; the astral, the stellar, the celestial; the insubstantial, the ethereal, the unearthly – the heavens and the heavenly, with all their shady frills and rills.

'No . . . oo,' mused the Padre.

'I mean, how will we know when it has burnt its last ember and gone dark up there? We won't, not until we see this light coming at us like a rocket and then whoomph! – suddenly there's nothing behind it but blackness. Right?'

'Hmm.'

'I mean, we'll know it's died. But not before another million or two years, so we'll never really catch up, will we?'

'No . . . oo.'

'I mean, supposing we had a big enough telescope we could reach back and see the light before we can see it now, that light at the far end wouldn't be the same light we'd be seeing when we take our eye off down here, would it? Cos the light at the far end would be more recent light, and the light down here would be older light, wouldn't it? So that means we can stand and watch light whizzing past us that left its star a million years ago, and then nip back quickly to the scope in time to see light leaving that's going to take another million years to get here! Right?'

'Ye . . . es.'

'But then, supposing we had a really big telescope, I mean, a real whopper, biggest ever made, we could see right back to the Beginning, couldn't we? Right back to when it all started! Eh?'

'Well . . .'

'Logical, isn't it? Stands to reason. If you agree on the first bit, you gotta agree on the lot!'

'I'm not sure it's that simple, my son.'

'Course it's that simple! Simple enough to me, Padre. It's only *you* blokes what want to make it difficult.'

'As you wish . . .'

The Sarge dallied, testing for a natural break.

'Look, that light there that's just passing us now – look, that bit, right there, whoosh! – it's taken a billion years to reach us. It must have left before we was even a twinkle in God's little eye. Before *He'd* even thought of inventing us!'

He banged his masterpiece. 'Amazing!'

'Careful!' warned the Padre.

'But where the hell's it going after it's passed? Heading for a brick wall – a dead end, a *cul de sac* in the Universe somewhere. Or will it just peter out like a dying candle? And if so, where will *God* be then?'

'Hmmm.'

'Won't be able to see much, for a start, will He?'

The Sergeant stamped his boots in the sand, and announced   decisively   but   not   convincingly: 'Gentlemen.'

'Makes you think.'

'Quite.'

The Sarge tried again: 'Reckon it's time for us all to hit the *cul de sac*, eh?'

Sextant ignored him but began to gather up his map and box of crayons and coloured pencils.

'You see,' he went on as he carefully folded his masterpiece, 'the way I look at it, Padre, is that once upon a time you had faith, right?'

'We always have faith, my son.'

'Right. But what I mean is, you *believed*. You didn't really *know*. You believed instead.' He gestured to the heavens above. 'In the stars and solar systems and things spinning and turning and making their music and the sun going round the earth and so on.'

'Move it now, Sextant,' said the Sarge.

'And now we've worked it out that it's the other way

round, haven't we?'

The great coloured view of heaven was now carefully packaged like a Christmas present. 'We don't have to pretend anymore cos we've *proved* it, right? Proved the belief. That we were right all the time!'

'Ye . . . es?'

'So what that means, Padre, is that all Science must have been Faith once upon a time!'

'Hmm.'

'So, I mean, it all works out in the end, don't it, whatever happens?'

'Yes, my son.'

Sextant shook the sand from his box and looked around to make sure he hadn't dropped anything. Then, placing his box on top of the large folded map, he added:

'But you need maps, Padre.'

'Time, gentlemen, if you please,' said the Sarge.

'Got to know where you're going, you know.'

At 8.50 the following morning we're moving steadily to our objective, veering right to the big wadi. If we take that we've done our job and got ourselves shelter too. Then suddenly we see Sextant up ahead of us in the thick of it and at the last bloody gasp he's brandishing his clipboard and screaming: 'Left, you stupid bastards, left, left, left, left! Heads down and follow me, me, me, me!' Doesn't tally, cos our best laid schemes and plans tell us the deep one's to the right. In fact there shouldn't be *any* to the left. Then the Sarge screams: 'After him!' and we get the heads down to rat level, kneecaps scraping our teeth, and tear to the left instead, when the world goes up on both sides – desert, dirt, dung, muck, manure, rubble, rubbish, junk, trash and litter – showering down like Noah's deluge: packs, rifles, boots, clobber, metal, gear, and bodies tumbling on top of each other like bloody great turnips tipping out of a wagon into a ditch and everything that's lain buried in the sand for centuries – bits of old Roman roads and, by the weight and smell of it, a whole legion's hard-tack rations.

We lie there for ages trying to breathe and work out if we've come through or is this it at last and the heaving smell of stinking armpits and rotting camels and centuries old sand is the real green pastures after all.

Then we start to move and begin to sort out the quick from the slow. We've got ourselves into a sort of mini-wadi, to the left of our main objective, more like a hidden rill for a secluded stream to pass through. Impossible to spot. Couldn't have been on any map. Only someone like Sextant could have known it was there. And sure enough, there he is, stretched out behind us at the entrance gazing up at his blessed stars, only there aren't any to see now, and he can't see them anyway, and he's clutching his coloured masterpiece all covered in dirt and dust, wafting in the breeze.

Over to our right there's nothing – the wadi we should have gone for – one ginormous hole, a hundred feet deep and ten times as far round. Jerry's supply dump and arsenal. He must have packed in everything and sent it up to Kingdom Come at the last second when he knew he couldn't hold it. And he'd blocked the inlet to a mini one on the left with a handful of booby jobs, enough to set the alarm off in case the map reader makes a mistake and leads us in there instead. Sextant had gone for it, but not by mistake. He doesn't make mistakes with maps. Must have known it was our only way to safety. But first one in buys it, unless he takes time to work out where the mines are and sits down quietly to defuse them. Not a lot of time for that on a surprise skirmish.

'Poor bugger went east instead of west at the Pearly Gates,' said a voice. 'Lost his bearings at the end.'

'No,' says the Padre. Usually you never saw sight of

the Padre until it was all over and we were washed and shaved and cleaned up and presentable again or being buried and he was doing his praying bit. But he's up with the crowd this morning, kneeling beside Sextant and unlocking the Divine Chart from his grip. 'No, no,' he says. 'Trooper Blake would know where he was going.'

WOOL SAC

Tripoli, January 1943

And they beat their cast-offs into woolies and spun garments into new raiments and sent them into the fields of conflict that the gladiators might not perish, neither from the damp of the ditches nor the drought of the dunes. And by the act of fate or the Law of Sod some fell on unprepared ground . . .

Thirteen

'Checking out at midnight, lads,' shouts the Sergeant. 'Just grab what you can, will you?'

It's Saturday night and Jerry's after us. Another retreat's on.

'Only the bare essentials,' he chivvies us along, eager to get a move on. 'Everybody out on the stroke.'

'Steady on, Sarge. It's Sunday tomorrow. We got to look our best.'

'Well, there are Sundays and Sundays, Cunliffe. And this one can do without the dressing up.'

Except for Wool, of course. There'll be ceremony in it for him alright. Him and his precious bundle of Sunday bests.

It was a bit damp around Tripoli that January.

'Must have been like this during the early days of the Somme,' said Shakes, our poet in residence. 'Wouldn't get much verse written in this weather.'

But it was much worse over in the west. Operation Torch had started as far back as July '42 when the Allies decided in their boffin wisdom to invade north-west Africa instead of opening a Second Front in Europe. They'd meet up with us pressing in from the east and we'd squeeze the daylights out of Rommel. Supposed to be a fast mobile operation, with the Yanks tearing across the desert in pursuit of the hounded Fox like Campbell on his Bluebird. But it got dampened down a bit when the rains came and turned the ground around into mush.

'Must *look* like the Somme an' all with all them sodden trenches.'

But for us, the attack on Buerat along the coast came first. The next big prize would be Tripoli.

'We're the spearhead, lads,' we're told jovially. 'Preparing the way to Tripoli. You'll like Tripoli. Nice shops.'

'Been there, then, Sarge?'

'I'm not taking questions yet, Wimpole.'

But first we had to flush them out at Beurat. 'Routine stuff.'

'Might get started when the rain eases off. Then the rest'll be a doddle. Mark my words.'

Then suddenly we're retreating. Some 'diversionary tactic'. Some 'tactical diversion', even. Some 'strategic foil'. Some 'deft decoy'. Some 'calculated deception'. Boffin brilliance. Never mind the spirits of the PBI.

'What about the "morale factor", Sarge?'

'Later, Wimpole.'

Saturday night, Christmas not long past, New Year still ringing in our ears, and guess what? – just when we're getting used to advancing and winning, we're on the retreat! Us, that is. Nobody else. *Us.* Alamein's a million miles behind us, we're almost into Tripoli and now we're turning our backs on it! Everybody else is advancing except Rommel, and then suddenly, just when we're getting over the seasonal festivities and the Wise Men have gone off back home, along comes another Three Wise Wonders from out of the mysterious east of Brigade HQ – Captain, Staff and Scribe – and we're doing what no one else has done since Rommel was a raw desert lad – withdrawing!

'Well, it makes a change, lads,' says the Sergeant, 'somebody has to give them a chance.'

'Thought we were on the victory trail, Sarge, give or take a freak thunderstorm or boffin.'

We should have known. We'd been at it long enough. All the way from Dunkirk and beyond, it had never been anything else but a Botcher's war: 'all do-it-yourself, make do and mend, try all and error,' said Shakes. 'Why should it change now?' We should have known.

We knew the patter by now, the Sarge always smoothly covering up for the rulings of the Three Wise Men, and them only ever turning up when they wanted something or to egg us along. Like Christmas cards. You know the spiel: *Hope you are well. Have a smashing time. See you in the New Year. Must get together soon. Good luck in all you do.* And then gone until another crisis or Christmas.

'C'mon. Move it!' pleads the Sarge, eager to press on. 'The minimum's all we want. The *bare* minimum, remember.'

Except for Wool, Private Wool Sac. There would have to be dressing up for him with his ginormous wardrobe. *Bare* and *minimum* were not in Wool's vocabulary.

Comforts for the Troops was the greatest contribution The Home Front made to the War Effort.

There were lots of campaigns by the 'folks back home' to assist the 'boys at the Front' at that time. Like *Dig for Victory*, inciting people to devastate their front lawns and back patches with acres of potatoes and carrots and turnips and any other root that might one day grow up into a square meal. Gardens, lawns, any old strip of meadow or fallow field covered in a wisp of grass that hinted at soil underneath was ripped up and planted, usually with potatoes for a start, 'cleanser and teaser', followed by any other root that looked even remotely capable of survival.

Or the *Save for Victory* campaign cajoling everyone

into buying special stamps to help build a tank, a battleship or a Spitfire so that us creatures of sand, sea and air could 'deliver the goods'. Billboards, classroom walls, public hoardings and private windows displayed vivid posters encouraging, even threatening everyone from the very old to the very young to 'Give us the stamps and we'll lick the other side!' 'Sacrifice and be saved!' they cried out to the nation.

But none of these 'campaigns' touched us directly. Except *Comforts for the Troops*. *Comforts* reached right out from front rooms and back kitchens, upstairs bedrooms and downstairs cupboards, up from damp, cluttered cellars and down from cold, scattered attics, into bare, Belgian ditches and over cold French beaches, across desert wadies and through treacherous dunes. *Comforts for the Troops* got next to our skin. Literally touched us. We could *feel* it.

'Retreating then, are we, Sarge?' asks a jaded voice stuffed with a yawn.

'No, we're not *retreating*, Barraclough. It's a tactical withdrawal. Re-establishing positions. Now get your case packed.'

'What's the difference, Sarge?' asks Barraclough, meticulously dusting the sand from the threadbare lapels of his undervest.

'Difference is it's strategical,' said the Sergeant with a strong emphasis on the *eegakal*.

'Oh! Thought you said *tactical*.'

'Oh, we're very sharp this evening, Mr Barraclough, aren't we? Had a good siesta then, have we?'

'But you *did* say a *tactical* withdrawal, Sarge.'

'I did. It's a bit of both, see?'

'No.'

Anyway, whatever the Sarge calls it, we know the patter. You have to admire him. He never let up. Covered up for everyone. Loaded everything with importance and significance. Justified any botch-up.

'An object lesson in loyalty and duty, our Sarge – and stubbornness.'

'Patter par excellence.'

'Perfect.'

'Pristine.'

'And priceless.'

But, however much he struggles to soften the blow, the point is Jerry's after us and tactically *we're* doing the packing and strategically we're moving out, 'midnight, on the swat'. And losing another Sunday too.

'Satisfying some other general's vim, are we, Sarge?'

'Move it, Pentonville!'

It looked exactly like any other late Saturday night at the movies with the main feature ended and the lights going up and the national anthem playing us out, except most of us in the one and nines are standing up roughly, bloody roughly to attention, more out of habit than respect. We're dazed and numbed by the stuffy atmosphere, bewildered that the fantasy's over already and we have to start shuffling out into the real night. Everyone's stretching and gazing around bleary-eyed at the rest of the audience edging out dead reluctant to start the long trek home.

Well, it's not exactly home, but it must be in the general direction. Benghazi, maybe, Alamein even, Cairo hopefully? And we're not exactly rejoicing because we know there'll be no warm welcome waiting us wherever we go. 'Don't matter if your withdrawal's tactical and heroic, or your retreat's strategical and celebrated, Sarge,' said Cunliffe, in a rare fit of oratory, 'they seldom serve champagne when you get back.'

All over Blighty the nation sat up night and day making things for us to wear. Old women, old men, young wives, sisters, daughters, small sons, kids, toddlers, everyone got co-opted or coerced into sewing and

knitting, weaving and warping, altering things and
making things and parcelling them up and sending
them off to us. Anything anyone could rustle up, mess
up or dream up, got unearthed or made, discovered or
remade, and packed up and despatched – scarves,
gloves, socks, mittens, pullovers, vests, caps, helmets.
Anything and everything that could have the faintest
hope of being of any use to a serving Botcher got
dragged out of bottom drawers and top attics and
garden sheds and cupboards under the stairs.

Cottage industries sprang up in schools and clubs,
masonic halls and scout huts, pub bars and tea shops:
the litany ran and rhythmed like the dum-dee-dum
commentary of those worthy documentary films of the
dark days that always preceded the main feature,
projecting visions of Brave New Worlds of cotton
pickers in Bihar, tea pickers in Ceylon, and hardy
harvesters of the Steppes and Plains, striving for a
better world against evocative black and white sunrises.
Back home a whole, equally brave Old World was at it,
desperately trying to ensure their own brave New One:
spinning, knitting, sewing, stitching, darning, patching,
manufacturing, and delivering to the WVS Centre to
send off to Our Boys to put on or lie on, cover up or
protect, wrap around or pull over – or even use for
ammunition. *Comforts for the Troops.*

'Tactical's what we're doing now,' the Sarge explains
ungraciously.
  'Retreating?'
  'Withdrawing!'
  'Oh, right.'
  'And what we do later's strategical.'
  'So, what's that mean, Sarge?'
  'What's *what* mean?'
  'Strath Teacha Ghoul.'
  'I just told you, Barraclough. It means it's *planned*.'

'Who planned it, Sarge, us or Jerry?'
'Fancy staying behind to mop up, Cunliffe?'

Comforts caught up with us in all weathers and campaigns, all theatres and stages, all sectors and zones. You could wait days for a meal, nights for a cuppa, weeks for a fag, months for a letter, ages for an Enfield, and yonks for a tank. But, no matter where we got to in muddy France or steaming Egypt, sodden Flanders or stewing Libya, the crates of Comforts always got through. *Comforts* was like a conspiracy that operated far and above the powers that waged the war, far and above even the might of the Geneva Convention and the right of the Red Cross, far and above the whims of crazed Hitlers and the ploys of flamboyant Churchills. It was as if army commanders on all sides were programmed to hold their fire, impose a truce, and muster up a makeshift armistice, whenever the Comforts wagons trundled across the battlefield, oblivious to the conflict raging all around them.

These wagons always appeared from nowhere without any warning, materialising out of mists, thrusting through sandstorms, sweeping aside downpours, surfacing from floods; and driven by anonymous men who seemed to belong to no regiment or flag; and always at the crux of the conflict. Then, after dumping their load, oblivious to the rumpus going on all around them, they drove off and were never ever seen again. Even ambulances were identifiable and knew their time and place, waiting for a lull in the fighting before going in, and under mutually agreed supervision. But not the Comforts wagons. Nobody ever made any signal. They carried no specific markings. There was no particular mention of them in any rules of engagement. But everyone on both sides had this sixth or seventh heaven sense that you held your fire while the wagonloads of socks and balaclavas and mittens and scarves and sundry deliveries trundled through and past and on and on again off into oblivion. To hinder a Comforts wagon would breach immutable laws. Definitely not cricket.

Even down in the depths of the ocean submarine commanders and U-boat captains alike operated according to the same unwritten *Common Comforts Agreement*. Like the Seven Seas themselves, the veneration of *Comforts* took precedence over the ships who sailed them and the nations that sent them. *Comforts* rose above all other considerations of tonnage and supplies, nations and flags, victors and medals. *Comforts* was the War's cricket – you played it only according to rules that needed no encoding. So that beneath the oceans submarine commanders, tracking convoys and scanning ships through their undetectable periscopes, would pause instinctively, stayed by the gentle hand of providence brushing their shoulders, and stand back and say: 'No, Number One. Hold your fire. *That* vessel's carrying comforts.'

Back at the dune, we start taking down the beach tents, rolling up the windbreakers, shaking the sand off the towels and cossies, and collecting our buckets and spades.

'No point overdoing it, lads,' says the Sarge edgily.

'Got to leave the place tidy for Jerry, Sarge.'

'Not sure he's that fussy, Cunliffe. Besides, he'll be bringing his own gear.'

'But it's Sunday, Sarge!'

'Maybe for you, Cunliffe, but Jerry's not so religious as you, is he? Otherwise we wouldn't be here in the first place, would we?'

'That's not very nice of you, Sarge. You make him sound positively evil.'

'Well, there are Sundays and Sundays, Cunliffe, and there'll be precious little ceremony this one.'

Except of course for Wool Sac. There would be precious ceremony for him alright, with his precious bundle of Sunday bests.

The instinctive reverence for these 'Comforts for the Troops' was embodied in the personal nature of the goods. Each 'comfort' was individual. Each sock, mitten, vest or scarf, bore a note and the name of the sender: Mrs Amelia X . . . Miss Jennifer Y . . . Master James Z . . ., together with the hope that it would be of some small 'solace and comfort' in our 'hour of trial'. 'Solace and Comfort' boxes, we called them Sacs for short. And we preserved them for our Hots – hours of trial.

Only, something went wrong in Wool Sac's case. All the way through the mud and sleet of Flanders during the winter of '39, and all the way through the rains and winds of North France during the spring of '40, right on to the beaches at Dunkirk, Wool got parcels of *tropical* gear. Silky this, satiny that – aerated vests, cotton shorts, sea-island underpants, fine-spun socks, sweat-bands for the neck and wrists, and boxes of the green eye-shades they wear at Wimbledon.

And then, the second he sets his sandals on Egyptian sand, the sequence changes. Everything is now heavy-duty wool. Scarves, pullovers, gloves, long johns, knee-length socks. Two-ply, three-ply, every bloody ply. Hot, heavy, smelly. You could still taste the mutton. And instead of open sandals, it's thigh-length fisherman's wellies and lace-up climber's boots. You could sniff Wool anywhere. And to be able to sniff out one man in Cairo in high summer takes some sniffing.

It didn't irritate him in Flanders when we were all young and carefree lying among the poppies writing our immortal verse, tolerant of man's blunders and imperfections, as if he regarded it as a perfectly acceptable botch-up. But when he stepped off that troopship at Alexandria and saw the crate of balaclavas waiting for him on the quayside, Wool went dead calm and dead white, stared, hollow-eyed, and shivered – 'like when someone walks over your grave'. Something mysterious passed over him and he just stood there, quivering slightly. Then he stooped down, picked up the lot, and took it with him. Faced the fact like it was a Revelation.

From then on, he could never escape. Months in, year out, the woolly socks and scarves kept coming. Any wadi, any oasis, any dune, any dugout, the wodges of wool tracked him down. 'Swamped by circumstance, he was,' said Shakes.

We began to wonder if Operation Torch had got themselves really bogged down, stuck even, so that the strategy wasn't going too well and someone else had botched it by not listening to the weather forecasts.

'You'd think the Yanks could have worked it out. I mean, I'd expect it from our lot, but not the Yanks with all their smart gear and jeeps and things.'

'Well, they got their Botchers too, you know.'

'Straight up?'

'Look at Pearl Harbour.'

'But that was surprise. Attack on the innocents. Treachery!'

'Well, if you ask me, mate, they botched it too. Mightiest navy in the world, with all that gear lying around, and they couldn't keep an eye on it. Sounds like botchery to me.'

That made us even more suspicious. If they'd botched Torch with all that ballyhoo and build-up, then *we* might be in a right mess this side. If Rommel didn't have to worry about his back in the west, maybe he'd dig himself in at Tripoli and come at us again.

'He'd do it too, the Fox.'

'Not the type to sit around and wait until the rain stops.'

'Naa. No mossies on old Erwin.'

'Faith,' said Wool, 'you gotta keep faith with them, you know.'

In each parcel Wool got there was always a little note, and always in a kid's hand, hoping that this latest mile of scarf or tower of balaclava or marathon of sock would be of some solace and comfort to him. 'They're relying on us.'

And he never once disowned them, never once sent them back, never once dropped or ditched them, never once so much as complained. Dragged them all over Egypt and into Libya, advancing against the Eyetie, retreating from Jerry, crisscrossing the Western Desert like a haunted nomad leaving woolprints in the sand – Wool humped the lot. Needed special transport in the end, and of course the Sarge arranged it. Cost him a lot of patience, it did, and time and energy too. Whole battles were held up while Wool got himself ready.

And Rommel waited for him too.

'Well, he would, wouldn't he? He knows the game.'

And from that first momentous revelation on the quayside, the Sarge and Wool did it all without a murmur, like it was the most natural thing on earth. Never a word of thanks or complaint between them.

'You'd think the War's about old Wool's Sac – or Burden – as much as anything else,' said Cass.

Not long before midnight the order comes to stand to. We're nearly naked except for our boots, floppy shorts, netting vests, steel helmets and rifles. All that rain then suddenly one of those freak desert nights. Decides to get warm and getting warmer by the second, so much so even the sandflies decide to leg it.

'Well, they know there's not much left of us to carry them.'

*

Each time a parcel arrived, Wool picked out the flimsy
little note tucked inside the sock or up the sleeve and
read it aloud: 'Dear Mr Soldier'. Or 'Dear Grenadier'. Or
plain 'Dear Sir'. Followed by a brief explanation of the
nature of the garment, how it should be worn and
when, basic washing instructions, suggestions for
suitable soaps, recommended ironing temperatures. All
that, plus a kind of 'social-economic history' of the
article explaining how the actual wool itself had been
discovered in some other attic manifestation, then
rescued and revived, ripped down and reconstituted
into another form, so that Wool received garments
which, if not manufactured for him personally, had
been resurrected from someone else's wintry past and
recreated in his own image.

'See,' he'd say, 'you can't disappoint a kid like that,
can you? 'S what we're here for, isn't it?'

He knew that Comforts were sacred, hallowed and
untouchable: 'created by man from rags and stitches for
his fellow man in his hour of need', he said nobly once
when we questioned his inflexible loyalty. Comforts
soared above all mundane concerns.

After each reading, he'd fold the letter carefully and
add it to his collection, the way we all kept our letters
from home. Then he'd send back his reply 'with grateful
thanks from me and all the boys out here for your
sterling work with the needles. Good luck. Yours etc.
Sgnd.'

It's going to be a sweaty dash back to wherever we're
going.

'It's got to be a hoax,' said Cunliffe. 'Some crazed
officer's dream.'

'How's that, then?' someone asked.

'Well, we're winning, aren't we? It's all downhill

now. Everything's melting in front of us. Not many medals around now. So somebody up there's probably dreamed up a little diversion to keep us on our toes and him in the limelight.'

'Reckon?'

'Blimey, where you been since Dunkirk?'

A sweaty dash and fatal to carry a surplus ounce. Everything else we leave behind. Cunliffe gets detailed to stay and blow it all up when we're at least a hundred and fifty yards over the top and well down the A1 to Cairo.

Except Wool. He's over there in a little dune all by himself with his monstrous pack. And slowly but surely he's emptying it and pulling on the lot. Glove upon glove, sock upon sock.

'Chuck it, Wool!'

But Wool shrugs, shakes his head and selects another garment. 'What God has knitted together let no man rip asunder,' he says.

'You'll never make it!'

'The kids,' he mumbles through the layers of plain and purl.

'You'll either fry or flop!'

'Can't blame them if the Post Office gets it wrong.'

'You'll never get out of that bloody dune, far less back to Cairo!'

'How could I face them?'

'You'll never even get *near* them again!'

'War's one thing,' he said, 'and not very nice, but you wage it according to certain rules. And the first commandant of war is ''Thou shalt not covet another man's comforts.'' ' He pulled on another glove and said defiantly: 'I'm not leaving *this* lot for Jerry.'

'But *he'll* never use them!'

'It's the principle.'

Then the signal comes. A quick rattle of gunfire towards Jerry covers up the Sergeant's whistle. And we're off, slithering and floundering in the sand, mad to get away before Jerry rumbles or Cunliffe panics and the lot goes up behind us.

A hundred yards out and there's this mighty 'Kee-rrr-ummmmppp!!' The whole desert lifts off the ground like the top layer off a cake and blots out the moon. We drop in our tracks and desperately chew the sand to make sure we're still alive. Jerry must have chucked over something the second Cunliffe took the plunge. Or chucked it before Cunliffe got started and they both went up together.

The boom lasts a long time. It seems to encircle us up there on our sand castle in the air, reverberating and throbbing, rumbling and thundering. Then it becomes other sounds too: the cracking and rattling and pounding and thumping of guns, the screaming and shouting and yelling and moaning of men – all variations on that first crump. Jerry's right on our tail.

We raise our eyes to check if the coast's clear enough to try another dash.

And then it comes. A Monster in the Desert Moonlight. Out of the Chaos. Out of the Ages. Out of the Ark. A great, dark floating King Kong of a ghost soaring across the dunes, somewhere Middle East of Eden.

There never was much of Wool – 5'7 maybe, 9 stone – but you'd never have guessed that night. He was transformed. A Mighty Mammoth swathed in every yard of Solace and Comfort his blessed kids had ever created for him, drifting over the sands through cloud and dust and lead like a cross between a Desert Nymph on her Magic Dune and a Knitted Witch on her Enfield Broom.

Never ever saw Wool again. None of us. Searched every dune and wadi between Cairo and Tripoli for the next year for a trace or a rumour of him. All the way back through Tobruk and Alamein and on to Cassino. But no. Not a dickie bird or a vulture. Not a mitten or a sock.

Not a strand or a ball. Not a stitch or a thread. Not a dropped plain or a passing purl. Not one. Wool had simply melted away. Suppose that's all he could have done, really.

We even searched the skies. Funny thing, but you know how you often get them clouds that look like woolly wads of unwrapped knitting? Well, every time we looked up and caught sight of one of those formations, we'd glance at each other, shy like. Never *said* anything, of course. Just looked.

ART THROB

Medenine, March 1943

And lo, the images dispatched to him were graven upon his envelopes, and he understood them not, admiring but not knowing. And the Servant of the Legion vowed verily that his eyes be opened before the first whistle, never mind the last trump . . .

Fourteen

'Wilberforce!'

The name thundered out over the Western Desert like a challenge to Rommel himself, who'd been flexing his muscles for one last heave to dislodge us.

'One for you, Wilberforce!' But it was only the Sergeant distributing the mail and waving on high a letter as elaborate as the battalion's colours.

They always used proper names on occasions like handing out the mail – civilian ones, that is, the ones we'd left behind when we settled for a life under the palm trees. Otherwise no one used them anymore. We had our own names for each other. So when the name 'Wilberforce' rang out that beautiful morning in March, only Art Throb ran forward to collect the flamboyant package.

'Another one from Hannah,' the Sarge said, as Art took the packet and squinted myopically to make double-vision sure it was his. It was usually the Corporal's job to call out the names but the Sergeant always took over when there was one for Art Throb. 'Bless her loving heart.'

Handing it over the Sarge sighed and said loudly and admiringly: 'Work of art that, Art.'

Medenine sounded like something the doc gives you when you've picked up Benghazi Belly, except that Medenine's in Tunisia and we'd left Libya behind us a month before. But we took the feeling with us.

Crossed the border the first week in February, in driving rain of course, and took Ben Gardane and Medenine with their precious little airstrips a fortnight later. Now we were having a few nice mornings to relax in and contemplate the next job – the main assault on the Mareth Line which the French had built and where Erwin was regrouping his *Panzerarmee Afrika* for another big stand. All the old familiar stuff.

'War can get bleedin' boring, you know, Sarge.'

'That's why you got me to keep you lot on your toes. Much gratitude I get an' all.'

But instead of waiting for us to come at him at the Mareth Line, Rommel was just as likely to get up and have a bash at us while we were feeling smug about Medenine. Whatever he did, it wouldn't be the obvious. You wouldn't expect *Rommel* just to sit back and wait for us. Not his style.

'Keeps you guessing all the bleedin' time, does Erwin. Whoever named him the Fox must have known him well.'

'Probably the missus.'

'Barraclough, Greatbatch, Snipcock, Bigglesworth!' The names rang out over the desert air like God calling down to his chosen – '*Samson, Gideon, Jephthae, Batak!*'

You wouldn't have thought we were waiting for Rommel. It was more like a prize giving at school. But he was over the ridge there alright, working himself into a frenzy, and the rumour was that if he didn't dig us out this time, he was due for the chop. Course, he'd have to wait a bit because we weren't budging an inch until we got our mail.

'Funny time to dish out the old mail,' said Noblesse, although it didn't much matter to him on account of his never being able to read his letters anyway. But that was another story. But he had a point. Mail wasn't something you gave out a short while before 'going in' or waiting for the thump, certainly not when it demanded a line-up like the one the Sarge had called for. 'Still, anything that puts off the evil moment,' said Tight, and we dutifully fell in and waited for the Sarge to do his lucky dip routine, which he always did whenever there was a package for Wilberforce – or, as we knew him, Art Throb.

'Telford, Latchforth, Wallasby!' – *Noaboth, Muppiom, Jubal!* The names boomed out and the guys who owned them stepped forward because only they remembered the sound of the originals. No one ever knew, or wanted to know, who the names applied to, except the Snipcocks and the Bigglesworths themselves. So, you could never tell an Anderson from a Cogsdale, but you never ever mistook a Tight Hold for a Con Brio or a Sextant Blake for an Art Throb. Your identity belonged to the unit and the war only. Like we'd left our proper names behind for safekeeping until we got back home, when we'd put them on like Sunday bests and walk down the street in them feeling good again.

'Found you again, has she, Wilberforce?' the Sarge went on as Art Throb clutched his package and studied its complex decoration.

Art was a timid soul by nature – and quivered more than lived. Spent all his time fretting and brooding, not just about war and action but about being down here in the first place – on the planet, that is, not the desert. Seemed as if he'd landed on Earth by mistake and was always anxious and edgy to get off again. Until Hannah's letter arrived.

'Methinks you won't get shot of that one with such ease.'

Art kept mum, a mixture of fear and confusion, never quite understanding the meaning of the Sergeant's comments. He peered disbelievingly at the envelope as if mesmerised by the wonder of it.

It didn't matter how many Wilberforces there were in the desert, or if Hannah got his number and rank and postal number all wrong. Her letter would always catch up with him. Because it wasn't just *for* Art. It *was* Art. Her vision of him.

'You won't have time to read all that before Rommel comes, will you?'

Art waited for a moment before returning to his place in the line and we held our breaths as he lifted his eyes from the package.

'But it don't matter about *reading* it, Sarge,' he said. 'This is enough for me.' And he lifted the package and tapped the ornate motif.

'That's what I mean,' said the Sarge, not the least put out by Art's out-of-character, if mild rebellion. 'But, like I'm always telling you, it's more than a painting. It's Hannah's you. *You* are Hannah's *you*.'

'Well, then.'

Proper names still appeared on all our letters and documents marked OHMS: *'Oh, Help me, Sergeant!'* But none of us ever used them. Each man was who he was only in relation to the rest of us and not to some mum or wife or kid we didn't know anything about because it was none of our business.

'What you mean,' said one corp. who passed in the Benghazi night, 'is it don't pay to get too personal with anyone. He mightn't last that long.'

Knowing each other's proper names might compromise us, weaken the resolve. We couldn't afford sentiment. So we made up our own disposable ones and got on with what we were doing, like having meaningful relationships with mosquitoes and Rommel. And we called Rommel Rommel, not because we knew it was his dad's name, but because that's how he sounded to us – a Rommel. He had to fit into our scheme too.

So each man had two identities: his original, which he

kept to himself, and the unit's. Except Art. He had three: the original, the unit's and Hannah's. Everyone just *had* to know who Wilberforce was, because every time the mail arrived and the Sarge roared out 'Wilberforce!', Art would dart forward and grab the packet like it had come straight down from Heaven. But when the Sarge called out the name, it wasn't because he'd read it on the envelope; it was because the envelope carried such an elaborate design that he could only recognise it as Art's *because* of the design. To us, of course, he was Art Throb – because he was the one who vibrated when the mail arrived.

'So what do we look like *this* fine morn, Wilberforce?' The Sarge peered over Art's shoulder at the sumptuous pack.

Hannah's work was a canvas. Each time she sent Art a letter she composed his name anew. And not just his name – *him*. She took the basic form of the Wilberforce and allowed her vivid imagination to run wild and free, creating it differently each time, depending on how she was seeing Art, and what she was feeling about him, at the moment she put her pen or brush to paper.

'What I want to know is,' said the Sarge: 'What hidden aspect of our Art has Hannah uncovered today?'

But Art only blinked and clutched his precious envelope. He'd never been able to see it that way. He knew Hannah was not writing for Wilberforce, the Sarge's version of him; nor for Art Throb, our version of him. And certainly not for his own, because he never seemed very sure what that was. He was overwhelmed by Hannah's talent but never fathomed the Sarge's comments, or discerned any significance in Hannah's art beyond that talent.

'I mean, what has the all-seeing eye of Hannah revealed *this* morning?' And he stabbed his forefinger at Art like a schoolmaster hoping he'd coax out an answer *this* time. Art ran his fingers over the envelope, desperately trying to find the starting point and his way into the maze before the Sergeant put him on a charge for malingering or neglecting his homework.

'*This* morning?' said Art.

Clutches of officers stood hanging around at a respectful remove, occasionally stamping their feet and clearing their throats, sometimes whacking their thighs with their batons and turning to look generally in our direction but staring above or to the right instead, pretending they weren't obsessed with what was going on over our way.

Enraptured, Art clung to Hannah's symbols. He didn't have to open the letter. It was enough to gaze upon the strokes – like gentle caresses in charcoal, pen and ink, watercolours, brush and wash, even oils, depending on her mood, with which she orchestrated 'Wilberforce'.

'D'you know what that means?' the Sarge stabbed at the glistening design. He seemed much more involved today. He always was when he found a cause he had to get stuck into, but more so this morning.

'Reckon he senses Art's on the way.'

The Sarge had a seventh sense for blokes on the edge. He'd been uncanny about a lot of chaps who'd eventually gone over the side, or just plain gone.

'Like he has premonitions.'

'Could be himself this time.'

The Sarge rubbed his chin and tried again:

'Do you *really* know?'

'What, Sarge?' Art wasn't seeing that Hannah didn't just *write* him. She *defined* him.

'Get it?'

Art shrugged. Anyone could tell Hannah was bloody good with the brush.

'Thought so. Too bleeding good for you, she is.'

The Spring silence was broken by an irritated

rumbling from Rommel's direction as if the Great Fox too was becoming impatient with Art's stubbornness. The Sergeant had tried hard on many occasions to make the breakthrough but Art resisted tenaciously, and it didn't look as if there would be time this morning to force the final breach. Maybe the Fox was impatient for another reason. His days were numbered: Alamein lay a long way behind. It looked as if Art's enlightenment might have to wait.

'D'you know what, Wilberforce,' said the Sarge, finally lifting his awestruck gaze from the intricate drawing as if he himself had suddenly had something revealed. 'You are the only man in the entire Eighth Army who is *literally* an artist's impression!'

Again a rumble from Rommel. Less irritated, this time, more long-suffering.

'What's that supposed to mean, Sarge?' Art said carefully, not sure if the Sergeant's tone hinted at mockery or admiration. He kept his eyes on the sweeps and lines that made up him as Hannah saw him – this time, this morning, this light, this mood, this tone: a work of art, God's or hers: Hannah's impression.

Now the Sergeant took a deep breath. 'You know how artists always used to illustrate battles in the old days, don't you?' he asked.

'Nope.'

'Well, they did. Long before they had cameras, armies used to drag their artists around with them.'

'Oh?'

'Course they did. Right through history. All over the great battlefields. Somme. Agincourt. Bannockburn. Thermopolae. All them big clashes. *You* know!'

'Nope.'

'Well, they did.'

'What for?'

'Well, for one thing to show people back home what it was like.'

'What they want to know that for?'

'Cos they couldn't come and see for themselves, could they?'

'Before photographs, you mean?'

'Well, that too, yes. But an artist's work was always more, well, personal like.'

'Oh, yeah?'

'Like Hannah's.'

'What you getting at, Sarge?' Art was curious now.

'They drew blokes in action, see. Made them come alive. Caught them for posterity.'

'Had to be bloody quick, then,' said Art morosely, twisting and turning the envelope to catch the artwork in different lights and shade and savour Hannah's many nuances of him.

'No, they didn't!' the Sarge scoffed. 'They just came out to the Front, had a quick shufti at the shambles, made some scribbles on their sketchpads and went off again to do their impressions back home, didn't they?'

'Why not do them out here?'

'Too messy. Too much noise. All them shells and mosquitoes and you lot squabbling all the time, and Jerry not being much help – couldn't concentrate, could they?'

'Dunno.'

'Course they couldn't!' The Sarge scoffed again. 'That's the whole point! They'd only get a rough idea out here then they'd go back and do the finished article at home – through their *mind's* eye. Get it?'

'Well . . .'

'That's the *art* bit, see. The bit that makes it different. Unique, like.'

'Oh.'

'Like what Hannah does.'

'Oh.'

'And that needs peace and calm and concentration, don't it?' The Sarge looked around the lot of us. 'Not much chance of that with the likes of you lot and him over there,' and he gestured over his shoulder in the general direction of Rommel. 'Don't know what's got into him this morning but he's being bloody bad mannered, if you ask me.'

He cleared his throat and resumed his lecture on Art.

'I mean, imagine your Hannah having to hang about here in this mess.'

'But she wouldn't be here anyway, being female,' said Art mutinously.

'True,' the Sarge nodded sagely as if acknowledging that Art really had a point there. Rommel coughed again, the idling officers whacked more thighs, and they both went back to studying the pattern on the package.

The ciphers W I L B E R F O R C E stood out like a challenge, a signal, of distress almost. Or even a beacon, a lighthouse to guide you by. It wasn't a simple sequence of letters which, when put together in a particular order, duly denoted that the contents of this or that envelope or page were for somebody called Wilberforce in another manifestation. They were a sketch of a *particular* Wilberforce, of a certain Art – and not ours or anyone else's – *hers*.

'See!' The Sarge tapped the envelope and tried again. 'That might say Wilberforce to me or someone else who knows the code. But to you, Art my boy, it says something totally different. It says *you*.'

Art shrugged.

We were all involved now. Crowding around. We had only ever been impressed before, admiring but not enlightened, so to speak. But we'd never had a chance to study Hannah's art, far less have it pointed out to us. Like a school trip to the Art Gallery with the teacher trying to explain surrealist or cubist paintings. But any excuse for a day off school or a dodge in the desert and we were all dead keen. Far better than Maths or Rommel.

But we could see you couldn't take in the artwork at a glance. You needed time to study it, to see what she was getting at. It wasn't just the name you had to figure out, it was the whole intricate setting, all the shapes and shades she saw him in and felt him in.

'Neither a civvy name nor an army handle, that is,' said the Sarge.

Again the impatient coughing came from Rommel's direction, and now a few officers of our own joined in. We could quite understand Rommel's point of view. He had to get on with it. After all it was *his* job that was on the line.

Art pursed his lips and lifted his eyebrows so that his face reached upwards in a *you-could-have-fooled-me-there* expression and went back to tracing a finger through the elaborate design.

'But just as Hannah made you – in her own image.'

The ordinary brown envelope stared back at them like an engraving. As if she meant it to last.

A runner came scurrying over to our lines from the group of officers irritatedly whacking their palms and legs with their shining batons. He mumbled something to the Sergeant who looked up surprised, glanced at his watch, then cocked his ear as if trying to catch the sound of Rommel's cough on the breeze. An enormous roar of artillery deafened the entire wadi then died away again on the desert air. The Sergeant nodded wisely, mumbled something in reply, and the runner scurried off.

Art always came back into focus with Hannah's letter. Between mails and before and after each bit of action he tended to fade a bit, to de-focus. Then, when Hannah's canvas arrived, he would drift back like a figure emerging from a mirage.

'Did them artists go in 1914 as well, Sarge?' he asked now, perking up, as if suddenly able to imagine the scene for himself.

'Course.'

'In the trenches, with camouflaged palettes?'

'Course.'

'And army-issue easels?'

'Course.'

'Battleship grey ammunition boxes crammed with regulation brushes?'

'Why not?'

'And bullet-proof tubes of paint?'

'Maybe.' The Sarge was looking slightly unsure.

'Yeah,' Art squinted and squeezed his eyes tight as if to get a better picture.

'Can you see them now?' the Sarge went on. 'Trenches at the Somme and Verdun, lined with rows of easels and stools and artists in big floppy hats strung along the hills overlooking the battlefield?'

Art squeezed. 'Not many hills overlooking the Somme, Sarge.'

'Mounds, then?'

'Mounds, yeah, that'll do.'

'Standing tall above the war far below them like them umpires at Wimbledon. Aloft. Judging.'

'Yeah. I got them, Sarge.'

'That's it, then, you got it! Just like your Hannah!'

Art hesitated, and opened his eyes.

'But Hannah's not up there, Sarge,' he said, coming back to earth or sand again and pointing to the far dunes.

'Ah,' said the Sarge, 'isn't she, now?'

For a few moments of informal armistice, the war paused in the Western Desert at Medenine. 'Like an extra Stand Easy,' said Tight.

'In her *mind*'s eye, remember.'

Art squeezed hard again and Rommel held his breath.

'Watching over you, Art, keeping an eye on you. Somewhere over there.'

We all turned to where the Sarge was pointing, to

Hannah in her floppy hat, high up on the far off ridge, scribbling, sketching, outlining, shading.

'And occasionally sending down a runner with one of her rough sketches in a brown envelope.' He tapped Art's package. 'Studies of *her Man at War*.'

Course, all that coughing from Rommel was a bit of bluff too. After all he didn't have a lot of stuff to throw at us. If the attack came it would be the second phase of a counter-attack which began the previous month at Kasserine Pass, but he messed it up a bit by running an offensive in Tunisia at the same time that came unstuck. The result was Monty had had time to get more reinforcements in through Tripoli and he probably had twice as many tanks as Rommel and better air power now with the forward airfields to lift them off from. So maybe we were in a far safer position than we allowed ourselves to think. And maybe the Sarge knew that. Maybe he *did* have time to sort Art out this morning.

'Aw, c'mon Sarge!' Art resisted.

'Aw, c'mon, no!' the Sarge retaliated. 'In her *mind's* eye, remember. It all happens up here.' And he tapped a general area between his eyes and temple.

Art de-focused again: 'In position at least fifteen minutes before commencement of battle, eh?'

'On their marks.'

'All spruced up?'

'Immaculate.'

'Credit to King and Regiment?'

'Did it naturally, too, them old soldiers.' The Sarge picked up the cue. '*Real* troopers in more ways than one.'

'Eh?'

'Not like you bleeding lot, always scratching and complaining.'

We all dutifully scraped the sand with our toecaps.

'Easels propped up and proved.'

'Yep. Just like Hannah does.'

'Brushes primed and poised?'

'You got it.'

'Ah,' said Art drifting back into focus but not yet pin sharp. 'And the Poor Bloody Infantry going over the top, again and again and again?'

'Dutifully, as befits a soldier.'

'Like film extras!'

'In a way,' said the Sarge, hesitating.

'You mean, on and on and on until the artists get their impressions right?'

'Well, it's a painstaking exercise.'

'Or until it gets so bloody dark they can't see the canvas no more?'

The Sarge sensed something a bit off centre.

'Or they can't find the enemy lines to run straight at and they're messing up the composition?'

The Sergeant eyed Art carefully.

'That's what we are, Sarge!' cried Art, thumping his package and pointing to the distant dunes. 'Artists' bloody extras.'

'Well, in a way.'

'Ordered by the box.'

'No, no, no, ordered by the *artist*. Seeing you – not just *in* the picture, but standing *out* in it, see?'

'Not just a design?'

'A design *within* a design.'

'Yeah,' said Art, blinking, dazed by his own efforts and the painting on the envelope.

'Now I reckon,' the Sarge added, 'that's really something. I mean, that's *unique*, that is.'

Jerry's artillery coughed and rumbled like old Fords trying to start on a frosty morning. There was much shuffling in our ranks. Just as well we didn't have any

Xs, Ys or Zs in the unit. Wilberforce was the last name. A great hush descended over the gathered host, like the hush that always comes before the whistle blows – only more so.

'You know, what, Wilberforce?'

'Sarge?'

'You are above all this!' Stabbing his baton at Art's package, then lifting his hands, the Sarge gestured over us comprehensively, and the desert contemptuously.

His eyes focused on remote mounds of sand and a legion of faraway Hannahs sketching Arts in their floppy hats. The first barrage erupted but it sounded no more than drum rolls. The impatient officers gave up their impatience and ceased whacking their thighs, and we knew that Rommel wouldn't dare strike at a moment like this. He knew the rules.

'This is it. The Patter bit.'

'He's already done it.'

'Thought he'd flipped.'

'Thought it was for Art.'

It was the sergeant's night-before-speech, except it was morning-of this time. He hadn't done it the previous evening on account of the heavy mossy count. So he'd held it over until after breakfast. And the mail too. No one ever handed out mail immediately before action. And because the post brought Art the perfect package, the Sarge had got his perfect theme. We ought to have known. Patter impeccable.

'The great design *is* you,' he was saying. 'You exist elsewhere, Art, not just here, but somewhere else, somewhere your Hannah has created.' But he wasn't looking at Art.

'*You*,' and again he swept his arm across all of us, 'you are above all *this*.' And he gestured to the desert disparagingly, but we didn't look round. We'd seen it before.

He held his position for a few seconds while his voice

floated off to fade away on the desert air. Then he came back into focus and said firmly: 'Right then!' And we all shuffled back from mental Attention to At Ease.

'You know what, Wilberforce?'

But we had forgotten the coda.

'Sarge!'

'A diamond in the sun, my son. That's what you are. One of the many facets of Hannah's life – shining in the desert.'

'Sarge!'

'You are the vision of Hannah in the wilderness.'

But by now Rommel had had 'genug'. He struck while Art was still overcome by the import of the Sarge's words and contemplating his package in disbelief and revelation as if gazing into a mirror and being fascinated to see what he really looked like.

You couldn't blame Rommel. He had to get moving. And, like the Sarge, he'd waited long enough for Art to get organised. When the shell arrived Art was still studying Hannah's artist's impression.

'Went off into oblivion,' said the Sarge, 'with a total understanding of who he was.'

GREAT SHAKES

Mareth Line, March 1943

And the muse was upon one of their hordes, and he descended among them and sang psalms for their beloveds, definitely not from his stinginess but verily from his heart. But he did labour so hard he lost his gourd and sang of love to his adversaries too . . .

Fifteen

When Xmas comes, from desert dune
I send my heart to you in tune,
And dream of times when there will be
A wonderland for you and me.

Great Shakes wrote all our Christmas cards. Or rather, he composed them: wrote them in verse. And more than just Christmas cards: he'd tackle any name and every occasion: Christmas, Easter, Birthday; Valentine's Day, Engagement, Wedding; Birth, Christening, Death. 'Just give me the subject and tell me who it's for and I'll give you a personal poem,' he'd say, throwing down his offer like a gauntlet. 'The whole range of human experience, I cover.' He sounded like a barrow boy flogging off surplus Granny Smiths. 'And I do it for love.'

It was true. There wasn't a man in the regiment who hadn't benefited from Shakes' talent and generosity. We flocked to him with our own 'very special requests', and Shakes listened, reflected, and turned them out. 'Not for nothing, mind. For love.'

But something happened shortly after Alamein.

If you could catch a glimpse of me
And I of you, who knows,
We two might lifelong buddies be
Instead of mortal foes.

He started writing them for Jerry as well.

'He's flipped, Sarge,' said Splints the Medic.

'Well,' said the Sergeant, 'you never can tell with these creative guys. Funny things happen out here. Maybe it's the heat.'

The Mareth Line was Rommel's last major defensive position before Tunis. When we breached that, the way would be clear because there weren't many more major defence works to stop us.

The line lay about a hundred miles inside the border between Libya and Tunisia and stretched from the sea due south to the Matmata Hills. The French first built it against the Italians in Libya, and it consisted of barbed wire, artillery positions, anti-tank ditches and miles of minefields in front. Of course when Rommel came along he reinforced it to a far more formidable fortification than the French ever built. Cracking it would be tough enough – 'another one of those nuts, lads,' the Sarge said, 'so you'll need all the sleep you can get.'

> *I think of your birthday*
> *and the hope it will give*
> *to your husband and loved ones*
> *as long as you live.*

Shakes was a poet. 'Not just a rhymer of Christmas cards, you know', he assured us, but 'a genuine, beduine poet', a very apt description for someone hard at work composing in a sand dune on the way to Tunis on the night of the 25th of March, 1943.

'First day of spring tomorrow, remember!'

> *I never thought that I would sing*
> *Above the sands my song of spring;*
> *But spring is neither brown nor green,*
> *A state of mind it's always been.*

*

'When I was called up,' Shakes told us, 'I put down poet as my preference for a trade, but they said they didn't have any vacancies. Besides, they said they thought "Poet" sounded a bit too grand for the likes of me. Usually poets were commissioned chaps only, like artists, see, and Padres. Posh blokes.

' "Well," I said, "how about 'Bard', then?"

'So they thought about it and thumbed through their lists, and said: "Barber do? Near as we can get." And I said "No, thanks. Try 'Rhymer'."

'So they went *thumb, thumb, thumb* and said: "Reemees do? Sounds nearer, more like your number. You look like the kind of bloke with a long fuse. Besides, Reemee has a certain lilt to it, don't you think? Although there's music in barber too, in a way. You know, bar . . . ber. No?" '

But Shakes opted instead for the PBI – 'flows well, see, and got a lot more potential for rhymes' – and thus became the voice of the man in the dune: our very own bard of the wadi and desert minstrel – troubadour to the troops.

As usual Rommel wasn't just sitting waiting for us. We'd tried a few of our forays to soften things up but the going itself was soft enough, the mines were 'an absolute pig', and Jerry's artillery never stopped hammering us. The Americans were in the north, the New Zealanders in the south and an awful lot of us lot in the middle.

And as usual we kept plugging away and falling back to recuperate, then off again, and in between Jerry would thunder away with his artillery and dare to mount the odd counter-attack or two – 'to keep us on our toes'. Familiar enough stuff, but draining. The kind of relentless slogging that made more than Shakes think again.

> *Oh distant daughter, far off son,*
> *I sing to you now day is done*
> *A song of love you safe to keep*
> *And bless you in your birthday sleep.*

As well as birthdays and weddings, Shakes wrote before and after each engagement, jolly rhymes we could send home to reassure them we'd come through, another way of celebrating. 'Better than a long letter when you're too damned bushed to put quill to parchment.' Shakes' way with cards was a quicker greeting and, like he said: 'a bloody sight more effective than a dozen pages of you lot's prose'. And at other times he'd say: 'a card's better than a disc with an address on it, you know.'

He never wrote the same verse twice. 'Oh, no! That would be cheating. Downright disrespectful. Them shop cards on bereavements and weddings and anniversaries all come from some hired hack and get sent out to anyone and everyone. All *general* cards. Nothing particular or personal. But not mine. Oh, no, self-directed, they are. Straight to the person.

'My poetry's different, see. I mean, Old Shakespeare wrote for the world. I write for the people in it. Same message, though. His stuff's much longer. I keep it short, so you can call me Shakes. Someone gives me his story, sob or joy, and I listen, like the Padre, take it all in, absorb it and digest it, like, and it comes out like a piece of music in the words he'd have chosen if he'd had the gift.

> *Never fear that they won't hear*
> *Your voice amid the crowded sphere;*
> *Your heart will ring out strong and true*
> *For I will sing your song for you.*

'You know what the Great Book says, don't you? "They shall cry out but there shall be none to hear or

help them.'' Well, they can't say that now. As long as
I'm around, you'll all have your voice.

'Difference between me and Shakespeare is they can
understand me. The difference between me and the
Padre is I give them their own voice.'

The wadi we'd encamped in was a shambles. It was part
of the greater Wadi Zigzaou that was proving such a
brute with its sodden carpet and mosaic of mines. Wadi
Hamtah was a sort of offshoot or mini-wadi and looked
as if a squadron of bulldozers had been out scouring the
desert for rubbish and had shovelled back everything
they could find into our little refuge hole: petrol cans,
ammo cases, tyres, oil drums, tools, tents, tarpaulins,
pots, poles, pans. And now after one futile attack when
we hadn't breached anything except the rules of decent
language we're dumped down right in the midst of it
and told to sort ourselves out and find a complete kit
before another go the following day – 'Pee, dee double
queue!'.

'Which attack, Sarge, theirs or ours?'

'Moo-vve it, Beaucoup!'

'But every bleedin' bleeder's knackered here, Sarge!'
said Mersey, admiring the litter.

Not a lot of poetry in Wadi Hamtah.

'How about this one, Sarge?' Shakes called out from the
debris of 'the world's most welcoming wadi':

> *Now Rommel's gone back and called it quits*
> *We're left on our tod to pick up the bits.*
> *But we should go home to count up instead*
> *The cost of the peace, the price of the dead.*

By the time we reached the Mareth Line Shakes'
sentiments were definitely not for us alone.

'Well,' said the Sarge, assessing Shakes' latest effort at
reconciliation. 'You might have something there.'

Five months and 70,000 casualties after Alamein, the Old Fox Rommel had been summoned back to Berlin: 'He's on Headmaster's report,' said the Sarge. 'His homework's been slipping. And that's double bad news for him, cos his old man's a schoolmaster.'

We're a bit peeved about that. It wouldn't be the same without Rommel. And now we're to be left to cope with a couple of unknowns: von Arnhim and his Eyetie oppo, Messe. Not even consulted.

'Then again,' said the Sarge, ruminating further, 'aren't you maybe, how shall I say, *overdoing* it a bit on the Jerry side?'

'Can't help it, Sarge. Poets are moved by other forces, see.'

The Sarge surveyed the shambles of Wadi Hamtah and said 'Hmm.'

'They sense things on the wind, see.'

'Really?'

'Yeah. They tune in to sounds and vibrations ordinary blokes can't apprehend yet.'

'Ahhh. . .'

'Ahead of their time, see.'

'Well, stone me. . .!'

'Oh yes, we see beyond, see. We *warn*. We sense the way the wind's blowing and the tide's flowing and send messages back to you lot.'

'Ah, hah. Could have fooled me, Shakes.' And again surveying the shambles, the Sarge added: 'So what do you sense or smell on the wind *this* fine evening?'

'I sense we have to look at things differently now, Sarge – now that we're winning.'

'Ah. . .'

'When you think about it, it's not very bright to fight each other in the sand a thousand miles from home, now, is it?'

'Hmm.'

'I mean, what's all this sand got to do with it,

anyway? I bet Jerry'd rather be building castles in it with
his bucket and spade, just like the rest of us.'

'Ah, more compassion, you mean?'

'Well, if you need a big word, Sarge, yeah.'

'Well,' the Sarge recovered and looked again at
Shakes' latest contribution to international reconciliation. 'I'm not sure if it'll cut much ice with them he's
left in charge.' And he gestured over the ridge in the
general direction of Tunis. 'Different blokes, them.
They'll need to make their mark.'

'Well, you never know, Sarge,' said Shakes, 'they got
their Christmases and weddings too. Might bring a
change of heart if I keep at it.'

'I wouldn't bank on it, Shakes.'

'Talking to each other in the tones and tunes of the
spheres, that's what it'll be. It's what *I'm* fighting for,
anyway.'

'Fair enough, Shakes. As I always say: "every man to
his own trade". But I'd make sure your rifle's in tip-top
condition before tomorrow, if I were you. Safer than a
get-well card.'

Everyone else spent the day fly-ridden and mosquito
bitten, unwashed and smelly, coughing and bitching,
moaning and groaning, spluttering around searching
through mountains of sand-clotted gear to see if we
could rescue anything that might prove useful in case
old Arm'im and Messy decided to come at us before
we'd got the reinforcements and supplies of food and
weapons that were always 'coming up right behind us,
lads' across five thousand miles of desert.

But not Shakes. Grubby, oiled and ragged, he sat on
an upturned ammunition crate like a man possessed.

'He's on a mission, Sarge.'

'Hmmph.'

'The muse is on him. "Verily inspired", as he would
say.'

Shakes scribbled away, no longer looking up at the Sarge and his Corporal as he spoke and wrote.

'Seeing the wadi in a completely new light, I reckon.'

'Well, he's lucky. He'll get a lot more written tonight, then.'

The Sarge turned to survey the rest of his flock, morosely nibbling away at the desert leftovers.

'Promise, lads,' he shouted to cheer us up, 'the refreshments'll be up shortly. Clean underwear, new shirts, fresh socks, glistening rifles and buckets of ammo.'

Nobody took a blind bit of notice.

'Even as I speak,' he pressed on, borrowing a little inspiration from Shakes, 'the golden goodies are winging their wondrous way across the silver dunes like blue birds over the white cliffs of Dover. Just you wait and see.'

Shakes paused and looked up. 'What you say, Sarge?'

But the Sarge was walking off now to supervise the scavenging.

'Watch it, Shakes,' said the Corp, 'there's competition around. A touch of the old muse in that patter, I'd say.'

Course, it was a safe bet the goodies hadn't got to Cairo yet, but we'd have felt cheated if the Sarge hadn't kept up his patter. After all, he'd been at it since before Dunkirk.

A little flock of clouds go down to rest
With shepherd winds that shook them in the West

Shakes got his inspiration from a little book he carried around with him like a Bible: *A Treasury of War Poetry*, packed with poems from the First World War which he read aloud to us under the stars as we sat with the sand in our socks and pants and the creepy crawlies in all the other places.

And when the war is over I shall take
My lute a-down to it and sing again

'They were always writing poetry in the First World War,' he said, 'because they had the time, see, sitting in them trenches for years and years with only the odd Somme or Passchendaele to break the monotony. And if you read these guys something rubs off.'

'Nick their ideas, then, do you, Shakes?'

'No! Not that! Just means you get a kind of fellow feeling.'

'Gets you started and underway, then?'

'Yeah, guides me along, if you like. Inspiration, they call it. Means being breathed upon,' he said.

'Don't strike me as particularly wonderful.'

'Why not?'

'Not with the kind of blokes we share our tents with. Socks is bad enough.'

'Not the *breath*! The *ideas*! It's like playing football with star players.'

'Ah, yes, raises the standards, eh? I used to get that from my old boss. Master plumber, he was. Always did better bends when he was around.'

'Right. That's why these First World War blokes turned out so much. They were *all* at it, sitting around their trenches composing all the time – breathing on one another, inspiring each other.'

'Not like you, Shakes, trying to compose all on your own with us lot and all this turmoil going on all the time. Beats me how you do it.'

'Well. . .'

'And always on the move, covering thousands of miles.'

'True.'

'Composing on the wing.'

> *The little lark adoring his lord the sun*
> *Across the corn the lazy ripples run*

Shakes read aloud to us from his little book – all about distant corners of foreign fields looking forever like

England with rosy bushes and apple blossoms and running streams and thrushes' songs.

> *or 'tend the carefree lark in summer skies*
> *and feel the brush of zephyr in the wings*

'They sang about the places they loved back home,' said Shakes, 'all them green fields and wide valleys and high larks and mill streams they wanted to get back to.'

'Where was that then, Shakes – Eden?'

'No, England!'

'Could have fooled me.'

'You know:

> *where nature blossoms richest 'mid the long*
> *morns of warming loam and "spiring song".'*

'Well, I heard about mean back-to-backs and meaner front-to-fronts,' said Stripes, 'and I seen steel works and cotton mills and pit villages and terraced houses and outside lavs, but can't say I can recall . . . what was that line again?'

'The agile waterfly wrinkling pools.'

'No . . . doesn't seem to ring a bell.'

'Flowers gray and dun?'

'Doubt it.'

'How about: buccaneering bees proving busily?'

'Again.'

'Buccaneering bees proving busily!'

'Don't think so.'

But obviously Shakes had seen and heard them all in Walsall.

> *O distant daughter, far off son,*
> *I sing to you, now day is done,*
> *A song of love you safe to keep*
> *And bless you in your birthday sleep*

But over and above all his First World War infatuation and serenading Jerry, Shakes' first duty was still to us.

Oh, dear Grandpa, from distant sand
I touch the contours of your hand
That held me close and helped me grow,
Now thou art gone and I am low.

'Better in verse, see. More intense. Then I stick the RIP bit on the front.'

'Rest in Peace?'

'No. Revered in Perpetuity.'

'Oh. That sounds nice.'

'Adds a bit of dignity, see. Rest in Peace is old hat. It's more a vocation, really. A calling. I give voice to the inner feelings of the common bloke in the dune.'

Whatever inspired the poets on the Somme, there wasn't a lot of it in Wadi Hamtah. But Shakes kept at it.

'How about this one, Sarge?' he shouted, thrusting out another card he had just run off.

Because we've been at war so long
We can't distinguish right from wrong
And if that's so why do we fight
To try to judge twixt wrong and right?

'Hmm.'

Shakes was composing for Jerry instead. 'Or this:

'You and I are not so grand
We cannot deign to sleep in sand,
But you'll agree it's not the best
For hero heads to come to rest.'

'Hmm.'

'You said there was new stuff coming up right behind us, Sarge, so I thought I'd fill in another card for Jerry while I'm waiting.'

'Well, you know, anything can happen in the desert, Shakes, so why don't you find yourself a bit of rifle as well?'

'But how will I clean it, Sarge?' said Shakes, looking

morosely down at the grime and dust encrusting his hands.

'You can find something, Shakes! Exercise a bit of that fertile-reptile imagination.'

Holding his hands out in a gesture of despair, Shakes looked genuinely lost.

'I mean,' the Sarge pressed on, 'you're a very ingenious person, Shakes. . .'

'Eh. . .'

'Talented.'

'Oh!'

'Maybe you ought to apply some of it to rummaging around this little lot. I mean, with a gift like yours, you could make requisitioning creative.'

'But I'm doing it another way, Sarge.'

And he pointed down at the large ammunition box at his feet chock full of cards.

'This way we might never need the ammo, see?' And he handed Sarge another one:

> *If I could catch a glimpse of you*
> *Or you a sight of me;*
> *We'd find we're nowhere half so bad*
> *As we're cracked down to be.*

'Bottle's gone, Sarge,' said Sparks.

'Another beaver berserk,' said Speed.

'Think it's the heat?'

By late afternoon there was no sign of supplies and the rummaging was becoming futile and irritating. There's not a lot you can do with scrap in a desert except stare at it and wipe off the sand.

Shakes was still scribbling, adding to his supply, oblivious to the accepted chaos and futile activity going on around him.

'You know,' said the Sarge, coming round on another tack, 'that's a very nice thought about Jerry, Shakes. But

for a start he's not going to understand it, is he, him being
an uncouth and uncultivated kind of kraut – not blest with
the pure tongue of the King's English like us lot, is he?'

'Well, he'll get the idea, Sarge, and he'll know it's
poetry cos the lines are in the middle.'

'Well, please yourself, mind, but I'd do a bit more
rummaging around this lot, if you ask me.'

'I won't, Sarge.'

'No telling what you might come up with, a creative
chap like you.'

Shakes stopped writing and contemplated the grime
and the mayhem around him. Then, as if in another
flash of inspiration, he was off his arse like a shot,
charging around the wadi scrapyard, burrowing and
scraping amid the debris, heaving and turning over
wheels, tracks, pistons, gearboxes, ammo boxes, crates,
barrels and shell cases, scratching materials from the
debris, dragging them to the far end of the wadi and
piling them up into some sort of last-line-of-defence.

'Told you he'd flipped, Sarge,' said Splints.

'Well, as I say,' said the Sarge. 'I seen a lot of them
creative guys in my time – Khyber Pass, North West
Frontier. Kurds. Thugs. Pathans. 'Sides, there's got to
be something in what old Shakes says. We been at this
caper since the cave days. Could do with a change.'

> *And if in days as yet unseen*
> *We shall stay joined as we have been,*
> *Then we may build from out this sand*
> *A safe and surer homemade land.*

The love of Shakes reached out far beyond the war.

'See, the way I figure it,' he said, 'is it always comes
down to this in the end,' waving his hands around the
world. 'It's all a kind of war – living. Now, when I get
out of this mob I'll be working in one of them big
Government Departments – and the whole business of

government and people will blossom into something much more beautiful. Like advising the Income Tax, see, on compassion and style:

> *'The year upon its axis turns*
> *And once again the date comes round*
> *When you must pause and give account*
> *Of every deed and every pound.*

'I call that one Many Happy Returns.'

Shakes kept at it but no one paid much attention.

'Think he's flipped. Sounds ripe for it.'

By sundown he had constructed a huge facade like a cross between a shop front and a proscenium arch, lashed together out of spare planks, duck boards, dismantled ammo boxes, ration crates, and sundry metal struts and pipes, all flanked by sheets of tarpaulin folded to give the effect of drapes.

The Sarge kept a wary eye on him at a distance but said nothing. He always kept a wary eye on the 'edgy ones', at a distance. But by sundown his curiosity was too much.

'What's this, then, Shakes, the wall to put our backs against?'

'Nope. It's a gift shop, Sarge. A welcome for Jerry if he takes us.'

'Very well. And if we take him first?'

'Then it's all over anyway.'

'Now there's a nice paradox.'

'No, Sarge. A kiosk.'

'Ah, well, you're the literary gent. So if we win, it's lost?'

'The way I look at it, Sarge, we're both lost anyhow.'

And Shakes worked at it well into the night.

Before sunrise the following morning Jerry pushed first and called our bluff, and we were out of that wadi like rats from a sinking barge. But we held him, even with our make-do-and-mend supplies, until suddenly he gave up. Just stopped coming and scarpered back to his Mareth Line. Must have had a change of heart or thought our defences and supply lines went deeper than they did. In fact they went no deeper than Shakes' Shack. And that was only a front.

When we slipped back into the wadi again for a shave and a hot bath there was no sign of Shakes. The desert was like that. Some chaps just seemed to evaporate. Sarge said it was the mirage effect: 'probably never been there in the first place.'

Now, for the first time we got a sight of what he'd been up to all night. He had constructed his own version of a mobile shop front like you find on any seaside promenade, and decked it out with hundreds of cards, each one welcoming the buyer in verse. They fluttered in the morning breeze like bunting on Coronation Day.

> *Now that the Fox has come and gone*
> *And sand blows o'er his traces*
> *Come join the Rats and sit ye down*
> *To share his fares, and graces.*

And in bold letters across the front of the facade he'd painted:

SHAKES' PIER

Promenade Poet

And underneath:

Help yourself

And he'd surrounded it with buckets and spades.

Inside, or rather behind the welcoming facade, he had stacked the other thousand-odd cards he'd been composing since Alamein, like:

*If you agree there's nothing grand
In dying for a grain of sand,
Then you like me might wonder why
We've come this far to vie and die.*

We selected cards from his massive collection to send home. Well, we didn't have to select. They were all appropriate – singing of goodwill to Grandpa, Jerry and tomorrow's Tax Man.

As Shakes always said: 'Sing it to them, lads. Remember, there's a lot more mileage in madrigals.'

INTERLUDE 3

Sixteen

Mon . . . Tay . . . Caa . . . See . . . No

The sound of Monte Cassino brought everything together for us. Or the music did.

By the time our father came home, we knew all about it, but when we first heard the name, we recognised it immediately. Recognised that we had heard it before, had been hearing it right from the beginning – not just the name, the sound:

'Oh, Monte Cassino,' we seemed to be saying. 'Of course.'

'It's where we'd all been making for right from the start,' he said, easing over to select another wound to rest on, and squashing his precious scroll.

Chronologically, Monte Cassino didn't come into our life until 1944. It must have been February at the latest, but we had been aware of it some weeks or months earlier while the Allied armies struggled to get footholds on the slippery beaches and mountain paths of southern Italy and assembled their forces and supplies for the awesome assault on the awesome mountain on the road to Rome. Awesome in size, awesome in import:

'Tampering with something else at Monte, we were,' he said.

There must have been talk of it before then, probably whole chapters in the *Botchers' Book*, because Monte was a 'stubborn nut to crack', and didn't fall – presumably down from Heaven – in a day: 'four months in fact'. Nevertheless, the name couldn't have been there during the Readings of the early years.'

'Really started looming after Alamein. Could feel it coming at us across the dunes. Heard it on the wind, worried at it like a bone, without knowing it, long before booking up for Sicily. Right lads, that's the sand bit, now for Monte. Then off home.'

For us, it was like the sound had always been on the tip of our minds, butterflying, fluttering around but never alighting. A sound rather than a name that we kept flicking at, trying to swat or pin down. Not just for a few weeks or months before or after the battle, but for years. Since the beginning, in fact. 'Maybe as far back as that Clapham Recruiting Office.'

Mon . . . Tay . . . Caa . . . See . . . No

The vibrations had always been there. And the echoes.

The sound of Monte Cassino was like the sound of Morgan the Mighty or Mersa Matruh or Dai Fox, of Enrico Caruso, Con Brio or Signor So-So. The theme and variations were there already, mentioned occasionally in his dispatches, featured regularly in his Botcher letters, as if running through Crosby's croonings and Caruso's strains, as if we'd always been hearing the sound, or listening for it, so that when it did finally emerge, in so-called *real* time, we recognised it immediately and felt a great sense of relief that it had turned up at last and openly declared itself.

Monte Cassino was the Holy Grail, the Crock of Gold, the End of the Rainbow, the place where everyone in the story was heading. No one had known its name before but everyone had set out to look for it, believing that 'when we find it, we'll know.'

For us the entire music of childhood derived from the sound of Monte Cassino. It sang out as beautifully as

any name from the *Bumper Book of Botchers*, any hero
from the *Famous Five*, any character from *ITMA*, or any
phrase from our gramophone, except perhaps 'Sweet
Fulfilment', which seemed roughly the same anyway.

Mon . . . Tay . . . Caa . . . See . . . No

Its music brought together all the diverse sounds of
those years:

> *'o sole mio*
> *st nfronte a te!*

> *Wo Du nicht bist,*
> *Kann ich nicht sein*

> *So inspire me with passion*
> *In dreams and fond illusions*
> *And castles in the air!*

and

> *O, no, it isn't perfume*
> *It's love in bloom*

Sweet fulfilment . . .
Mother's voice reading the letters 'from the Front':

> *And, lo, it came to pass, that a certain Botcher . . .*

which seemed the only place to read them from
anyway;
the roll call:

Con Brio, Mona Lot, Heddle Nash, Toby Rook, Signor
So-so, Enrico Caruso, Bing Crosby, The Wolf of Kabul,
Tight Hold, Mrs Mopp, Richard Tauber, The Black
Sapper . . .

the quartet:

> *Our Father, with chart in Heaven*

presumably the one who finally botched it at Monte Cassino;

and the name itself:

Mon . . . Tay . . . Caa . . . See . . . No

The sounds of that time were our basic musical language, but they had been resounding in our veins in a turmoil and needed a theme to bind them together and impose a structure, to provide the rhythm and make sense of the whole piece. The five notes of Monte Cassino did it: the long, uninterrupted, uninterruptable call of

Mon . . . Tay . . . Caa . . . See . . . No . . .

like the distant cry of a train pleading with the darkness.

'Like another way of listening to the world. Like hearing the Promised Land.'

It didn't matter when he had first talked or written about Monte Cassino. We knew about it like we knew about his Margins.

'Might have been the eighth wonder of the world,' he said, balancing on the top of one of his wounds.

For us it was the ninth.

NOBLESSE O'BLEECH

North Africa, Saturday, 10 July 1943

And they spoke with the tongues of angels, but father and mother heard him not nor he them, for the powers of thickness drew a blue veil across their utterings. Until there appeared rips in the raiment and the music came through and he rejoiced he'd cracked it. . .

Seventeen

The night we left for Sicily, Noblesse O'Bleech announced he was off to post his letter.

'You're off to do *what*?' seethed the Sergeant.

'Post my letter, Sarge.' O'Bleech blinked innocently. It was the opaque eyes that did it: so pale, so light blue, you could see through them – 'like looking through polished glass', said the MO – only there was nothing on the other side and no reflection either. Noblesse O'Bleech was *transparently* innocent. He would always look young.

'Post it *where*?' asked the Sergeant, more curious than angry now because the look of O'Bleech was enough to melt the heart of any NCO. '*If* you don't mind my asking.'

Funny the kind of calm that hung over us that night. Not the lull-before the-storm kind, nor the all-packed-and-ready-to-go kind. More of an emptiness. 'Like the day I left school for the last time,' said Cass, 'and hadn't any idea of what to expect next. Alone. Hollow.'

We seemed to have been embarking for weeks, with all the Allied armies turning up to join in or wave goodbye. You couldn't see the sand or the quays for troops and trucks. The desert itself was blotted out.

'Makes a change at least,' said Edge. 'Thought the world was made of sand.' Until it began to dawn that what these thousands of men and tons of steel were covering up was exactly that – the sand that had tortured us for three years, soaking up more than our sweat and blood and tears.

'Never liked us from the start.'

'Dogged us all the way.'

When the ships were loaded up and only a few stragglers left behind to tidy up the mess we'd made of it all, even the desert looked deserted.

'Hated our guts for years,' said the Corp. 'Now she's suddenly looking bloody lost without us.'

'The Field Post Office, Sarge,' said Noblesse.

O'Bleech we called him, Noblesse O'Bleech, on account of his colouring and his pedigree. His mum was Danish and his dad Irish, so he wasn't just fair, like non-dark, but a blend of pure blond and ginger that varied according to the angle of the desert sun. If it was early morning or early evening and the sun was below forty-five degrees and the colour either warming up or reddening down, then the pink bits on his skin popped up like freckles, his hair looked rinsed and the irises disappeared into sightless spots, like on a photograph taken with a flash. But when the sun was higher and he had a bit of moulding to his features, he looked golden. Not sunburnt like we got – you know, either raw-peeling or fisherman's brown – but golden. Like one of those Egyptian kings – *flax*-golden.

Facing the Sergeant at sunset the night we embarked, O'Bleech's hair was pink-rimmed.

The Sergeant's eyebrow stretched up slowly towards the peak of his cap. 'And where, Mr Hans Christian O'Finnegan,' he asked in his soft, enquiring tone, 'where, may I *humbly* ask, do you expect to find one *here*?'

Sarge had a sort of distant *place* of understanding where he could always find room for the weaknesses of every one of his charges when it mattered, that is, right up until the instant we went through the 'veil of hail'.

'Then it's up to you,' he said. 'Then you're on your ownsome. Then it's anarchy.'

O'Bleech blinked and said confidently: 'Oh, I'll find one, Sarge,' while the Sarge cast a sceptical eye across the million desert rats swarming over the quays and dunes and beaches.

'Will you, now?' he said, squaring his shoulders and pursing his lips. He looked around at the disbelieving group gathering about him, hanging on his decision, but he took his time, waited for the shuffling and murmuring to die down, then rubbed his chin thoughtfully. When it seemed he'd got as much attention and as little disturbance as he could hope for, he began: 'Well, then.'

Here we go, we thought.

We'd no real idea why we were embarking at all. But then we were never consulted. The rumour was it was Sicily, which didn't mean or help much.

'They might have *said*.'

'Scared we'll nip out and ring Rommel.'

'Shhh.'

But we knew it was the beginning of the invasion of Nazi Europe. Which didn't convince us much because it seemed a bloody silly idea anyway.

'Expect they're trying to open up the Med. Clear a way through.'

'Through what – Italy?'

'Dunno.'

'Not much point going there – too bloody narrow for a start.'

'Difficult to get a foothold, yeah?'

'Difficult to get a bloody *toe*-hold!'

'Especially with them boots.'

'If you ask me, it's because we're here. Handy.'

Seemed a weird decision. Just because we'd driven Rommel out of North Africa, it didn't follow we should jump across the Med and chase him up through Italy.

'Plenty of other places to start a Second Front.'

'And better.'

'Well,' said the Sarge, 'you never know what goes on with them general types.'

'Think it's the heat, Sarge?'

'Now, then,' announced the Sarge. 'We all know what's on tomorrow, don't we?' And with that onerous introduction we knew the decision on Noblesse and the Post Office would have to wait. 'Not exactly *tomorrow*, of course, but one of the tomorrows coming up soon.' He looked around his congregation. 'The task ahead. What your King and Country expects from you.' A dangerous groan threatened the platoon, then wisely subsided. This was it. The ultimate Patter.

We settled down for the time-honoured custom – the Sarge's into-the-breach-dear-friends sermon to the assembled host, ie 'you lot under my bleeding charge'. His own personal rallying call aimed at inspiring us. Always neatly timed for a few hours before we went into every action, usually the previous evening, as we were very keen, or he made us keen, on early morning assaults – 'sunrise surprises', he called them, except that very rarely had we ever surprised anyone.

This time, because we were already packed onto the vessel with loads of other units, it was going to be difficult for him to find any space to get it in on time. But Noblesse had given him his opportunity. We had all shuffled together to hear the great man's judgement on the letter posting, so he had literally cornered us. He saw it as the best chance he'd get, and took it.

'My friends . . . dearly beloved . . .' The call to attention. Soft. Compassionate. But still the call. All scratching finally faded away.

'As you will have observed during our years of trial together passing through this wilderness, it has been my custom, whenever faced with the unknown tomorrow, to deliver unto you a few words by way of sustenance and encouragement, at once enhancing your faith and at the same time inviting you to take heed and beware the pitfalls of wayward unreadiness and downright insubordination. . .'

He cleared his throat, indicating the introduction was over and giving us implicit permission to clear ours. Whereupon a great retching rent the evening stillness before it descended into peace again.

'Now, as you will doubtless have observed, we are leaving behind us tonight the scene and source of all our trials and tribulations of many months.' And he signalled in the direction of the dunes cowering behind the military machinery and lying exhausted after another day's torture, but hushed now in the evening sun, and looking, as the Corp so elegantly put it: 'bloody lost without us.' We all stared in the direction he was pointing and suddenly realised we were looking upon the source of all our torment for the last time.

'Wouldn't bank on it,' said Mort. 'By the look of this old tub we might never get away.'

'And as the Padre has so rightly informed me . . .' The Sergeant paused weightily to acknowledge the presence of Padre Felter, standing sheepishly by his side as if receiving official thanks for the contribution he had made to the recent desert festivities, ensuring that a good time had been had by all, and without whom they would not have been such an unparalleled success. He paused for the 'Three cheers for the Padre!' to ring joyously through our minds, then pressed on: 'As he has so eloquently put it, we have "wandered together in deserts, and in mountains, and in dens and caves".' A murmur rumbled through the congregation and the Padre looked suitably thanked. 'As you pass through that vale of fear, that fiery curtain of shell and sand and smoke, you will pass out of my orbit into another world all of your own.'

Low murmur. He was off. We knew the rest. Not all the details, perhaps, because they had to vary slightly each time, but the rhythms. We could have recited it like the Lord's Prayer.

'Some have called it the veil of anarchy. I call it the veil of hail. Whatever, on the other side you are yours . . . and maybe divine. On this, you are mortal . . . and definitely mine. Only *you* can decide what you do through that dark vale, *and* what you achieve. You have your choice, and you have your freedom.'

Pause. Cough. Shuffle. Sentiment over. Now the admonition:

'Howevah, my brethren, until that supreme moment, until that final frontier, until that twinkling-of-an-eye rendezvous with your wretched little destinies, you are *mine*, and *only* mine. Here on earth reigns *my* dominion, and *only* my dominion.'

The heel clicks resounded above the engines as we instinctively came to attention.

'And heaven help the bastard that lets me down!'

Mock-shock pause. So far, so familiar, patter verbatim. Now for the coda. New every time. The particular, personal motto of the moment.

'And *I*,' slowly, menacingly, 'and *only* I, decide who goest to the Field Post Office, and at what appointed hour. Certainly not *you*, O'Bleech!'

'Sarge!'

'Right then.'

'Sarge!'

'Now bugger off!'

'Sarge!'

'And mind you're back before the ferry leaves!'

'Sarge!'

The Noblesse part of the name, the pedigree bit, came from O'Bleech's old lady. She'd been a Countess or Something Grand in Denmark and had travelled with

Princess Alexandra, the daughter of the Danish King, when she came to England to marry the Prince of Wales (the future King Edward the Seventh).

Very upper was Mrs O'Bleech. Had to be. Some job. Only the best and toughest need apply, the real thoroughbred kind who'll stick it through thick and thin and sacrifice everything for duty. Couldn't just choose any old Kirsten, Karen or Ingrid. Top drawer. That was Noblesse's mum.

When she arrives in London, the first thing the Lady Viking does after she unpacks down the bottom of the Mall is mosey around the Palace stables. 'Understandable enough,' said Shade, who'd done a lot of time for doing dubious deals on horses and dogs. 'Them upper folks are always fascinated by horses. Like bookies, they are. That's why bookies have to wear checked jackets, so you can tell them from royalty. Otherwise you might start placing your bets with the Queen, see?' And what does she find there but this pure, bona fide Paddy, this Irish geezer who looks after all the Queen's horses. Well, one touch of the blarney and she hands in her notice. Grabs Seamus right in the middle of grooming his fetlocks and ups and offs to the bogs with the gay galliard from Galway. Chucks in the lot! Scandal's all hushed up, of course. Not a word to *The Times*

Course, it's high treason, isn't it? And sure enough her noblenesse gets herself excommunicated. Out. Disgraced. Cut off. But does she care? Not a bit of it. She's off having the wedding of her life in the emerald west. And before she can say 'Stuff your Crown Jewels anyway!' little Noblesse is on the way and the couple are back in London, cos times is bad then and even the best of lovers have to break it up occasionally and make a living.

'Must have done that trip every evening since Cairo,' said the Corporal as we stood contemplating Noblesse swaggering across the quay toward the desert in search of his Field Post Office.

'He has.'

'But an hour before embarkation!'

'All the same to O'Bleech.'

Which it was, except that Field Post Offices were usually only a few dunes back from the lines, and were never more than a corporal with an outsize bag and an upturned ammunition box under a mosquito net. You couldn't fail to find them. But finding a Field Post Office in a seaside town in North Africa teeming with half the men and most of the steel the Western Allies could muster was definitely something else. Except of course for Noblesse.

'Noblesse sees things nobody else does,' the morose corporal says as we watch him work his way through the crowds and artillery on the beaches to reach the sand dunes and the open desert beyond. 'But mostly Field Post Offices.'

It was true. Noblesse's eyes were all distance. Always looking through and beyond you, always focused on infinity. Just didn't notice the ordinary people and props that make up the everyday scenery.

'He's *elsewhere*,' said the Sarge, savouring his new expression. 'He might *live* with us but his *life's* not with us. It's *elsewhere*.'

You meet a lot of blokes like that in the Army, but they're usually the really disturbed lot – you know, the kind that read Sanskrit or Calculus at breakfast and do Arabic crosswords at Stand Easy. We were always bringing some poor sod back down from his Mount Olympus to our humble little wadi to help him get his arse blown off.

Never seemed fair, really. Schoolboy fair. Cricket fair. They never seemed part of anything *we* were involved in; they were just out there, as if by mistake, keeping the head down, minding their own business. Course, the war was supposed to be *all* our business, but it always seemed it was *ours* and not theirs. Like they were alien and out of it and helpless. Whereas we were supposed to be made for it.

'That's us,' said Beef. 'Made for it, we are. "What you want to be when you grow up, son?" they used to ask me as a snotty kid. "Train driver. Royal Prince?" Naw, I used to say, none of that commonplace lark for me. Going in for war, I am. Taking up arms, that's me. Great career, that is. Lots of travel. Deserts, dunes, beaches. Couldn't wait to grow up and get stuck into wadi life, I couldn't.'

It was like war was supposed be our lot. We were just *un*-qualified misfits. The Sanskrit Brigade were the real thing.

'There's something else about Noblesse,' said our morose corporal. 'Operates in a twilight zone, he does. Two languages, two countries. Well, three, really. And he floats between them.'

Noblesse's Dad, Seamus, gets himself a job with a farrier in Kilburn and he and Kirsten find a room round the corner so he can nip back regular to keep an eye on the mother to be and, when she's been, on the mother and child. And that's how Noblesse was born: sired by a ginger Paddy from the golden west out of a blonde dam from the icy north with a touch of the nobles. And with a mixture like that he has to have a dash of the gent and a splash of the bleech. So we stuck an O on the front for Old Ireland's sake and came up with Noblesse O'Bleech.

'Got a magnet for Field Post Offices in his brain, he has,' said the Sparks as we watched Noblesse plodding away over the fourth or fifth set of dunes as if guided by radar before it's invented.

'Or a periscope in his mind's eye,' said Signals.

It was true – Noblesse could detect Field Post Offices over and above and through and beyond the natural wavelengths of sound, smell and instinct. 'Can home in on them like a pigeon to its loft, except he's never been to any of them places before like pigeons have.'

Yet during his entire army service he was never able to read any of the mail he received from home.

At the time Noblesse was born there was a little Irish ghetto up in Kilburn – of secret men very wise in the lore and language of horses, who kept their knowledge and their tongues to themselves. Seamus worked among them and spoke only Erse.

Kirsten stayed at home and talked to her son – in Danish. She couldn't say much to the other mums in the neighbourhood, so she talked to the young Noblesse instead and he grew up completely fluent in his mother's language. And as Seamus could only talk to him in Erse he grew up completely fluent in his father's language too. Then, when he started to meet other kids in Kilburn, he learned English. Trilingual was Noblesse. Never noticed differences, just communicated in whatever way people wanted him to.

'That's his problem,' said the Corp. 'Brought up by a couple of aliens in a place foreign to both of them. Has to be the outsider par his excellence, hasn't he? That's why he's never actually *there*, where we are.'

Noblesse always seemed to be passing through everything. And as he only ever communicated with his mum in Danish and his dad in Erse he worked on two very separate, extra-dimensional wavelengths, sniffing them out like a thoroughbred dog.

Until the war came in '39 and he joined up and started to write home.

Waiting for Noblesse seemed the only thing to do that night. Leaning over the guardrail of our craft in a line, there wasn't much else for us to do but smoke, mumble, and gaze.

Out there beyond the docks, the desert looked positively abandoned, the strange hush heavily emphasised. The Sarge's time-honoured speech had only stressed its loneliness. All the Agincourts he had ever done the nights before had concerned that desert, but the one he did the night before Sicily looked to tomorrow in another place.

We were leaving behind our tormentor. For three years that desert had asked no quarter, and given none, resenting every moment of our time there. 'Couldn't even raise a smile at one of our jokes.' And not one grain of compassion, not even in our finer moments. Apprehensive as hell, we were, about what lay ahead, but still in terrible awe of what we were leaving behind.

O'Bleech's dad couldn't go back to live in Ireland because there wasn't any work to support the three of them. And his mum couldn't go back to Denmark because she'd blown it, turned her back on her own kind and let the side down in the eyes of another country. That was double sin, that was.

Noblesse turned out to be the only product of the union. 'Just one big love, see!' His father kept a low profile in north west London, looking after horses for a number of businesses, because it was horse power all the way then, and if you knew horses backwards as Seamus did, having come from a long line of stables himself, you could be sure of a steady and secure living, and if you fell out with one boss, you only had to walk round the corner before you fell in with another. And M'Lady pressed on, intent only on nursing and nurturing her two beloved boys.

'Maybe he won't find one in time,' the Corporal moped.

Noblesse was well gone into the evening sunset by now but we still thought we could catch the pink edging around his head from the sinking rays. We'd got so used to his halo we imagined it was always there.

'He'll find one,' said the Sarge, 'empty desert or crowded beachhead.'

Then again, maybe we didn't want to lose sight of him because we all had a personal interest in him. We were concerned with Noblesse in a way we weren't with anyone else. No one ever wanted to know anything about anyone else's civvy street and pretended that everyone's personal history only began when he joined the regiment. But it was different with Noblesse. We were all involved. We all knew about the censors.

'He'll sniff it out.' The Sarge had always allowed Noblesse to go in search of his Post Office. After all, he was the only man in the British Army who received a letter every day of the week and couldn't read a word of it.

The problem started in 1939 because Noblesse could only write to his mum in Danish and to his dad in Erse. Of course the censors suspected him of subversion and time and again hauled him before them to explain why he insisted on writing in code. And Noblesse explained it wasn't code, it was the only way his mum and dad wrote and spoke to him. And each time they said yes, they understood, but it would help the War Effort if he wrote in English instead. But Noblesse said he was very, very sorry for the War Effort but that was impossible. And the censors said his parents must understand *some* English and Noblesse agreed that they did and could write in it too. 'Well then,' said the censors, but Noblesse stuck to his pens and said but that wasn't the same thing at all. Communication, especially between families and loved ones, was much more than just words and he couldn't possibly deny them that and what's more he wouldn't. He also said he was very, very sorry for Mr Churchill and his noble War

Effort and that he would do all in his power to help it, even as a genuine alien – might even *die* if really necessary, although, he had to admit, he'd have to think about that one – but he couldn't give up his inalienable right to write to his parents in the only tongues they understood each other in – after all that's what they were fighting for, wasn't it, and he was sure Mr Churchill would understand that too. 'Oh, very well, then,' said the generals, 'please yourself, O'Bleech, but you know the consequences.' And hostilities broke out between Noblesse and the War Effort.

So Noblesse carried on writing in Danish and Irish and the censors carried on scoring out every bleeding word of it. There was never a censor in our neck of the dunes who could decipher either, so they couldn't take any chances. Would have been easier to throw the letters away but by law they couldn't deprive the poor sod of his regular mail. And so Noblesse went on receiving letters in Danish and Erse and went on replying in them, and the censors went on drawing blue pencils through everything so he never got any news from his mum and dad and his mum and dad never got any news from him either. The only thing they did get was pages and pages of thick blue pencil and what Noblesse called 'vibrations and things'. But he scanned studiously through each one of them, line by line, as if he could actually detect something through the blue. It wasn't the words, for sure, but he kept at it. Obviously he must have seen *something*.

'Well,' he would say, folding the pages neatly after a long stint of poring and peering, 'at least they know I'm here.'

It was getting very late and we were dangerously close to casting off. O'Bleech hadn't got back yet and we were staring out over to the desert horizon to see if he was going to make it.

'Might be legging it back to Cairo if he doesn't find a Post Office in between,' said Sparks.

'Knowing Noblesse,' said Signals, 'he'll do it too.'

Noblesse never once got angry about what the censors did. It went with the staring-into-the-distance look. He seemed to see over and above all the ordinary things, all the whims and foibles of sergeants and censors. Not arrogant, just different. We used to think it came from the Countess of Copenhagen, noblessed as she was, but after a while we got to thinking maybe he took it from Seamus as well, because after all he came from a long line of generations who lived fetlock by fetlock with 'them noble beasts', and royalty beasts at that.

'*Something* must have rubbed off.'

And when Seamus came down in the world and ascended up into Kilburn to groom Clydesdales and Shires and Suffolk Punches instead of Arabian thoroughbreds, 'he'd have taken his inheritance with him, wouldn't he?'

'So it's not just a story about the Princess and the stable lad, then?'

'Naa, they both got their finesse from different places, but it's the same finesse, isn't it?'

As Seamus himself had said, grooming away cheerfully beneath a Clydesdale: 'They're all aristocrats, you know' – in Erse, of course.

And Kirsten stayed happy in her one room in Kilburn, never once regretting what she'd done, and never becoming bitter. Some of that must have rubbed off on Noblesse too.

'Censors don't worry folk like Noblesse,' said the Sarge, quietly scanning the horizon.

The din coming up from the engine room warned us we'd soon be off on the road to Palermo or wherever.

'Only place *I* know in Sicily.'

'Well, sounds fine to me.'

'Not like you bleeding lot, always moaning,' said the Sarge. 'Folk like Noblesse know there's a war on. They know their duty. And if that means they can't talk to each other for a few years, then that's how it is.'

That just about summed it up. Noblesse's world had nothing in common with ours. In fact he had no other world to compare it with. 'Out on his own, he is,' said the Corp. 'Not just on a limb. Whole bleeding anatomy.'

On the quay below us a few stray dogs and Military Police sniffed and shuffled around and stared up at us, obviously bloody grateful they weren't coming too.

'There's that hush again,' said Troop. And we shivered, but not because of the air – the *air* air, that is, but because of the *other* air. Got quite maudlin staring out over that empty scene, waiting for Noblesse.

'Well, we'll remember it, but it won't remember us. Couple of nights' wind should cover up our tracks.'

'You like to feel you've made some kind of mark on a place, don't you?' said the broody corp. 'Like you like to feel a person will always remember you for *something*.'

'Yeah, well, not that lot.'

'One breeze and we're gone.'

And then he appeared – a frantic blob on the horizon, like a ghost, running and shouting and waving something in the air. Came rushing over the dunes and down onto the quay through the MPs and dogs, shouting at us to hold on, like a schoolboy running for his bus. Noblesse wasn't so young, not like some of the trainee Acnes we'd had to get along with, but he always *looked* young. Colouring, the golden flax tinge.

Somebody threw him a rope and he leapt over the edge. We swung him aboard and dropped him on deck and a great cheer went up as he landed laughing and beaming and the Sarge greeted him with: 'Cutting it rather neat tonight, aren't we, Mr O'Bleech?' Noblesse said he was sorry but he'd had to go a bit further back than he had estimated but anyway he was here and he promised the Sarge he'd 'make up for it in the morning.'

Then he held up his letter. As usual it was covered in long thick strokes of blue pencil. But he was excited about something else and kept stabbing at points on the page. We looked closer and sure enough we could see that the blue lines were all beautifully chopped up and spaced out, with the white lines shining clearly between. Some censor, out of malice or kindness, had gone through the whole ten pages painting his blue pencil along the words, meticulously avoiding the blank spaces as delicately as a sign writer. And he hadn't removed one single item of punctuation: every comma and semi-colon, full stop and exclamation mark, was left intact, shining out boldly from the blue.

'See', shouted Noblesse, 'there's nothing in the rules about punctuation marks!' And he held up the pages to the dying sunlight and shouted: 'Look! He's left in the music!'

And the evening sun shone through the flimsy paper so that the punctuation marks and the white lines stood out gleaming like notes on a scored page of music.

'They couldn't write to me,' he rejoiced, 'so they sent me a song!'

Noblesse was glowing. He'd gone along with the censors and the despair through thousands of silent nights without one word to read from home. But he'd stuck to his guns, hadn't broken any rules, and finally he'd cracked it.

'Can't ever predict, can you, now?' he said. 'I mean, nothing ever *quite* works out as you imagine.' Not for the censor either. Probably never dreamed about the patterns and music and mosaic he was creating. But it had come out like that.

Noblesse began to hum some weird lament that sounded just what a mixture of Danish and Erse should sound like, and with his eyes closed and his head swaying from side to side he serenaded us off the coast of North Africa and out into the sunset Mediterranean.

'Well done, Noblesse,' said the Sarge. 'Now get some bleeding kip.'

As it turned out, Sicily wasn't too bad a landing. We began to suspect something when we weren't getting any flak before coming in, unless they were waiting until we hit the water.

Course, you couldn't have told that to Noblesse. He was fired up. This was his occasion, his moment, his war. He'd show them. He'd waited for years for this and he'd be giving it a champagne go. He'd have torn down the doors themselves if they'd stuck.

Must have been first off. Couldn't have slept much. Passed him on the way in. He looked very content in dawn's early light with his pink locks flowing and his head still swaying on the morning tide and his lips pursed as if he was still humming.

TIGHT HOLD

Salerno, September 1943

And he held fast to his faith and anything else he could reach to succour him, and the marks of his clasps were upon his hands, until he beheld the contours of salvation in Siren Land and went for it, soaring in body and spirit . . .

Eighteen

'Getting a nice day for it, aren't we?' he shouts down to us, staring up at the blue skies of the Med from high up on the landing craft bound for Salerno.

It's early morning, very early, not long after dawn, and we're well on our way. It's September and still high summer in the Med, although edging a bit on the autumn side. But not the kind of bit we are going to let worry us. The heat of the Med's the heat of the Med and the first week in September's still a far cry from the week after Bank Holiday in Cleethorpes.

'Nothing like getting the day started, is there?' he calls down, flexing his shoulders and rubbing his hands as if to encourage us by his example that he's raring to get off and frolic up the beaches of Italy and make a day of it. By the time we embarked for Salerno, Tight Hold must have been the only man in *any* invasion fleet still affected by the romance of it all.

'What the hell we doing here, anyway, Sarge?' someone asked when we boarded the landing craft and found out where we were going.

'Orders, lad,' he said. '*They* know.'

But long before we embarked for Salerno we knew that whenever the Sarge said 'They know', he knew we knew they didn't know at all. Or as Clogs put it: 'They *know*, but they don't know *why* they know.'

What we did know was that we were landing all over

the place in Sicily and Italy, setting up all sorts of operations with fancy names like Baytown and Husky and Slap-
stick and Avalanche, like some frenzied rabbit in a field
desperately looking for a hole to get back into his burrow.

'Helluva long way to come from Tripoli and Bizerte to
end up in this mad scramble to get ashore, let alone
hold on.'

'Can't they read a bleeding map? Any fool can see it's
the messiest bloody place to try to land on anyway!'

There were all sorts of nooks and crannies and bits
and bends in a triangle like Sicily for a start, but we were
trying to go round the corner to the toe of Italy as well,
and over to the boot, *and* under the bleeding heel, *and*
back round to the shin again.

The time it took to get to any of these places, far less
find a decent foothold, Jerry could see us coming and
was ready for us. Just had to sit and watch the struggle
we were having to hold on. And with some of the
mountains in the south and that narrow band across the
middle to defend, he must have thought his luck had
really turned.

'No bleeding room for manoeuvre, this way! You
want a bloody great wide front to go for so you can
change your mind if you have to. Not all them piddling
little, pinching little, stabbing little heres and theres –
and we're trying to get a whole bleeding army ashore!'

It seemed mad to us, but then, as another philosopher
warrior put it: 'complaint is the purgative of the poor'.

What we did know was that it cost us a lot to get into
Europe through these side doors, and even when we
got through, where were we anyway?

'Yeah, where the bleeding hell's Germany? Thought
that's what we were aiming for!'

'We could have suggested a few more direct routes.
They only had to ask.'

'Bloody sight cheaper ones too.'

But all we got was the ever loyal 'They know, lads,'

from the steadfast Sarge. Same old dedicated patter, but then if he hadn't kept it up all these years a lot of us wouldn't have been on that landing craft anyway.

'Could be a really nice day by the looks of it!'

Up above us Tight Hold seemed not just romantic but positively *keen*!

He might have been right about the weather, although we were still a long way off and it was a bit early to tell. But not about getting the day started.

'I'd settle for a much later start, Tight,' shouts one dark voice from the interior. 'So much later it wouldn't be worth starting at all!'

We had a few left like Tight – or Tight that morning, because he wasn't always like that. The kind that are always humming and whistling and singing the first lines of their tear-jerking versions of First World War songs – like 'Ma'ame's so swell her charms are dear, barley brew' and 'It's the wrong way to tickle Mary' and 'Jack up your Bubbles' – picking up where their fathers left off in rain-sodden Flanders and needing to believe war's a jolly good romp when all prayers are said and done and the rest of us are six feet under. And it's always only the first line they sing or hum – never ever the words of the second.

Then there's the hearty outdoor kind with their Boy Scout haversacks and hiking boots sunbathing on the deck to get themselves in trim for the desert as far back as the troopship to Alexandria. Carried along by Jeanette Macdonald and Nelson Eddy on their Desert Love Song and the dreams of camel charges with Gary Cooper. You know the kind of thing:

'Ho . . . nalay a luvvvv . . . song . . . da da da dee da, da da deeeeeh!'

or

'Loooovvvvveee, love only you, looooovveee when the day is through . . . '

Lots of them knew lines like these and went on from humble troopship beginnings to serenade whole wadies and deserts with them. Only *first* lines, of course, but marvellously adaptable, they are, easy to slip into a tum-tee-tum hum, or phew-hew-hew at the end.

'Yep!' shouts Tight after we'd thought he'd dropped off, 'looks really promising, it does.'

Tight Hold's way up there somewhere above us, shouting down his running commentary on the state of the sea and the sky and the prospects for the day ahead, all of which sounded more like a wireless someone switches on too early in the morning when you're struggling for another hour's shut-eye and this guy keeps feeding your dreams with details of fishing prospects north of Finisterre or west of the Western Isles and the south of Shetlands, and east of Tyree.

Tight was a weather man, among other things.

Apart from a general disagreement with the powers that be about the wisdom of entering Germany through Italy, our little group were still smarting at being on this Salerno run at all.

'We done our stint in Sicily, Sarge.'

'They think we're special, lads. Used to beaches now, see.'

'Flattery'll get you nowhere.'

'Straight up, credit's where it's due. Besides, we got to help these new Commando chaps. Show them how it's done.'

'We're special alright, Sarge. Cos we're here. Pretty bloody special to me.'

'Our's not to reason why . . .'

'Why not? It's *our* arses on the line.'

'Imagine, the whole of bleeding Europe to choose from and we go in here!'

'There'll be a reason.'

'But no bleeding rhyme.'

*

It's getting on in the war now. Not exactly late, but well after half time and we're running out of breath and memory. The romance really began to wear off somewhere around Benghazi and Alamein, or maybe Dunkirk. Most of us had gone through our Biggles stage long before leaving Aldershot, but the rest had grown out of it during Jerry's attacks on the convoy through the Biscay and the Med. Some stubborns still clung on through the dunes of Egypt and Libya, and a few indefatigables held out doggedly into Tunisia like inspired schoolboys with a craze for comic heroes. We had all sorts out there – blokes straight from the *Wizard* and the *Hotspur* and the *Boy's Own*. But not many left now.

Tight Hold was one, or so we thought. Never at peace, always keen – *dead* keen. Whatever was driving him, it was difficult enough trying to resist his tiring enthusiasm in the middle of *any* night, far less the one before Salerno. Trouble with these overkeen enthusiasts, like train spotters and stamp collectors, is they never grasp that the rest of us are just *not* interested in their games, not because we're not very good at them, but because we're simply desperate to get through life without them.

'I'd say it might even be a proper scorcher,' Tight shouts down. 'Hundred in the shade soon.'

Clouds and barometers were Tight's hobby. God knows what kind of enemies he's expecting at Salerno but he's definitely not making many friends on the way in, although he's up there where the crow's nest might have been if they'd had one, too far away for anyone to have the strength to get up and silence him. You know the feeling when you want to heave a wardrobe at the cat wailing on the dustbin, but you can't even muster the courage to get out from under and heave the window open.

'You can tell a lot from weather, you know,' he explained often enough, 'more than from horoscopes and tea leaves.'

He wasn't called Tight for nothing. Everything about him was tight – attitude, grip, temper, outlook.

'Life's all about weather, see. All about wind and rain, sun and cold, hot and dry. You can always tell a man by the weather he keeps at home. Now you take wind . . . very interesting is wind. Changes a man's moods, it does, influences them, like. And just think of all the weather things we say: a rainy day, a fair wind, blowing hot and cold, feeling a draught, being under a cloud. We *think* weather, see. We're *shaped* by weather. Isotopes, millibars, barometers – they all affect us, they all take their toll. They all *shape* a man – or a woman, for that matter.'

'Well, we all have our hobbies to define us,' the Sarge said often enough.

War apart, we seemed to live in a perpetual night-school world where boys and men like Tight and Sextant escaped from the abodes of women to pursue their private obsessions – their hobbies. As if they were out here at war passing the time until they could get back home to them. You might have thought it was the wife and kids they longed for. Not a bit of it. War teaches you that. True love to a man is something else – pigeons, stamps, fretwork, stained glass . . . A man *is* his hobby. The rest of the world, including war, just happens around him. The Sarge knew that.

'D'you reckon generals and politicians have *war* as their hobby, Tight?'

'Nope. Hobbies are solitary, and come from inside. War doesn't come from *inside* – comes from out. And it affects others. Real hobbies only affect yourself.'

Well, we knew generals and politicians can't get on with war by themselves, but we hadn't taken it to Tight's extremes.

'If they think of war as their "hobby", they haven't learnt about it *inside* yet. Now, if they got themselves a *real* hobby they wouldn't have time nor interest for war, would they?'

'Well, pigeons or paper hanging, Tight,' said the Sarge, 'hobbies maketh a man. And if yours is wind, so be it. Just don't keep pushing it our way.'

On these occasions when we were 'going in', train spotters and Crosby whistlers and romantics like Tight expressed themselves in lots of different ways. Some sang sentimental songs, some recited plaintive First World War poetry, and some settled for whistling the national anthem: 'God Save the Queen', 'Land of My Fathers', 'Scotland the Brave' and 'Danny Boy'. One bloke did imaginary football league scores – four Divisions plus two Scottish; and another recited all the English Test teams since Test Matches began, like rosary beads. There were times when you had to admire them for their unquenchable spirits but others when you prayed they weren't so unquenchable. And there were times when you had to envy them for their cheerful perseverance but others when you felt there were less boisterous ways of handling the impossible, 'making light of the coming night', as Shakes our poet once said.

Well, we're steaming along with Tight's weather forecast droning down our ears when suddenly he changes gear and shouts out: 'Here! You lot! Anyone down there know the date?'

It didn't make much sense or impact at first. We just shut him out. Let him ramble on. We always left off when someone got the rambles. Something to do with premonition. Con got it. Tarzan had it. Wool sensed it. Sextant divined it. Art rumbled it. Shakes twigged it. Noblesse knew it. We called it the rambles – others call it the rattles, but that expression never cottoned on. Too harsh. But nearer, of course. As Shakes put it, contemplating one soggy battlefield around Crusader time: 'Nearer, my Sod, to thee'.

But Tight had got the bit between his rambles. 'Oi, someone, *anyone*, down there. *You*! The date!'

Course we knew what day it was. Salerno Day. That was enough. No other meaning.

'Hey! You!' he shouted again. 'What day is it?'

We still didn't pay attention. 'Any idea? Eh? Any of you, you down there?'

We roused ourselves to look up, slowly forced our eyes to focus in the general direction of this desperate voice. He's wedged in way up on the far side of the guard railing with his arm around a flagpole or mast or something and scanning the horizon like a ravenous hawk.

The real reason we called him Tight, as in Tight Hold, was that he gripped hard on everything, just like he was doing up there now, as if life would get away from him the moment he dropped his grasp.

'Hey, down there, anyone! You lot! Wakey, wakey! Got any idea?'

He's shouting almost non-stop now and everybody's rousing, desperate to throw something at him and shut him up. Then we notice Tight's shout has something extra in it, something worrying, definitely edgy, like he's spotted a periscope.

'The *date*! Anybody know?'

Course, even when we realised he'd changed his commentary from the weather forecast to the calendar, no one gave a dickie, cos no one wanted to know it was *any* day yet, far less one that had a name or a number on it. And dates was a completely new one from Tight.

Weather. Millibars, yes. But dates, no.

'Anyone? Eh? Any idea?'

Romantics or romaniacs. We called them Beavers. Fever Beavers. Never relaxed. Never let go. Tight was one. The rumour was his real name was Beavers too.

'Real?'

'Well, civvy.'

'So we're all kind of marked from the start?'

'Or *before*.'

Anyway, Beavers was a general name, so we had to find something different. And it became *Tight*. Tight *Hold*. Because he was a bit special with his phobia, clinging onto life 'like it's a great Alsatian dog always straining at the leash to get away from him.' Great weals on his wrists, he could get. And he was clinging on desperately now.

'Going to be one of them days,' says Cass, cool. 'You can always tell.'

'Yeah, but *which* one is what he wants to know.'

'C'mon!' screams Tight. 'Someone must know.'

'From this angle I'd say it'll probably be blue, Tight,' shouts the duty comedian through a haze of Capstan Full Strength.

'*Not colours*, you clots! Dates!'

You hear about those weird geezers in India or Borneo and places, coming down from mountains or tramping out of jungles or stepping out of rivers, turning up with holes in their palms and feet, and tears in their sides or barbed wire scratches round their heads. You get a lot of *them* in the Army too. Spend all your waking and sleeping time jam-packed together with other Botchers like in a tin of khaki sardines, and then all of a sudden your next floor mate's gone and got himself air-holes in his feet, or crisscross stitching round his forehead, or a matching pair of see-through palms.

'Stigmas!' they claim, defiant, challenging. 'Stigmas!' Superior too. And they slap in for an immediate home posting on religious grounds.

'Stigmatas,' Steeple corrected. Steeple was good at stigmas. Better than the Padre. Told us some weird tales about martyrs and flagellation and how blokes would mess about with their bodies and cut and slice and whip them as a punishment for all the wrongs they'd done and sins they'd committed – 'doing it themselves to save the Good Lord the trouble'.

Judging by some of the untouched bodies we'd got with us, we reckoned the Good Lord had already figured out their intended sins and dished out punishment in advance.

But as the Sarge summed it up after a rash of applications before Alamein:

'Stigmas, my arse! Soon nail these buggers!'

There was always another Botcher seeing the blinding light and plunging into total conversion and sprouting another 'stigma variation', as Con once called it. Until somewhere after Alamein, we saw Tight's wrists and them horrible lesions.

At first the ICs – the Instant Converted – were usually too overcome, or shy, to flash their stigmas, but Tight couldn't hide his in time. That's how we rumbled.

'From the strain of the dog's life you been leading,' said Lance, uncharitably. 'I mean, thorns on the head's a bit old hat, isn't it? And holes in the feet. But lesions on the wrists! Definitely something else.'

'Original, Tight is.'

'Not much to expect someone to know the day and the date, is it?' Tight continues to shout down. 'Ignorant bloody lot.'

'You're on your way whatever the bloody date!'

'Thinking of going down in history, then, Tight? Or just style?'

We're well on our way now and the Carusos have started on their 'Come back to Salernos'.

'Well,' says the Sarge, ostentatiously waving his diary, 'if it makes any difference, Tight, it's the ninth.'

First there's this strange lull, followed by the flash of the Sarge's words, and then the clap of thunder. Tight whips round, galvanised, and shouts: 'I knew it! It had to be! It's me mum's birthday!'

Another lull, another storm – then up goes one almighty cheer into the Mediterranean sky, rocking the boat and shaking whoever's waiting on the beach.

> *Happy Birthday to you*
> *Happy Birthday to you*
> *Happy Birthday, dear Missus . . .*

'Beavers!' screams Tight, 'Beavers!' reminding us of his true name, but no one's listening:

> *. . . Tight Ho . . . oold!*
> *Happy Birthday toooo ooo you!*

Then a great cheer followed by:

> *Hip, Hip, Hoooo . . . raa . . . ay*

And another:

> *Hip, Hip, Hoooo . . . raa . . . ay*

And another:

> *Hip, Hip, Hoooo . . . raa . . . ay*

'Getting a nice day for it, isn't she?' he calls down.

We look up, thinking his sense of humour has come back. Tight never had much: 'stigmatas don't half take it out of you'. Then we rumble he means it. His grip's tightening so hard on the rail it's almost controlling the rolling of the craft. He's off.

'The fever's got the Beaver, Sarge!'

We look to the Sarge. Tight's not the kind of bloke

you want to have with you on your day out on the beach, is he? Sure as hell he'll mess up the sandcastles or go in at the *No Bathing* end and some other poor sod'll have to risk his neck getting him out.

But the Sarge doesn't say a word, just looks straight ahead.

Tight's rocking back and forward on the guard rail, getting himself real roused and his stigmatas worked up and reddening. He's taken our mind off the coming landing.

Down below we strain to detect the sound of Salerno cafés opening up, shutters coming off, awnings being pulled down, and croissants crackling and the whiff of coffee.

Then Tight screams out as if stuck through the arse with the next bloke's bayonet. 'There she is! Over there! 10 o'clock!'

One or two of us can just make out the very far corner of the approaching beach. Still well distant, a few thousand yards yet, there's a special little cut-off cove, all nice and smooth and sandy by the distant prospect of it.

'That's her!' shouts Tight. 'She remembered!' he screams, banging the rail in excitement so the boat's lurching and his wrists are raw and red.

A couple of thousand yards to go.

'Always took us to the beach on her birthday!'

The Sarge squares his shoulders.

'Last trip of the summer!'

Now he's clambered up as high as he can go, like a sailor on the rigging in *Mutiny on the Bounty* or a high diver going for the top board, and carrying full kit too.

Then he goes all gentle. All the straining at the leash evaporates. The rigid grip and Alsatian domination melts away. The fever drains off. Suddenly he's a young lad again all set for the beach with his bucket and spade. And his calm falls over all of us. Because Tight Hold, Fever Beaver extraordinary, has spotted Salvation!

'None of your straight-up-the-shingle-and-onto-the-beach-dear-friends for me! No, sireeeeer.'

The Sarge moves slightly and lifts his rifle. 'Bags that cove!' Tight screams down. 'It's mine!' and brandishing a blood-red fist, he warns: 'Keep clear of that one, you bastards!'

'A moment, lads,' says the Sarge. 'Get your bleeding thoughts straight. And heaven help the bastard that lets me down!'

'Five. Four. Three. Two. One ... Doors awa ... aaay!!' And they start going. Or they start grinding. They don't fall clonk, do they? Ho, no! Not the ones on *our* craft! All that build-up for hours, miles and years, and when the command comes and you're poised to leap off into glory or infinity, all you get's a grinding, badly oiled, cranking, sandpaper-scraping trundle. British made, see. Botcher built.

But it's an ill wind and all that: 'Awaa ... aaay!' The sound soars out across the Mediterranean blue. The delay gives Tight his break. And he takes one almighty lunge out into the great blue Salerno yonder – clouding over now, of course. Soars away like an inspired eagle in a high wind and regulation boots. And for one miraculous moment everyone forgets the War and the beach emerging slowly as the doors drag themselves down.

He seems to gain maximum height and then hover. And at that apex point of no momentum before the drop, the choppy waves start to pull back below him – like a conjuror whipping off a tablecloth and leaving the dishes intact, or a clown snatching away the trapeze artiste's safety net.

And there it is, spread out like a welcoming carpet across the sea floor far beneath him: one ginormous great underwater field of barbed wire, all coiled up neat and snug and innocent like great balls of Granny's knitting.

And still rejoicing, Tight drops – straight down into it, as the waves race back in after him like a shoal of starving sharks.

Never knew what finished old Tight – the wire, the waves or the wops.

CASS

Monte Cassino, May 1944

And they came upon a city built on a hill to celebrate their covenants; and being the first to recognise it, one of their number prepared himself finicky-like for entry, wrapping himself in scrubbed finery and taking great pains to camouflage the creases and consulting the glass just once too often . . .

Nineteen

The day we set eyes on Monte Cassino was the day we knew we'd arrived. And nobody appreciated it more than Cass.

'All the rest were rehearsals,' he announced. 'This is the performance.'

We knew then that Monte was what we had come for.

Not that the generals would have seen it that way any more than they could have justified being there in the first place. Sicily, Anzio, Salerno, none of them made any sense to us. After years of slogging across North Africa, Italy seemed the last place you'd choose to invade even if it *were* reasonably close. Any schoolboy with a map could tell you that – long, narrow and tight, easy to defend if you want to, appalling to attack if you dare. We'd been beefing about it all the way from Tripoli.

Jerry noticed too when he saw us struggling to get a toehold from our reach-me-down landing craft, getting ourselves hemmed into tight little Calabrian corners. 'Must be laughing all the way back to the tank!'

But by the time we reached Monte Cassino we had long since given up expecting reason from above. 'Got to make our own sense of things, chaps,' said Cass.

As we crawled around that last bend of battle-beaten road, the whole column checked, lurched to a halt, and stopped right there, dead in its tracks. And not just *our* column. As we pulled up short, it seemed the whole Allied Army stretching all the way back to Dunkirk stumbled into us like a pack of cards.

There she stood, towering far and away and above us, sublimely aloft on that exalted mountain, up there all on her heavenly own, queen of all she surveyed:

'That's it,' Cass announced. 'The raison for all our d'êtres.'

And there he stood. Tall, lean as a beanpole, still immaculate despite the long trek that had turned the rest of us into a shuffling shambles, rooted to his spot and waiting for the curtain to rise.

'The past is prologue,' he said.

He was right about the performance. Everyone seemed to be gathering there. All the way up from Syracuse and Anzio and Palermo and Salerno, and from all corners of the globe, the regiments kept coming – British, Americans, Indians, Gurkhas, Poles, Canadians, French, Algerian, Tunisian, Maoris, New Zealanders. And the top billings of course – Alexander, Clark, Leese, Kesselring, Vietinghoff, Mackensen.

As we stood there, awestruck, a dreadful silence descended. You could hear it. Even the puffs of air switched off. Like in a cathedral or a catacomb. Like the first time you see the Pyramids or the Taj Mahal. Like something else is there. An extra presence. Not that time is standing still, more that something has stopped it in full flight, and it's holding its breath for a moment, awaiting the cue to move on again. Like the world's a carousel the showman has stopped while one lot of kids get off and another climbs on. Like when a Caruso makes his entrance or a Garbo fills the screen.

With the barest of movements, Cass lifts his hands to his left breast pocket, draws out his gleaming brass mirror and peers into it. Like a king arranging his crown, a Derby horse waiting for the gate to open, he adjusts his tie, tucks a few straggling hairs under his cap, brushes the dust off his shoulders, and looks back up at the clouds. A beat, a deep breath, as if bracing himself on the wings for his entrance, then:

'Royalty in the audience tonight, chaps.'

To say that the day we reached Monte Cassino was the day we knew we'd arrived isn't so Irish as it sounds. Monte was about the Promised Land, although we didn't know until we saw it.

Maybe no one knew. Maybe Monte was never anything more than another milestone – another strategic position, but only another. But *we* knew. First time. Exactly like looking at a girl and knowing immediately – 'Ah, that's her!'

We'd been searching for Monte all the way from the shores of Dunkirk to the docks of Tripoli, through the sands and wadies of Egypt and Libya and Tunisia, the dugouts of Alamein and Tobruk, the beaches of Sicily and Salerno, the mountains of Calabria, and the mud and rivers on the road to Rome. For four years we had plodded over fields, ditches, gutters, trenches, grooves, ruts, bogs and beaches; through brushes, brawls, fights, feuds, skirmishes, scrambles, scuffles and scraps – never really knowing why but trying to put them all together to calculate the grand total that would add up to a whole war – complete, finished, audited, over and done with, closed. Whatever the generals didn't tell us, we needed to find Monte for ourselves.

And to say that Cass and Monte were meant for each other is not so romantic, either. If we'd called him Cass after Casanova because he was the regiment's dandy, it would have been right. If we'd called him Cass after Cassius because of his lean and hungry look, it would have been right. And if we'd called him Cass after Cassino, it would have been just as right, because of his style: grand and golden. Funny how you sometimes hit on a name that's dead right from every angle: everything fits, everything slots in, everything adds up. Doesn't matter when you choose it.

We chose 'Cass' long before we ever heard of Monte Cassino, and yet when we rounded that bend and first set eyes on it, there wasn't a man in the unit who didn't think 'Ah, *that's* the reason!' Cass and Monte were a perfect match.

'You know, Cass, I been thinking. Maybe that's how you play wars.'

'Play?'

'Yeah. Someone gets an idea, scribbles it down, drums up some cash, puts it on and performs it. Then dishes out rifles and spears and tanks and swords and things for the rest of us, the hoi polloi, to run around shouting with. But not them what stages it and stage *manages* it. They get all the nice parts and the good lines. And everybody else does the screaming bits. Maybe that's what wars are – plays for others. *You* know.'

Everywhere else had been a shambles: everywhere we'd been and everywhere we'd fought, every time we'd advanced and every time we'd withdrawn, every Jerry we'd met and every one we'd dodged – a shambles. Mud and drizzle, grime and rain, heat and dust, sand and flies; drab dunes, mouldy mounds, wobbly huts, teetering tents; tatty towns, withered villages, crumpled camps. Dan Kirk, Sid Barrani, Ben Ghazi, Mercy McTrew, Try Polly, Sally Erno and a thousand dunes and ditches that never even got a fancy name, only a scratch on the Sergeant's map where they might have been, or a title from Sextant Blake telling of something much more personal.

Cass summed it up for all of us. War was always a bit beneath Cass. Far too dirty a game for a man of his flair and finesse. Not *dirty* dirty – you know, ugh-stuff – but messy dirty. Definitely not his style.

'But if the cause be not good,' he said now, distantly, his eyes on the resplendent monastery, 'the king himself hath a heavy reckoning to make.'

'Eh?'

'If these men do not die well,' he went on, studying the clouds, 'it will be a black matter for the king that led them to it.'

'What you on about, Cass? What's the bleeding King got to do with it?'

'I mean,' said Cass, coming down from the clouds, 'if you have to fight a war, you want to have something you can identify and respect, don't you, when you're climbing out of a ditch or stumbling over a beach?'

'You're right,' said Zig, 'nothing ever *means* anything in this bloody war. To the generals maybe, but not us.'

'Yeah,' Bunce agreed. 'Nothing ever *adds up* to anything, does it?'

'All we ever do is attack, repel, destroy or run away.'

'When they tell us.'

'Right.'

We never had any sense of the geography of war – the political geography, that is. Sands, yes, but lands, no. No idea of the landscape of war, only the particular fields and trees and ditches.

'Something bigger than what you've known before, you mean?'

'Well, otherwise, what's the bleeding point?'

'Right.'

Decaying French ditches, steaming Egyptian dunes, drenching Flanders mist, blinding Libyan sun – not a lot to admire or inspire, not a lot to do with freedom and dignity, nothing whatsoever to do with the grand theme, the great idea, the magnificent proposition of WAR. Not for us.

'More to the point,' Cass added, 'what's the point of *dying* for them anyway?'

But Monte Cassino was different. They first built the monastery in the year 500 and something. You could tell. Not that it was crumbling. It just looked as if it had been there in the Beginning. Part of the fittings. Like one of those mediaeval paintings that comes straight from the painter's imagination, not showing the real thing like a photograph does, but revealing his unique way of seeing. You recognise it's a castle or a town or a landscape, but it's not *true*, like we call true, except to him. It's done in the proportion *he* saw things, emphasising the things *he* took to be paramount – another way of looking at the world.

That's why we stopped without a command for the first time in four years. Monte Cassino was different.

'I don't care for this place,' said Rasp the REME, gazing around at the scenery on that road to Cassino. 'There are some places you shouldn't be fighting in or on, you know.'

'Kind of sacred, you mean?' said Sharpers.

'Yeah. It's like you degrade them by squabbling over them.'

Mad to be fighting in Italy, it was – or obscene. Not a land to be brawling about or battling over. Not grubby enough for a start. And far too romantic.

'Maybe certain places have a kind of *precious* thing about them, you know – as if you shouldn't tamper with them.'

'Which ones would you choose to fight on, then?'

'The un-precious ones, I suppose.'

'Like what?'

'Well . . .'

'The Wirral?'

'Well . . .'

'So, you try telling them folks in the unprecious lands that you've selected their back gardens to fight in cos they're not so good as your Wirral.'

'Yeah, well . . . put it that way . . .'
'But you're right. We shouldn't be touching this.'

'Keeps himself as clean as a new grenade pin, does Cass.'

There was always far too much grubbiness around the war and the world for Cass's peace of mind and soul.

'Looks after himself like he's his own valet tending to someone else.'

Cass was Cass's job – more like a mission – to care for his body: wash and scrub it, scour and scrape it, rinse and flush it; launder and press it, spit and polish it, shine and furbish it; clean out its corners, oil the moving parts, and paint whatever was left over.

'Like a garage mechanic tending a Rolls. Slightest sign of a cough or choke and he's got his engine out for an overhaul. Slightest speck of dust or dullness on the bodywork and he's shining it off until dusk.'

'Tell you what, Cass is Cass's hobby.'

Sometimes we thought he might have been royalty in disguise, some minor member planted among us to see how the common man in the wadi lived with war. Like Henry disguised the night before Agincourt, only not for an evening stroll among us before nipping back to the comforts of the mess and leaving us to it in the morning, but to see it right through alongside us. Or maybe a black sheep who had mutinied against his own family and decided he was really one of us, so he'd come down from his regal tower to live among his fellow sufferers.

But wherever he came from and wherever we fought, Cass presented himself – like a tailor's dummy fresh from a month in the store and a week in the barber's.

His sense of the occasion and his quiet brooding to get himself in tune before 'going in' gave the impression that the only curtain he had ever gone through before and would ever go through now was not the Sarge's curtain of fire into the pit of anarchy, but the heavy drapes opening up the proscenium arch onto an audience – an enemy to be confronted and mastered, or somehow won over and judged by.

He treated all actions the same. They were all stages and all deserving of the same preparation and performance. You could see the star on his door and smell the greasepaint. And he'd sign a chit for an extra pair of socks like signing an autograph book.

'Actor manager, maybe?'

'Yeah, and all the leads – Hamlet, Macbeth.'

'Lear, Prospero.'

'Never heard of *them*.'

'And always out front.'

'Ten years before the cast.'

But Cass never said, and we never asked, any more than we asked anyone else about his private life, or why he'd stuck with us lot for so long.

'Must be a role in the old officers' mess for a bookish bloke like Cass.'

'At least a nice niche in ENSA.'

'Well,' Cass said, every time he spruced himself up, 'if you're going out, whatever the show, the least you can do is go out in style, with a clean cossie.'

Monte Cassino sparkled, nudged by whiffs of cloud that looked as if they'd been hung up when they built the place, part of the architecture. It was a fable and a fairy tale, Aesop and Hans Andersen in one, a castle in the air, a palace in the clouds – fit for a Queen or a God. The crock of gold at the end of the rainbow.

After years of scouring the ditches and dunes of Europe and North Africa, we began to think differently on the way up to Cassino.

'Must be the air.'

'Or the scenery.'

We were getting some time to breathe it in and think

of more than shells and socks.

'Maybe it's the end of the road.'

'Yes,' said Cass, rubbing his hands and contemplating the set, 'we deserve something with a certain air after all we've been through.'

That struck a chord. We'd only ever watched blokes buying it and getting shovelled in quickly so we could press on. Never ever stopped to consider whether they'd deserved a better way to go or a better place to leave from.

'I mean,' he said, 'if the only idea we've come up with in ten thousand years to settle our differences is to fight, we should be allowed the big vision once in a while.'

They said that inside Monte Cassino they kept the records of what we'd been all about since Bethlehem – a sort of 'museum of christianity'. We could tell just by staring. You could feel it was all up there, secured like a deposit box in case the world ended one day.

'If someone drops in from Mars after we've done destroying this little lot, he'll find out all he needs to know about the way we been doing things – up there.'

Head wreathed in cloud, Monte looked distant, but not aloof.

'How the hell did they manage to get it up there?'

'You wouldn't think anybody could have got up there to build it, would you?'

'Maybe some geezer came down.'

Cass used to sweep the sand out of his tent even when he didn't have a groundsheet. Then he'd wipe the brush and wash down the guy ropes. He even scraped the pegs with his penknife, like cleaning carrots.

Dirt, smudges, smears. Hands, face, knees. Shirts, socks, shorts. Tents, Jeeps, bikes. Rifles, bullets, grenades. Everything got the Cass treatment.

'Narcissistic,' said Wally the Reaper, who had picked

up the word in Alexandria and clung onto it until D-Day when he suddenly stopped reaping. 'That's what he is, *narcissistic*.'

'But Narcissus spent his time gazing into pools.'

'At his reflection, yeah.'

'Cass wouldn't waste time doing that! He'd dive straight in. Take a shower in a teaspoon, Cass would.'

Each time we went into action Cass prepared himself like an actor playing Hamlet. He carried this slim brass mirror in his left breast pocket like some of us others did, next to the heart as a kind of protection as well. But his wasn't like ours, all dull and smudged and fingerprinted, layered in dead flies, dried snot, and desert acne. It was burnished. Gleaming. Glittering. Radiating, yes, but above all, *burnished*. Spent hours rubbing it with paraffin or meths or petrol, and breathing on it.

Cass studied his image in it like a general poring over his maps. Every ridge and contour and pimple was observed, noted, marked, plotted, scrutinised, smoothed out. And he didn't just *study* it. He kept trying to change what he saw in it, a bit like an actor perfecting his make-up, or an artist worrying at his painting, but more like a landscape gardener or a woman: always trying to make a better job of nature. He'd go on and on right up to the final whistle, when the Sergeant would tip-toe up to his tent, tap his baton lightly and respectfully on the pole, and whisper:

'Three minutes, Mr Cass. If you please.'

'The logic stops here, lads,' said Cass, distantly.

'Don't know about the logic, Mr Cass,' said the Sarge, 'but you lot do.'

Not that there's any logic in war, but you pick up some ideas of why you're supposed to be fighting as you go along: 'King and Country', 'The Four Freedoms', 'World fit for Heroes', 'Inalienable Rights', all that awful codswallop they dish out to keep you happy and chivvy you along. All a con, of course, but you have to have *something* to go on.

'A man needs his raisons,' said Cass. 'This'll do me.'

Monte stopped any pretence at normal logic. No more line. No more bull. No more flannel. No more con. No more poetry. Well, no more *verse*. No more of all that 'if I should die' or 'corner of a foreign field' spiel, all that small-time, parish pump stuff. What was perched up there was bigger than all that.

'Poetry enough for us.'

Monte was what we'd come for, what we'd been all about for nearly five years – 'give or take a couple of thousand' – but the twist was it belonged to the enemy. And he was the enemy *because* he'd stopped believing in what was up there.

'So what are we supposed to do?'

'Teach him a lesson.'

'Even if it means blowing it to smithereens?'

'Well, that's war logic for you.'

The sun came through a cloud and Monte beamed.

'Well, I suppose, if you have to make a botch of it, better make it a *clean* botch. Not much point in a *botched* botch job, is there?'

Monte Cassino was the ultimate botch.

And Monte Cassino was Cass's battle. He knew it. We knew it. Spent hours on his make-up this time. All these years grubbing around in the mud and sand, putting up with other men's smears and smells, slumming around the rep theatres of the war, sprucing himself up for the bit parts. Yet never once letting it affect either his presentation or his performance, treating every role with the same reverence, however far beneath his talents he knew it to be: 'Remember your role and your audience, gentlemen. Whatever and wherever they are, West End or Provincial Rep, London Palladium or Cleethorpes Pier, they are *all* worthy.'

And now at last he'd got The Big One. When Cass set eyes on that set, long before he read the script, he knew. When he looked up at that gilt-edged box in the clouds that first fine evening that's what he meant when he said:

'Ah, Royalty in the audience tonight, chaps.'

You could argue, why bother to take Monte at all? And we did. 'I mean,' said Sandy Bay, 'it's up there, isn't it? All on its own. Harming no one.'

We could have got around it, bypassed it, besieged it, left it alone to starve and rot, and gone on up the road to Rome and home we were going to follow anyway. Whatever the strategists said we could have ignored it – 'come back to collect it later'.

'Or just starve the buggers out.'

We could have camped along the banks of the Rapido or put up in the Amphitheatre or Coliseum, and waited. There was no hurry. Nothing much pressing at home, nothing that couldn't wait a few more weeks or months that hadn't waited four years anyway. 'Besides, spring'll soon be here, and a prettier place to spend it in'll be hard to find.'

But that was too simple. You don't do things like that in a Botchers' war.

When the call came we did it. Or rather the Poles and the New Zealanders did it. And the Yanks and Indians, the French, the Gurkhas and the Maoris. And anyone else who was hanging about these slopes during these wintry months waiting for the signal to pull it all down. It was a long run. By the time the final assault came we'd destroyed just about everything else in sight. Took days, weeks and then months, plugging away to get it right, rehearsed, blocked and staged. Started in January and some reckon it only ended in June when we entered Rome. Four months and four separate battles.

'Enough to put you off war once and for all,' said Old Vic.

Every other battle or brawl was the same – a mad
scrabble and scramble, everyone keeping his head down
and charging God knew where and doing his own thing,
hellbent on just going on and on and getting somewhere,
*any*where. Every time we went in the Sarge would say:
'Now it's up to you, lads. Now you're on your ownsome.
Now it's anarchy.'

But with Monte it was something else. In the flat of the
desert it's as if everyone's on the same eye level –
exposed, yet on the same terms; give or take a dune or
two. Even if you can't see the enemy, you know you're
on the same plane. But Monte was a mountain. They
were up there; we were down below. And to get them
out and down *we* had to do the scaling. You couldn't
compare it to any previous action, and you couldn't have
trained us for it. All we could do was pray that Jerry was
just as mesmerised as we were. So, we had no choice, as
the books say – when the supreme moment came, we
just went for it.

And once you get started, the mind goes. Nobody
knows a bloody thing. Just one titanic shower of din and
darkness. Apocalypse? Sounded right – Monte Cassino
language.

We didn't know much about the final phase. Didn't even
know why our little lot were there at all. Seemed mostly
Poles on that last lap. But that didn't stop us getting up
there or Cass going through his little routine a hundred
feet from the top.

'C'mon, Cass, they'll never notice your bloody
make-up!'

He lowered his mirror and looked at us, eyes glazing:

'Band of brothers,' he whispered.

'What's up, Cass?' asked Drum.

He looked towards us but not at us, then down at
himself and up to us again as if comparing his immaculate condition with our tatters:

310   *On Yer Bike, Schweik!*

'But such a *ragged* regiment,' he sneered.

'What's he say, Bird?'

'Dunno. But sounds bloody offensive to me.'

'What, old *Cass*? Never.'

'Don't think he approves of how we're turned out this morning, Snatch.'

Cass waited, narrowing his eyes slightly as if not quite recognising us, then, dreamily:

'This day will gentle your condition.'

'Told you,' said Bird.

'What's it mean?'

'Dunno, but it's offensive alright.'

But Cass was off, raising his head and gesturing to the clouds:

> 'And Botchers bland in England now abed
> Shall think themselves accurs'd they were not
> here . . .'

Beat.

'You're right, Dudd. He's off.'

'Reckon?'

'Bottle's gone.'

'Ripe for the old exit, eh?'

'Entrance, maybe.'

Then he turned back to us:

> 'And hold their manhoods cheap while any speaks
> That fought with us upon Cassino's day.'

'C'mon, lads,' said the Corp, scrambling ahead. 'Leave him. He's happy.'

We could see the citadel, the fortress, the city on the hill. But the blood and sweat and dirt and smoke was like *nothing* we'd ever seen before. Course, you think that every time. Nothing ever makes sense or meaning. Tactics, plot, logic – it's all one ginormous jumble. And when it's over, you can't see *what's* over. Can't sort out *anything* in that unholy mess. Some of us never had to bother.

At Monte we knew because of Cass.

He must have got really messed about on his way up after we'd left him. Followed us after all, but in what state of mind we'll never know. By the time he reached the top he was in a right old shambles and badly put out when he came to take his last call. Couldn't enter the Cassino looking like that – 'or any little rep show for that matter. Remember, they're *all* worthy.' He'd have to look his best to play *that* house, and right at the entrance he paused to sneak a last look in the mirror. A quick comb of the sideboards – the Sarge had let him grow them for a fortnight before: 'but just this once, mind' – a tweak of the moustache and maybe even the eyebrows, and a final tilt of the helmet before bracing himself for his entrance:

'One minute, Mr Cass. *If* you please.'

When the din dropped and the smoke thinned out and the birds were doing their testing, testing, testing bit again, they found him. Trim, smart, elegant to the end, lying just below the last ridge – the edges of the wings – seconds from his final entrance onto the central courtyard, yards from the steps to the Pearly Gates of the Bramante Cloister, left hand clutching his gleaming mirror, and the neat little hole through the breast pocket where it should have been.

PATTER NOSTER

Somewhere in Italy, May 1944

And when they came down from the Mountain, they sang praises to their Servant who had led them to salvation — well, most of them — but he had scarpered in the night. . .

Twenty

The Sarge told us about our medals some days after Monte Cassino. *Some* days. We couldn't count. We took it as another bit of patter to soften the blow.

'Come to tell you we got a couple of medals for you, lads.'

'Oh, that's nice, Sarge. With ribbons?'

'Ribbons too, yes. Very proud, they are, of you.'

'That's nice, Sarge. Always good to feel appreciated.'

'Came good in the end, you did.'

'Aw, Sarge.'

'Didn't let me down.'

'What did we do?'

'Don't you remember?'

'Survived?'

'No point in giving medals for bravery in a Botchers' War.'

When we opened our eyes, we were still flat out 'under canvas' – martial lingo for makeshift Field Hospital – but all we could see was the Sarge's head and shoulders at the end of the bed. The first thought was that it must have been the only time we'd ever seen him sitting down. He only ever walked about, paraded around, faced us, addressed us, or towered over us, cajoling or admonishing, but always matching our 'attention' position, never sitting facing us or looking up at us, obeying his own rule that 'a Botcher copes by standing up – usually on someone else's two feet' – meaning his own. Anyway, he was sitting now, delivering his patter.

'What these medals for, Sarge – bravery?'

'Nope, botchery.'

'Oh, right, we'll have some of them, then.'

'You only get *one*!'

'But I got three kids. I can't have them fighting over *one*.'

'Now, don't be like that. They think you did a great job.'

'They?'

'The high ones.'

'How the hell do they know? They weren't there!'

'Botchers are there because they're not brave!'

He drifted in and out like a ghost at the bottom of our beds, but the lights were none too good in the tent or cellar or whatever. It was difficult to tell *where* we were. There seemed to be canvas all around and on top and yet there were dark walls when the drapes moved and a strong smell of mustiness and damp and alcohol and spirit and cotton wool and things, so we could have been anywhere except that the anywhere had something to do with hospitals and sick beds.

'Not seeing too clear. Can't make him out. Can you?'

'No, must be the aspirins.'

'Aspirins!'

'Never could say Anna's thetic.'

There was a stain on the ceiling so it wasn't a tent. Yet there was light coming down like from a shaft. Sunlight?

The first time he disappeared someone said: 'Did I dream he was there?'

'Well, you *would* dream about him, wouldn't you? Been around us for years – haunting.'

'Worse than Jerry.'

'Yeah. Jerry makes you afraid. He makes you ashamed.'

'Given us lots of patter about that.'

Lazarette or hospital, infirmary or charnel house, canvas tent or wine cellar, he kept coming out of this dream, no more than head and shoulders. Made the place even more eerie and ghost-like. Kept appearing and disappearing behind this white shroud like they were pulling a curtain across the end of the beds or the beginning of the Sarge when visiting time was over and he kept getting cut off or out or exorcised – obliterated, ghost-like.

'What's he saying?'

'Giving us the old spiel.'

'Talk the hind legs off a camel.'

'What's this about medals?'

'More patter, I suppose.'

'Maybe the heat.'

'Or the aspirin.'

In fact, it was a damp wine cellar in an abandoned farm.

'Make-do-and-mend right to the end, eh, Sarge? *Field* hospital, is it?'

'Wine field, yeah.'

After the next disappearance, the next vanishing:

'Patter merchant. Not flannel. Patter. Even when he's popping in and out of our aspirin.'

'What's patter mean?'

'Dunno. Patter, patter, pitter, pitter, like drip, drip, rain pattering down on a window in Manchester, maybe.'

Voices and screeching of rubber trolley wheels.

'Or pat, pat, like pat on the back, maybe, to cheer you up.'

'More like patter, patter, drizzle going on and on.'

'Hmm.'

More noises off.

'How about always having everything off pat?'

'Smooth tongued?'

'Could be.'

'Could be a lot of things, patter.'

'Ask the Padre. He knows about that kind of stuff.'

The ghostly head and shoulders emerged once more.

'Well, stone me, if it's not Old Sergeant Banquo again.'

'Brought them medals with you, then, Sarge?'

'No, but they're coming.'

'What's the hold-up?'

'FPO's out of order.'

'Franking machine stuck?'

'Something like that.'

'Couldn't even print out our medals. I ask you. Another botched job.'

'What went wrong – the King's Head side or the "for bravery" bit?'

'Neither. Perforation machine's gone down. Couldn't tear yours off the sheet.'

'We could have taken the whole sheet, Sarge. Worth more that way. First-day cover and all that.'

'We weren't there because we were soldiers. We were there because we were Botchers.'

The medics said he'd dragged us from under the rubble and down the hillside then tucked us up in this 'field' hospital the way he said he always did, and given them his bit of patter.

When he drifted back in we asked:

'Did *you* get a medal, Sarge?'

'Me? No. Don't give medals to the likes of me.'

'Aw, diddums. Why not?'

'Well, I'd need a special one, wouldn't I? to distinguish me from you lot.'

He sounded distant.

'You speaking through a sock, Sarge?'

'No. Haven't got one.'

'You keep fading.'

'Keeping the noise down.'

'If not a medal, what about a cross, then?'

'Couldn't bear that.'

'What you been doing all war, then?'

'A cross is for officers. They'd have to make something special for me – between a cross and a medal.'

'How about a credal?'

'Or a medoss?'

'A crossdal, even?'

'No, I fancy something more like a trophy. A cup, maybe.'

'Can't pin a cup on your shirt, Sarge! Look bloody daft at the Cenotaph.'

'Did all the other guys get one?'

'No, only a few.'

'Giving medals to a few Botchers only makes the rest look failures, you know. Put down. Terrible thing to do to a man.'

After drifting in and out for a few times or days with this shroud being pulled across him to mark the end of each patter performance about bravery and medals and pride and codswallop, he disappears completely. Just fades from the dream. Doesn't come back. That's when we knew for sure it hadn't been a dream. Because each of us had seen him in it. We saw the face enter and we saw it stop entering and we saw that it didn't come on again. Each of us at the same time. Couldn't have been a dream.

We mentioned this to the Doc.

'What's happened to our Sarge, then, Doc?'

'Been posted?'

320 *On Yer Bike, Schweik!*

'In a way.'

'How come?'

'Didn't make it.'

'Make what, a medal?'

'Took the huff, you mean?'

'No, didn't come through.'

'Through what – his medal ordeal?'

'Got messed up doing his fetching and carrying.'

'But he was here regular, visiting us. Flitting in and out, ghost-like.'

'He said he wanted to make sure you'd learned to stand on your own two feet at last after years of standing on his.'

'That's him.'

'So we had to keep wheeling him in to have a word with you.'

'Wheeling? Sarge as life?'

'Yes.'

'That why he was only ever head and shoulders?'

'Yes.'

'So . . .?'

'We weren't wheeling in very much.'

'How . . .?'

'Went back to fetch something and trod on a mine.'

'And bought it?'

'Botched it, *he* said.'

'You can't fail as a Botcher, see. A Botcher has already failed.'

'What's patter, then, Padre?'

'Patter? You mean, like rain?'

'No. Like the Sarge.'

'Oh, that's quite different.'

'Well, we figured it could be pitter-patter like rain on the Old Trafford Pavilion, or lots of pats on the back, or having something off pat like a smoothy.'

'Well, no, it's none of these, actually. It's from Pater

Noster. The Lord's Prayer.'

'How come?'

'Well, pater noster means our father, in Latin. And in Catholic Churches you'll find them saying it over and over again with their rosary beads. Like they say "Hail Marys". On and on repeating the Lord's prayer, their Pater Nosters. Doing their patters, see?'

And after the Padre had gone:

'Well, there you are, then.'

'Pater noster, eh?!'

'Neat.'

'Very complicated business, botching. Takes a lot of working out.'

FINALE

Twenty-One

'On yer bike, Schweik' were the last words we heard our father say.

The day he died was the day they dropped the Bomb on Hiroshima and finally 'mucked up the margins'.

'The Bomb obliterated the entire city.'

The News came through at 8 o'clock on Monday morning on our imperial Cossor wireless set which we had graciously carried upstairs to his bedside so he could ring the changes with our canary.

'It is estimated that the population of Hiroshima was 300,000.'

My first thought was that you can't just go around dropping things like that. If it was as big as they said it was, they should have taken a lot more care.

'The Bomb was accurately dropped over the centre of the city.'

Father lay silent, staring as if stunned. We had never seen him like that before, not even at his worst moments when pain forced him to twist from one wound hole to another.

When he arrived home we were told he was having the bedroom at the rear because there was 'more room for his wounds' there. They sounded like mementoes brought back from the Desert and Italy with his medals, and as he often described them as 'little keepsakes from one wadi or another', we were curious to see what they looked like. It was some time before we worked out that they were not separate objects he kept in a box and needed more room to spread out, but things *he actually carried around on him like the blotches on our fingertips, which we had from writing at school with pens that had to be dipped and always blotched, and from brass-rubbing medals at home through tracing paper with soft pencils.*

That way we discovered that 'blotch' and 'botch' were actually the same. 'Blotch' was the wetter, more sloppy mess that we made with pen and ink and soft pencil. And 'botch' was the drier, smoother type that adults made by not paying enough attention.

The 'blotch' covers the whole range of liquid messes a child makes from leaking pens and pants to running nibs and noses, so that children are fundamentally wet people. And the 'botch' covers the whole range of more mature states of general helplessness and inadequacy, so that adults are fundamentally damp people.

Blotches become botches, blotchers become botchers. Soppy fingers in children became butterfingers in adults. But they are both types of wounds.

Our father had obviously botched his wounds, too, by getting them in the wrong place, otherwise he'd have been much more comfortable.

But this morning there was no movement, no twitching of the eye lids, no sucking of the cheeks, no pursing of the lips or wrinkling of the brow. And nothing in the eyes. Nothing. He could have been dead for all we knew, because we'd no idea how a dead person looked anyway, except that it must have something to do with nothing – no 'thing', no moving inside.

'The Bomb successfully detonated 560 metres above the ground.'

Hee . . . rosh . . . eeemah

Another sound had come into our life:

Hee . . . rosh . . . eeemah

calling into the night as painfully and plaintively as

Mon . . . Tay . . . Caa . . . See . . . No

*You could close your eyes and feel Hiroshima – feel it, call it,
reach out to it – like Monte Cassino. Of course, it had to come
second. Monte had been there in the Beginning.*

*And yet, the more we heard the name repeated that day –
turned it over, tasted it and sounded it, the more we discovered
echoes. Maybe we'd been born with Hiroshima in us too.*

Hee . . . rosh . . . eeemah Hee . . . rosh . . . eeemah

'Now, then, children . . .'

The day our father was buried Mother conducted a
special ceremony for the three of us in the front room
downstairs, the 'Dark Room', as we called it.

It was the day they dropped the Second Bomb – this
time on Nagasaki – obliterating whatever was left of my
father's margins. And of course it was a Thursday.

*'It is estimated that the population of Nagasaki was
280,000.'*

We called the front room the Dark Room because it
was dark and because all the important affairs of the
family were developed there. Day-to-day living took
place in the other parts of the house: 'chores and
things'. *Real* living took place in the Dark Room:
'decisions and things'.

*'The Bomb fell for forty seconds and exploded 500 metres
above the city.'*

The Dark Room was full of miserable purpled plants
that thrived on darkness and cringed when any light
sneaked in, and the windows were flanked by heavy
dun drapes that were closed only when we had
important guests to feed or serious business to attend
to, like burying my father.

*'The Bomb weighed 4.5 tons and detonated 22 kilotons of
TNT.'*

My brother and sister and I stood dutifully behind the
heavy mahogany table draped with a thick, once-
white crocheted cover with ladies' heads inlaid like

silhouettes into the overall design. In my great grandmother's time the ladies in the family spent their evenings working together on one enormous piece of crochet instead of listening to the Readings or Tommy Handley – 'because that's what people did in those days.'

I pictured them carefully placed around the room like models in a painter's studio, patiently crocheting away their evenings by restless candlelight or wavering oil wick, heads poised over their intricate mission to construct a table cover for her grandchildren to put in their Dark Room for special occasions like burying her grandson-in-law. We must have seemed very far away from her then, further even than Monte Cassino.

'It is estimated that 30,000 people died in the first few minutes.'

But she was already dreaming about us. And as if to will a sign to us who would one day benefit from her lonely, reluctant labour, she left her signature, like mediaeval masons carved their marks on cathedral stones and martyrs gouged their names on dungeon walls – self-portraits in miniature.

'The plutonium bomb was twice as powerful as the one dropped three days ago on Hiroshima.'

I was studying Great Grandmother's profile when my mother came into the room carrying the medals, the map and the roll of poems.

'Now then, children . . .'

She had come in silently, but she couldn't have come in any other way because the house had been hushed for days and everyone was continually coming and going on tiptoe. Besides, there was a very thick carpet in the Dark Room which also came from some Great Grand-Someone or Other. We never seemed to have anything of our own, except the *Adventure* – even the canary came from the milkman, whose wife had had enough of his 'damned twittering'.

'Now then, here we are . . .'

We stood facing her, behind the table with our backs to the fire that never got lit – 'except on special occasions'. But there was never any occasion in our house so special that it deserved a fire to celebrate it. Not even our father's death.

'First, let me . . .' And she crossed over to draw the curtains, saying 'that's better'.

The blind had been lowered almost to meet the join of the sash windows. Almost. She'd told us the blinds were down because Father had 'gone': 'Because that's what people do.'

But there was a chink between the blind and cross-bar. Did she include Botchers? Had the doctors botched it? Was there still hope?

'Now then, I want you to take a last look.'

In her open hands, like an offering plate at church, she stood before us holding the dark-brown box of medals, the tiny folded map, and the well-thumbed roll of papers tied together with the army lanyard.

The three of us gazed helplessly across at the objects – limp, alone, lifeless.

'They're going with him,' she said, 'so we shan't be seeing them again.'

We had no idea what she expected us to do. Whatever it was, we didn't. We just stood there, staring. I longed to reach over and touch them, 'a last time', to feel the curve of the King's head on my palm, to trace out the letters 'for bravery' with my fingertips. I longed to run my thumb over the soft suede-like back of the map which always made me think of the tip of a dog's snout. As for the poems, I just hoped he'd got them finished in time.

My brother and sister remained rigid, and, in the name of harmony, I denied myself.

During that first long Armistice in the cold Dark Room I stared rigidly at the medals, map and bundle of papers until they began to move, circling slowly, then weaving in and out of each other, mingling with the ivory crochet and losing themselves in the intricate design of my great grandmother's heads.

And as they moved, they creaked – like doors swinging on unoiled hinges, stairs straining under centuries of feet, as the house swayed. My feet ached horribly as the nails drove down to fasten me to the floor so that I wouldn't fall over. The sound grew and grew until it reached an enormous 'Crrrraaaacccck!' in my head and I surfaced from my whirlpool to see my sister's shoes grinding down on my toes and the objects on the silent offering plate floating out of my sight. And I heard the door click softly as she carefully left the room.

'Funny, thought Monte was the reason why.'

When we came home from school Mother was going about her chores as if on tiptoe, indicating by her movements how we should behave without being told in words.

'Into August now. Caesar's lucky month.'

She was like that. She was far better at explaining without words, because she never got bogged down with the ones that make you despair because they won't fit.

'It was all about Monte, really.'

We gathered around the bed with Father propped up ashen-faced in his ashen nightgown like a Last Supper tableau.

'Peak of the year, you know. Takes eight months to get there. August. Got to make the best of it. After that, it's all slithering downhill to Christmas.'

The sun was still streaming down through the window and pouring all over our canary which stood transfixed as if newly cast in molten gold.

'Funny,' he said, squinting sideways at his 'winger' – his term for a feathered Botcher – 'whatever we got up to, the birds were always above it.' The canary perked up at this interesting observation and began to pipe with unusual fervour.

'We tried to silence the sounds of nature, roaring louder and louder to beat them down. But whatever we did to deafen and destroy, the birds always sang – afterwards.' Whereupon the canary struck out, stretching and swaying its yellow head like Caruso reaching for the high notes on our gramophone.

'Each time the thunder stops, the first thing that tells you you've come through isn't the tickling of sweat on the tongue but the song of birds on the ear.' Picking up his cue, the canary swayed back and forward on his perch, broadcasting his aria to a captive audience.

'How they ever survived what we did to the Earth, I'll never know. Where they hid and waited until we'd done with our madness, God only knows.' Left and right to the Stalls he sang and up to the Circle and Gods.

'But as soon as the ceasefire comes, a great silence covers the world like a heavy blanket to hide under when you've done something you're ashamed of.' The chirping died away.

He twisted and nodded towards the cage. *'Then the birds sing,'* he said, and the canary took off again. *'Long as he's singing, you're alright.'*

At 6 o'clock we listened to the News again.

'It is estimated that the population of Hiroshima was 300,000.'

'Monte was where we'd all been making for, right from the start.'

We sat solemnly clutching our mugs and comics.

'You have to make the best of August. Catch it while it lasts.'

He twisted to look past the canary and out of the window, as if August was just driving past.

'All the others were operations – bits, really. Bigger or smaller bits, more or less bits. Whimpers.'

'The Bomb successfully detonated 560 metres above the ground.'

'August's the high point, you see – when the sun reaches its zenith and the runs flow at the Oval.'

'The Bomb obliterated the entire city'.

A distant roar of 'How'zat!' and the chop, chop, chop of mild clapping followed the Newsreader's 'and now for the rest of the News.'

'Funny, thought Monte was the reason why.'

We waved him goodbye from the top of the steps in front of the light green door, the three of us lined up in the same order as in front of the darker green fireplace.

We stared down at the long black Rolls with its long dark windows shading whatever was long and dark inside and garlanded with flowers and blurred by the heads of the two men who had tried so hard not to creak upstairs.

Mother got into the car immediately behind the Rolls but she didn't look up to wave. In fact no one looked up to wave.

The second the engines started up and the row of cars prepared to edge forward, a platoon of filthy, camouflaged soldiers suddenly appeared from around the corner at the end of the street and came marching up towards us on the other side. They moved in such a rush they were almost opposite our steps before we registered them, as if they were desperate to arrive before my father left.

There must have been thirty or forty marching in threes, with another one out on his own in front. They were appallingly dirty, covered in splotches of mud from steel top to leathered feet. Their huge boots crunched noisily on the silent street and echoed between the houses on either side, like percussion cymbals smashing through the soft drone of the engines that seemed to be purring extra softly that morning. The desperate legion reached us just as the cars were edging away.

Suddenly the soldier out in front jerked up violently and screamed in great pain as if he'd trodden barefoot on a scattering of drawing pins:

'Plaaa . . . tooooon!! . . . Hiii . . . yezzzzzz . . . Right!!'

'He's the King Botcher, you see,' I heard my Father say. *'His job is to organise all the Baby Botchers. Trouble is, of course, you can't ever organise a Botcher – but* he *thinks you can.'*

I waited for the birds to start singing. Instead, all the Baby Botchers straightened up as if they too had reached the drawing pins and jerked their heads in our direction.

There was no doubt the King Botcher was saluting, and there was no doubt he was saluting us, because there was no one else in the street to salute that morning. But nobody on our side took the slightest bit of notice. We simply froze and stared back helplessly at the absurd mob of contortionists below.

'And the Lord God created King Botchers too but blessed them with one teeny-weeny flaw that they themselves can never ever see: A King Botcher doesn't know he's a Botcher too.'

You could tell by the mess they were all in that they'd gone to a lot of trouble to get there before our father left. So I lifted my arm slowly, held it for a moment, and then sneaked a glance at my silent sister and rigid brother. They were still very silent and rigid. I let my arm sink back again. But not too far.

Years later my mother told me it hadn't been arranged. They were not a special platoon sent to honour my father like they honour Kings and Queens. The soldiers arrived by chance, and when the King Botcher saw the hearse he naturally saluted the coffin, *any* coffin.

'That's just how they did things in those days,' she said.

'Another botch,' *he* would have said.

A long time later everyone came home.

Suddenly the house was full of the noise of people behaving like people instead of shadows, and talking instead of whispering. Whatever had happened elsewhere to make them all happy again, nothing had changed for the three of us left behind with nothing to do but wait for them to return.

I resented the tiny white sandwiches cut to look pretty with three corners instead of the usual four. But my sister said they had to be that size 'because of the occasion'.

My brother remained silent.

'You only make big ones when things are normal and nothing in particular has happened and you are just everyday hungry,' she observed.

I stared down at the miserable cut-outs that looked like shapes you wedge into a puzzle board and wondered if I put them back in the right order again and pressed them together hard enough, would they stick so I could pick them up with both hands instead?

'When things aren't normal and everyday,' she went on, warming to her passive audience, 'and you aren't hungry, you have to have tiny ones.'

I had learned a lot since my father died.

'Anyway, that's just what people *do*,' she said.

My brother remained silent.

At last my mother came into the room as silently as before. She sat down on the chair opposite us, lowered her hands carefully over one of the heads on the tablecloth, folded them neatly as if in prayer, then rested them on one of the silhouettes.

A strange embarrassment drifted over the four of us. It was as if we had been separated from each other for a long time and had now come together again and were unsure about how to begin. As if our peace and privacy had recently been wrenched away from us and had now been returned, and we didn't know how to behave. As if we were thankful to be back again but knew it was the wrong thing to feel.

My mother had come back to us, not from our father's funeral, but from another time – a time before the stretcher brought him home. We were back to where and how we had spent the five years of war – four of us, not five.

'It's all over now,' she said, as if she couldn't think of anything else.

It was as if everything that had happened since the blue men carried the white stretcher up the grey steps to the green door and on upstairs to the brown room with the yellow canary had been a separate time, neatly delivered into our lives like a carefully wrapped present, but now sent back – 'returned to sender'.

It was as if we had been on a long holiday, a tight, concentrated time when you live with other people and adapt to other ways, when you learn to set aside your own fads and tastes and accept their different styles and manners. You live differently and behave differently, because for a time you've become a different group. Until the day comes to pack up and travel home. And you arrive back to find it all very strange, uncertainly familiar, and you have to begin again to rediscover the ways you left behind, and the person you were before.

Now we waited helplessly in the cold front room as if about to pick up the threads and renew the relationship we had held so tightly during these years, grateful for the holiday, yet grateful to be back. As if we couldn't have taken too much more of his reality.

'Did they all go with him?'

My brother hadn't said a word since my father died.

Mother looked across and up at him.

'All?'

'The . . . things.'

She nodded.

'Why?'

'Well, they belonged to him. They didn't mean anything without him.'

'His papers too?'

'Of course.'

She waited. He was obviously wrestling with

something. Knowing my brother, it might take a long time. Knowing my mother, she would wait.

'They were poems, weren't they?' He finally made it.

'I think so.'

'Will they ever come out in a book?'

'Oh, no.'

'Why not?'

'Because they've gone with him.'

There couldn't possibly be a copy. He wouldn't have had the time. He'd been working on them right up to the last minute. *I* knew *that*!

'They belong to him, you see,' I heard her say, and in a flash the three 'objects' shone clear: the map to show him the way to go, the medals to pay his fare, and the scroll the homework he had to hand in. 'For his new dwelling place,' she added.

Well, that figured. In my Father's House there would be many Margins.

'The ultimate kybotch,' he observed from his pillows at nine in the evening.

Kybotch was another word that decorated these last six months, some kind of extra, super botch. It seemed to be something over and above a Botcher like Con Brio or a botch like Dunkirk.

We listened to the same News at 9 o'clock. Nothing had changed. Not even the wording.

'No more hiding places now,' he said, as if defining kybotch at last.

When the News ended, Mother rose quietly and deliberately, switched off the set, and said: 'Bed now, children.'

'Finito. Caput!' he decided.

And, with a deep sigh, he turned resignedly to pick up his bundle of papers. He smoothed out the curling pages, tapped them to a uniform shape, rolled them into a near perfect round scroll, took the lanyard from under his pillow and bound them together.

'That's that, then . . .' he sighed, placing the scroll on the bedside table and concluding his twelve hours meditation. 'No more margins.'

He settled back on his pillows, closed his eyes and said, quite distinctly:

'On yer Bike, Schweik,' on Monday, August 9th, 1945 – and went.

Epilogue

'Was Father a war poet?' asked my brother.

'War poet?' Mother smoothed the hair on her grandmother's head. 'Yes, I suppose in a way he was.'

She hadn't got the hair quite right, and had to use her other hand too. It took time. Like her own hair did.

'Were they about the war then?' he pressed on.

'No, not as *such*.'

She licked her finger and rubbed it gently over a smudge on her grandmother's chin. 'You see, there's no such thing as a *war* poet.' She smudged on. 'You can't be a poet if you only write about war. You can only be a poet.' She studied the effect. 'War is just something *else* people go into, and come through and out of. Or don't.'

'Did you read them?'

'Some.'

'Did he write them to you?'

'Some.'

'What were they about, then?'

'I know! I know!'

My left arm twitched violently, straining to swing up so that I could snap my fingers and force her to turn to ask me. Because I knew, if no one else in that frozen room did, that the answer was 'Botchers!'

But my mother only picked at my great grandmother's hair and said, 'Love.'

Warner now offers an exciting range of quality titles by both established and new authors. All of the books in this series are available from:
Little, Brown and Company (UK) Limited,
P.O. Box 11,
Falmouth,
Cornwall TR10 9EN.

Alternatively you may fax your order to the above address. Fax No. 0326 376423.

Payments can be made as follows: Cheque, postal order (payable to Little, Brown and Company) or by credit cards, Visa/Access. Do not send cash or currency. UK customers: and B.F.P.O.: please send a cheque or postal order (no currency) and allow £1.00 for postage and packing for the first book, plus 50p for the second book, plus 30p for each additional book up to a maximum charge of £3.00 (7 books plus).

Overseas customers including Ireland, please allow £2.00 for postage and packing for the first book, plus £1.00 for the second book, plus 50p for each additional book.

NAME (Block Letters) ....

ADDRESS...

....

☐ I enclose my remittance for _____

☐ I wish to pay by Access/Visa Card

Number ☐☐☐☐☐☐☐☐☐☐☐☐☐☐☐☐

Card Expiry Date ☐☐☐☐